T0244680

VINTAGE
BEST SERVED COLD

Bhaskar Chattopadhyay is an author and screenwriter. He started his career by translating Bengali and Hindi writers such as Rabindranath Tagore, Premchand and Bibhutibhushan Bandyopadhyay. He now writes mystery fiction and thrillers. He has also written several books on film-maker Satyajit Ray. Bhaskar's first feature screenplay releases in October 2024. He lives in Toronto with his wife and two sons and teaches screenwriting at York University.

Best Served Cold

A Janardan Maity Mystery

Bhaskar Chattopadhyay

VINTAGE

An imprint of Penguin Random House

VINTAGE

Vintage is an imprint of the Penguin Random House group of companies
whose addresses can be found at global.penguinrandomhouse.com

Published by Penguin Random House India Pvt. Ltd
4th Floor, Capital Tower 1, MG Road,
Gurugram 122 002, Haryana, India

Penguin
Random House
India

First published in Vintage by Penguin Random House India 2024

ISBN 9780143464228

Typeset in Garamond by MAP Systems, Bengaluru, India

www.penguin.co.in

[1]

I remember the events of that day quite vividly, for that was the day when this incredible story began. It was a typical September day in Kolkata—hot and humid, irritating to the core and threatening to spoil the fun promised by the upcoming festival. The world outside my window was teeming with people going about their day-to-day jobs. Children were being herded into yellow buses and green autorickshaws to be ferried to their schools. Anxious-looking men and women were trying to get to work by any means possible—their faces lined with a weariness that seemed inapt for such an early hour of the morning. Old uncles were returning from the vegetable market with the air of conquerors, the spoils of battle peeping out of their bags in the shape of gourds and pumpkins. The owners of shops and stores had begun rolling up their shutters, lighting their incense sticks and offering a quick prayer to the gods before going about their daily trade. There was a never-ending stream of traffic on the road outside my window, and everyone seemed to be in a rush to be somewhere. And there I was, sitting at my desk in my South Kolkata home, curtains half-drawn, staring blankly at a blinking cursor on a white screen. I knew everything there was to know about that flickering little devil—what it looked like, how often it came and went and what its exact position at the corner of the screen was. I knew every minute detail about it—tiny, insignificant facts that no sane person in their right minds would care to notice or pay attention to. But I? Oh, I knew. Because I had been staring at that blinking cursor on that blank page for the last three months. Every single day.

My dear friend Janardan Maity called sometime around noon, and I was glad he did. Because I had spent the better part of the morning trying to write one coherent sentence. But just like any other day, words had escaped me. Every now and then, I stared at the half a dozen books that I had written in my brief career so far, now adorning a shelf in my bookcase at the far end of the room. They seemed to stare back at me with mute reproach. All of them had done reasonably well, but now even they seemed to be wondering if they were the last of their coterie and if my career was over. I knew something was wrong with me, but for the life of me, I couldn't figure out what it was. All I knew was that I simply could not write. I could not put down more than three sensible words side by side. And it was a wretched, wretched feeling.

Maity's call lifted my spirits to some extent because he suggested that we step out. Not that he knew anything about my condition, though. I hadn't had the heart to tell him. What purpose could it have possibly served, other than to make me feel even more miserable? No, I was simply happy that he had called, and I looked forward to the reprieve. Unknown to himself, he had given me an opportunity to escape my living and breathing nightmare, albeit for a few hours. And that was good enough for me. At least for the moment.

There was a brief thunderstorm in the afternoon. But let alone bringing in some much-needed relief from the sweltering heat, it seemed to bump up the discomfort even further. Maity refused to change his plans, though. Like me, he was a big fan of the cinema, especially the classics. He adored the films of yesteryears and watched them over and over again. Having attended a screening of the classic 1922 German horror film *Nosferatu* at Max Mueller Bhavan, and then topping that timeless and fascinating experience by devouring the utterly delectable double-egg-double-chicken roll at Sher-e-Punjab, when Maity and I reached his ancestral mansion in Bhowanipore at half past seven that evening, his sixty-five-year-old manservant Mahadev—who had been with Maity and his father for at least fifty of those sixty-five years—announced that a lady had come to see Maity barely half an hour ago.

'Lady?' Maity seemed surprised. 'What lady?'

'I don't know,' Mahadev summoned a grimace of irritation on his face, which I knew was merely by force of habit and was not intended to convey any emotion, least of all irritation. 'She waited for some time, but when I told her that you might be late, she said she would come back again, and left in a hurry.'

'What did she look like?'

From Mahadev's description, we learnt that the unexpected visitor was a young woman, probably in her early thirties, dressed in a white shirt and blue jeans, had a head full of long, curly hair and she seemed to speak in a voice that was both soft and pleasant to the ear. The lady was apparently carrying a red-and-white packet, and by her appearance and manner, she seemed to come from a respectable family.

'Did she say why she wanted to see me?' Maity asked, as he took his canvas satchel off his shoulder and placed it on a rosewood table set against the wall.

'No,' said Mahadev, frowning intensely, 'I didn't ask her.'

Before Maity could ask him anything else, the faint whistle of a pressure cooker emerged from the interior of the house and Mahadev hurried out of the room, mumbling something under his breath. Maity let out an exhausted sigh, turned the regulator of the ceiling fan all the way up to five and plonked down on his favourite couch by the window. I sat in a chair nearby and looked around the room that had become so familiar to me over the last few years. Many years ago, it had been a parlour of sorts, used by Maity's father—who had been a renowned barrister in the city—as a waiting room for visitors, before they could be ushered into the main hall of the house. Maity now used it as a drawing room, because he had converted the entire hall into a library. There was no subject in the world that he did not read on, and I had even seen him read books on topics he did not believe in. The window next to which he now sat opened over a pretty little garden in the backyard, which Maity personally tended to. The room received ample light throughout the day and a cool breeze in the evening from the direction of the river. The couch itself once belonged to Maity's great-grandfather, who used to be a zamindar in undivided Bengal. Maity once told me it was made-to-order and flown in all the way from Montreux. The rest of the room too—like the rest of the house—was full of antique furnishings, drapes, vases, candle stands, paintings, chandeliers and the rarest of books.

'Have you started writing your new novel?' Maity asked.

'Not yet,' I replied after a moment's hesitation.

Maity observed me for some time with those keen eyes of his and said: 'You ought to travel more, you know? Get out of town, get away from all this noise and smoke and dust and sweat, and you'll be surprised to find your mind opening up. Like magic! Give yourself some space to breathe and some time to do nothing. Nature has this wonderful habit of soothing one's nerves, calming one down, recharging one's cells. Thoughts and ideas begin to flow the moment you come in contact with nature. Hell, the more I talk about it, the more I feel like taking a break myself and going somewhere nice and quiet. It has been quite some time since we have been to that little holiday place of ours by the sea, wouldn't you agree?'

Although I didn't say anything in response, I knew Maity was subtly prodding me, because he was right—the last time he and I had been out of Kolkata was more than a year ago, and we hadn't had much rest on that trip. Having come from a family of means, Maity himself had never had a 'job' per se, so there was no compulsion for him as such to stay in Kolkata. Unlike me, he could take off any time he wanted to. I, on the other hand, had my writing commitments to worry about. I was just beginning to wonder if taking a break would indeed help me overcome the writer's block that I had been struggling with for the last three months, when suddenly, the doorbell rang.

'Would you mind answering the door, Prakash?' Maity asked. 'It must be the lady who had come earlier.'

But it wasn't. As I opened the door, I found a tall, imposing young man smartly clad in an expensive business suit and a striped necktie standing outside with an iPhone in his hand. He was clean-shaven, and even his head was completely hairless and meticulously waxed. The man had a suave, professional appearance, and it took me a few seconds to take my eyes off him and notice the other gentleman—the one standing behind him at a distance. The second man was much older (easily in his seventies), tall and scrawny, hunched at the waist, slightly stooping over a walking stick, standing and staring at me with piercing eyes. He had a curved nose and a pointy chin; his skin was fair in complexion and his hair was long and silvery-grey. There was an aristocratic air about him, and although he now looked aged and shrivelled, for some reason, the old man's steely glance and uninviting countenance gave me the distinct impression that at some point in time in the past, he must have been the sort of man no one would have dared to mess with.

'Good evening! Is this the residence of Mr Janardan Maity, the detective?' the younger of the two gentlemen inquired.

'Yes, please come in,' I said, hoping in my heart that the man wouldn't make the mistake of calling Maity a detective to his face. I knew how much Maity hated that word.

I ushered the two men in, and Maity rose from his couch and welcomed them with his usual courtesy. I shut the door and joined them, and once everyone had settled down in their seats, Maity asked the visitors if they would like a cup of tea.

The old man betrayed an almost imperceptible gesture, which resembled a scoff. I caught on to it, and so did Maity, but before we could react, the younger man flashed an affable smile and politely declined Maity's offer.

'Very well, please tell me,' said Maity, 'how can I help you gentlemen?'

'Have I ever . . .?'

Before the young man could begin, the older one had suddenly uttered those words and was now staring around the room with a pronounced frown on his wrinkled forehead. He gave the impression of a man who was lost and was trying to find his way out of a labyrinth.

'I . . . we have been here before . . . haven't we, Mohan?' he somehow managed to say in a feeble, raspy voice. Although he looked rather frail and disoriented, it was that piercing look in his eyes that somehow made me uncomfortable.

The man named Mohan smiled at us apologetically, quickly extended a hand and patted the old man's wrist gently. 'No, sir. We're meeting Mr Maity for the first time. We spoke about this, remember? We're here to take his advice on . . . on the matter, sir.'

Maity and I watched the proceedings in silence, looking at the two men in turn. The old man's frightening eyes took their time to scan Maity's magnificent collection of artefacts neatly arranged across the room and finally came and rested on Maity himself.

'Hmm,' he quipped. 'Impressive!'

The young man now turned to Maity and said, 'You must be a busy man, Mr Maity, so I'll come straight to the point. My name is Mohan Sharma. I'm Mr Chowdhury's secretary and personal manager. I have been with him for almost six years now. Mr Jagat Narayan Chowdhury is the owner of several tea gardens in the Dooars region of Bengal. He has other business concerns too, but tea is the primary one. My employer is seventy-nine now. And for over fifty years, he has been in the tea-growing, tea-manufacturing and tea-exporting business. The tea from our gardens is not sold in India. It is of the finest quality, and we export it exclusively to certain specific regions in Europe.'

Mohan Sharma paused a little, Maity waited patiently, and I realized why the guests had declined our offer of tea.

'In his youth,' Sharma continued, 'Mr Chowdhury had been a dynamic planter. Much loved, much revered in his estates. Unlike the British, from whom he took over the business, Mr Chowdhury did a lot for the welfare of his workers. He built hospitals for the labourers of the tea gardens, schools and playgrounds for their children; he even built temples and churches for them. He ensured that they got clean drinking water, proper sanitation facilities and a safe working environment. Which is perhaps why the labourers literally worshipped him. And as a direct result of that, the production of our gardens has always remained unmatched by those of our competitors. But as you know, every successful man has his own share of enemies. Mr Chowdhury too did, although his enemies and naysayers could never get the better of him, and not for want of trying, I might add.'

I watched the old man's face closely. It looked tired and haggard, and his eyes were now shut, presumably with exhaustion. Although grand in stature, Maity's house was an old one, and the climb to the first floor took quite a bit of doing.

'Until now!'

Those two words from Mohan Sharma made me shift my attention back to him. Although his face was calm, his eyes were restless, and were darting back and forth between his employer and Maity. Maity had interlocked his fingers and was watching Mohan Sharma's face with a silent stare.

'Mr Chowdhury owns many gardens spread across the region, but he lives in the Manikpur Tea Estate, near the Chilapata forest range in Alipurduar district. He has his own bungalow there, right in the middle of the garden—a very picturesque place. The bungalow is situated around half a mile from the estate's massive factory, where tea is processed. Although it is a huge property with over twenty rooms, Mr Chowdhury himself doesn't live in the main bungalow. He prefers living in a small wooden cabin within the compound, which was originally built by the British for quarantine.'

'Leprosy?' Maity asked.

Mohan Sharma nodded with a smile, 'That's correct, Mr Maity. You seem to be familiar with the menace of leprosy in tea gardens in the past. There was a time when it was believed that leprosy was caused by the sap of the tea tree. It was also believed that the disease was contagious. We now know that neither of these are true, but back in the day, people were far more ignorant. The rumours were further fuelled by the fact that incidents of the disease were quite common in the gardens. And often, British planters would attract it themselves. Hence the isolation. Those days are gone now, as are the myths and taboos. But Mr Chowdhury prefers the solitude of the cabin now.'

'Too many people,' Jagat Narayan Chowdhury whispered, his eyes still shut, and an expression of agony now spread across his face. 'Far too many people. Coming and going, day and night. In and out. All the time . . . all those footsteps . . . I . . . I can't . . . tolerate . . .'

Mr Chowdhury's words trailed off. Mohan Sharma looked a bit embarrassed. He said in a soft voice, 'Although the bungalow is virtually empty—Mr Chowdhury's children are all settled in London—there are the servants, the cooks, the gardeners, the drivers, etc., who have access to the house. Mr Chowdhury moved into the cabin around six months ago. It's much quieter there, lots of trees, and there's a beautiful lotus pond right next to the cabin—he likes to have his breakfast by the pond, spends his mornings and evenings sitting there.'

'Where do you live?' Maity asked.

'I live in the bungalow. Only Mr Chowdhury and his personal butler live in the cabin.'

'I see. Please continue.'

Mohan Sharma cleared his throat and went on, 'Four days ago, on the night of the sixteenth, someone tried to break into the bungalow. Clearly, whoever the intruder was, he did not know that Mr Chowdhury had not been living in the bungalow any more, so luckily, he escaped unhurt. But for the same reason, we came to the conclusion that it was an outsider, and not someone from Manikpur. Because everyone in Manikpur is aware of the fact that Mr Chowdhury lives in the cabin.'

'What makes you think that the intruder wanted to hurt Mr Chowdhury?' Maity asked. 'Couldn't it have been an ordinary thief?'

'Well, we don't think so, and I'll tell you why. For one, the intruder climbed the drainpipes and made his way to a specific room on the first floor. He even tried to pick the lock and enter the room. That room used to be Mr Chowdhury's bedroom earlier. But even when he used that room, it did not contain any valuables. His important business papers, some gold jewellery pieces, petty cash, etc., were all locked safely in his office on the ground floor. The rest of it is all in bank lockers. This led us to think that the intruder specifically wanted to get to Mr Chowdhury, and that he wasn't interested in the valuables at all.'

I quickly looked at Maity from the corner of my eye, but Maity didn't say anything.

'And secondly, when the man was trying to pick the lock and break in, our chowkidar saw him from a distance and raised an alarm. The man jumped down to the ground below, ran for his life and disappeared in the dark before anyone could get to him, but in all the rush, he left a sharp dagger behind.'

'Do you have any idea who this man could have been?' Maity asked.

'None at all,' said Mohan Sharma. 'As I said before, a successful man like Mr Chowdhury has many enemies. Could have been any one of them. Could have been a hired goon too.'

'Do you have the dagger with you now?'

Mohan Sharma shot a quick glance at his boss and said, 'Er . . . no, Mr Maity. You see . . . I didn't want to carry it around when . . .'

Maity raised his hand and said, 'I understand. Have the local police been informed?'

'Yes, the very next morning. They came and interrogated the entire staff, including me. But to tell you the truth, Mr Chowdhury does not have too much faith in the police. He is of the opinion that their—'

'*You* will catch the culprit for me!'

Before Mohan Sharma could finish his sentence, his boss had opened his eyes and thundered those words. He was now extending his hand and pointing his forefinger straight at Maity. I noticed that the skin of his hand had wrinkled so much that it looked almost skeletal and otherworldly. His frame may have been frail, but the force with which he had uttered those words made me realize that the man still hadn't lost his mettle.

'My lawyers . . . they speak highly of you,' he went on. 'They say you are a useful man, a thinking man, a man who knows how to get things done.'

'But Mr Chowdhury,' Maity leant forward in his chair and began with a soft, respectful voice and a polite smile, 'in these kinds of cases, it is usually the local police who are far more equipped to—'

'How much?' The entire room seemed to vibrate with the force of Mr Chowdhury's roar.

Mohan Sharma looked somewhat embarrassed, but he made a visible effort to maintain a calm reserve. Maity, on the other hand, seemed rather taken aback. His notorious frown had appeared on his forehead.

'Excuse me?' he asked.

'Everyone has a price.' The old man had shut his eyes again. 'Name yours.'

Maity's face turned grave. The frown slowly disappeared from his forehead. He leant back on his couch and said: 'Well, that's where you are wrong, Mr Chowdhury. Not everyone has a price. I certainly don't.'

Very, very slowly, Jagat Narayan Chowdhury opened his eyes and looked straight at Maity. The man was obviously not expecting Maity's curt response and was clearly not happy to hear it. He sat in his seat in silence and fumed for a few seconds, staring directly at Maity all the while. Then he asked:

'So, you won't work for me?'

Maity crossed his right leg over his left and uttered a single word in a calm, firm and resolute voice.

'No.'

I looked across the room to find Mr Chowdhury breathing heavily. His right hand had grabbed the ivory head of his walking stick, his left had grabbed the wrist of his right hand. Both had begun to tremble.

'May I ask why?'

'Of course, you may.' Maity's eyes had not moved an inch away from the old man's face, and having said this much, he fell silent again. His dignified reserve made even me nervous; I wondered what it must be doing to the other two people in the room.

The old man made a gesture of intense annoyance and said, 'Well, why?'

'Because, you see, Mr Chowdhury, I help people who come to me seeking my help. I am an old-fashioned man—I believe in old-fashioned values. Values such as courtesy, humility, decency. I have nothing to offer those who come into my home and try to throw money at my face. There are exactly forty-five steps in the stairs outside that door you came through, and I regret to say that you have climbed all of them in vain.'

Mohan Sharma was silently staring at us so far. He now tried to say something, but was abruptly cut off by his boss, who rose from his chair with some amount of struggle, waved off an offer of help from his secretary and hobbled out of the door. Mohan Sharma turned to meet Maity's eyes with a helpless look one last time, before following his master out. For some time, we could hear the clacking of Jagat Narayan

Chowdhury's walking stick echoing through Maity's baroque stairwell. After a minute or so, everything fell silent. Maity rose from his seat, shut the door and returned to his couch.

'Obnoxious!' he remarked.

I didn't say anything for a few minutes. Maity sat fuming in his seat, shaking his head in disgust every now and then.

'What do you think?' I asked after some time.

Maity flared up in an instant, 'Even if I were to attribute the man's audacity and insolence to his age and agree to look into the matter, he wouldn't let me investigate in my own way. Did you notice how rude he was to his secretary? No, Prakash. I am convinced that he is the sort of man who thinks he can rule over people just because he has money and power. I have neither the time nor any sympathy for such people.'

Maity continued to grumble for a few more minutes, and in a bid to calm him down, I tried to divert his mind. It took some doing, but I finally succeeded. The atmosphere in the room gradually returned to normality. We spoke about the weather in detail, and about the timeless charm of German Expressionism, especially in cinema. Maity asked me to stay back for dinner, and we spent the rest of the evening chatting and laughing away to our hearts' content over Mahadev's delicious fish kalia and apricot custard.

But all through the evening, despite his cheerful façade, I knew Maity wasn't being able to get the incident at Manikpur Tea Estate out of his head. I had known him for a long time now, and I knew that contrary to what he may have said to me, throwing an old man out of his house was making him restless, especially when he knew that there was a threat to the man's life. Every now and then, he would fall silent and stare into the void, before resuming the conversation or returning to his food. This went on until after we had had dinner. Little did I think that something else would happen that night.

But as it turned out, it did. The grandfather clock in the drawing room had just finished chiming the Westminster Quarters followed by ten majestic gongs, a low rumble in the skies had conveyed the possibility that it might rain again, I had announced my intention to leave for the day, and Maity had just asked me my plans for the next day, when the doorbell rang. I opened the door to find a young lady dressed in a white corduroy shirt and blue jeans standing outside, holding a white packet neatly tied with a frilly red ribbon in her hand.

[2]

'I'm terribly sorry for having called on you so late in the evening, Mr Maity,' the lady said after she had settled down on the sofa Maity had offered her, 'but the matter is quite urgent.'

Mahadev's description of the lady had been quite accurate. But there were several other things that I noticed about her now. For one, although her voice was indeed soft and sweet, it was quite obvious that something was on her mind. It manifested itself in the manner in which she twisted her fingers every now and then, for instance. Or in the way she kept pausing between her words and breaking eye contact with Maity when she spoke. She was a good-looking woman, had sharp features and dark kohl-lined eyes. She had probably brought the packet as a gift for Maity, but had not handed it over to him yet.

'I have the deplorable habit of going to bed quite late,' Maity said with a shake of his head. 'So there's no need for an apology, Miss . . . '

'Sengupta,' the lady said, 'Mrs Mitali Sengupta.'

'Pleased to make your acquaintance, madam. This is my dear friend, Prakash Ray. He is an author.'

The lady nodded a brief greeting at me and then fell silent. Usually, when someone comes to know of my profession, they ask me about my books. She didn't. Something was obviously bothering her, but she wasn't able to express it. Perhaps she was finding it difficult to choose her words.

'Oh!' she finally seemed to remember, 'I got this for you. I run a small boutique bakery on Lower Circular Road. Just a few cookies and muffins.'

Maity accepted the packet, held it close to his face and sniffed it. A warm smile appeared on his lips and he thanked the lady profusely.

'How can I help you, Mrs Sengupta?' Maity said.

'Mr Maity, I've come to seek your help regarding a rather serious matter related to my husband.'

I glanced at Maity to find the smile still playing on his lips. He was obviously impressed by the courtesy with which the lady was speaking to him, as opposed to the haughty tone of our previous visitor.

'You see, my husband is a doctor. He has his clinic near Triangular Park. We were married around five years ago. We met at a common friend's party, and we developed an instant liking for each other. After a few months of dating, we decided to get married. By God's grace, it's been a happy five years, Mr Maity. We've had our ups and downs—his practice, my store—you know how these things are. But we've stood by each other at all times. Without exception, we have. And like any other couple, we've shared our deepest, darkest secrets with each other. He . . . he is a good man, Mr Maity . . . a sincere, hardworking man. A family man. He doesn't have any bad habits, and he thinks the world of me. He is also very emotional by nature. In fact, it wouldn't be incorrect to say that between the two of us, I am the one with the greater mental strength. He is more reserved, an introvert, a man of few words, a man driven primarily by instincts and emotions, and easily moved by them. But he has a kind and gentle nature. I have never seen him speaking to someone with a raised voice. He is a . . . a good man, Mr Maity . . . a *genuinely* good man.'

The lady said this much and stopped. The grandfather clock in the corner of Maity's drawing room was a silent one, which was why, other than the whirring of the ceiling fan and the faint swishes and honks of late-night traffic coming in through the window from the side of Elgin Road, there was no other sound in the room. Maity was staring at the lady fixedly. She had lowered her own gaze and was hesitating to say her next words. Finally, she seemed to summon all her courage and raised her head.

'My husband is about to commit a grave crime, Mr Maity,' she said, with a hint of desperation in her voice. 'And I've come to you, hoping that you would stop him.'

Maity remained silent for a few seconds and then said in a gentle voice, 'May I request you to be a little more specific, madam? What is the nature of this crime that you fear your husband is about to commit?'

'Murder, Mr Maity!' Mitali Sengupta's voice trembled a little. 'I'm afraid my husband is about to commit murder!'

For several seconds, no one spoke. Mrs Sengupta had gone back to fidgeting with her fingers nervously. Her entire demeanour had changed. Suddenly, she looked more anxious than she had previously seemed, as if she had shed her skin and the real person behind the mask of composure had stepped out in front of us. I expected Maity to say something or offer her a word of comfort. He didn't.

'In order to give you more details,' Mrs Sengupta finally said, 'I will have to tell you the entire background—and . . . I'm not sure . . . I mean . . . it's a long story.'

'As I told you, madam,' Maity said in a reassuring voice, 'I go to bed well past midnight, and so does my friend Prakash here. Please feel free to continue.'

Mrs Sengupta hurriedly finished the tea that Mahadev had served, the cup rattling against the saucer between her sips. Then she placed both on the table in front of her and said, 'It all began twenty years ago. You see, my husband grew up in a small tea estate called Manikpur, and he—'

'*Mahadev!*'

I had just raised my own cup of tea to my lips, and I almost choked on it. And almost immediately, in a bid to distract Mrs Sengupta from noticing my reaction, Maity called out to Mahadev, drew his attention to the fact that it had begun to rain and asked him to shut the window on the far wall.

I had gathered myself together by then, but my mind was still in a whirl. What were the odds? What were the odds of something like this happening?

'I apologize for the most unfortunate interruption, madam,' said Maity, as he turned back to the lady. 'Pray continue.'

After a moment's hesitation, the lady began again:

'Manikpur is a tea estate in the Dooars and my husband grew up there. My father-in-law was a clerk in the estate's office—he used to take care of the wages, pensions and gratuities for the labourers and other staff. As a young boy, my husband used to be very wild and mischievous. He and his gang of friends used to be so naughty that people of the village grew fed up with their antics. They would complain to my father-in-law, who would in turn rebuke him. But no amount of chiding would drive even a shred of sense into him. He would steal fruits and flowers from the neighbours' gardens, free the hens from their coops, draw caricatures of his teachers on the class blackboard . . . you know . . . the usual. But despite all of this, he always used to top his class— every single year, without exception. He had a sharp mind, he used to take part in the school plays and was a brilliant athlete too. He had lost his mother at birth, and my father-in-law had brought him up almost single-handedly. He was very close to his father, and was a happy and cheerful child. But when he was thirteen years old, something happened that changed his life forever. His . . . his father was found hanging by the neck from the branch of a tree outside the village. People said he had killed himself. But my husband knew that he had been murdered. Murdered by a man against whom he had raised his voice. A powerful man. A ruthless man who wouldn't bat an eyelid while removing every single obstacle from his way—including anyone who dared to stand up to his atrocities. It was this man who had my father-in-law killed, and then hung his corpse from a tree, making it look like suicide. That incident changed my husband forever. He couldn't bear the shock. The bright, jovial boy he was known to be was gone forever. What remained were the flames of an intense fire—a burning desire to avenge his father's death.

'For twenty years, my husband has burnt in this desire. Sometimes . . . sometimes I myself am afraid of him. There are days when he sits quietly for hours on end, without saying anything, without moving. Sometimes, I wake up in the middle of the night, only to find him sitting by the side of the bed, staring out of the window into the darkness of the night. Those are the days when I hardly recognize my husband. Those are the days when it seems as if a monster is living in my house. But there are days when he can be the gentlest, most caring soul one has ever met. An out-and-out gentleman; kind, caring, compassionate. I've been living with this dichotomy night and day for the last five years, Mr Maity. But so far, it was all restricted to embracing the man I had met at that party and cautiously keeping the monster at bay. To shower him with so much love that he would forget the scar that his father's death had left on his impressionable mind. And I did everything I could, believe me—as a wife, as a friend, I gave him all my love. And . . . and I'd begun to think that it was all over, that it was all behind us. Because I was seeing less and less of the man I was scared of, and more and more of the calm and soft-spoken man I had fallen in love with. He was happy, and so was I. But a few days ago, I realized I was grossly mistaken.

'A few weeks ago, my husband suddenly called me from his clinic one evening and said that he had something important to share with me. Something that couldn't wait and something that he did not want to discuss at home. I shut the store early that evening, picked him up from his clinic and we went for dinner. It was then that he told me that he was not alone. It was then that he told me about his three friends.'

Mitali Sengupta paused for a few seconds to catch her breath. There was a strange terror in her eyes—as if she was witnessing something horrific happening right in front of her, in this very room. Her beautiful eyes had widened even further, and her lips were trembling. She gave a slight shiver, which seemed to bring her out of her trance. Maity was silent. So was I. The rain was lashing away at the windowpanes, and I suddenly felt a strange chill, which could not possibly have been because of the weather.

'Imagine, Mr Maity,' she said, 'four friends. Four young boys, each scarred by a childhood incident that one man was responsible for—the same man, the devil, the beast. He who had ruined the lives of four innocent boys forever. One, whose father was killed and left hanging from the high branches of a tree. The second, whose sister's modesty was violated by the bastard. The third, whose mother was accused of a crime she did not commit—an accusation that drove her to take her own life. And the fourth: a little boy who was sexually abused by the devil himself, and who was found lying unconscious in the middle of the woods.'

'Who is this devil you speak of, madam?' Maity asked.

'Jagat Narayan Chowdhury,' Mrs Sengupta's voice sounded cold. 'He is the owner of the Manikpur Tea Estate.'

Maity and I exchanged quick glances. With a meaningful glance of his eyes, Maity prohibited me from saying anything about the evening's other visitor.

'All these four friends had, in one way or the other, been harmed by the same vile man,' Mitali Sengupta went on. 'He had destroyed their lives forever—plucked out their innocence in an instant. But they were young kids—these four boys—barely into their teens. What could they do at that tender age, when even the grown-ups weren't able to raise their voice against Chowdhury? Who would listen to them? Who would believe them? So, they did something unthinkable. They got together and took a vow: that twenty years later, no matter which part of the world they were in, they would return to Manikpur, and they would avenge the crimes that Jagat Narayan Chowdhury had committed against them and their families. And that they would do so . . . by ending his life.'

Maity was silent for the longest period of time; he seemed deep in thought. A thunderbolt cracked its whip somewhere pretty close by, but Maity seemed unmoved by its proximity. 'Did you not know this story before that evening?' he finally asked.

'I knew about my father-in-law's death,' Mrs Sengupta replied. 'I even knew about Chowdhury and his role in it. But I did not know about this . . . this pact between my husband and his friends.'

'And what was your reaction when you came to know of it?'

'I tried to stop him, of course. I explained to him that although I respected his emotions, what he was trying to do could potentially destroy him and everything we had built as a family—our lives, our careers, our home—everything. I told him that even if he were to avenge his father's death, it wouldn't change anything: it wouldn't bring his father back, or the years he himself had spent in misery.'

'And what did he say to that?' Maity asked in a calm yet grave voice.

'He didn't seem to understand. He told me that it was this desire for revenge that had kept him alive all these years. He told me that had it not been for this one goal, he would have been dead long ago. He said that he didn't expect me to understand but that he would have to do it anyway. And he said that come hell or high water, he would kill the man.

Nothing, he said, nothing could stop him, and that his whole life, all his years of struggle as an orphan, all the hardships and humiliations that he faced after his father's death, everything had been building up to this one point, this one moment, and he was not going to back out.'

Maity fell silent again. From the way he was cracking his knuckles, he seemed quite worried. I bet he was thinking about the intruder who had tried to get into Mr Chowdhury's bedroom a few days ago. Could it be one of these four friends? Mrs Sengupta's husband, perhaps? Or were these two totally unrelated incidents? I somehow didn't think so.

'Where is your husband now, madam?' Maity asked.

'That's what, Mr Maity,' Mrs Sengupta said desperately, 'that's the reason I mentioned right at the beginning of our conversation that the matter was urgent. You see, my husband already left for Manikpur a week ago. And as far as I know, so have his friends.'

[3]

The next day was a Thursday. Maity called in the afternoon to let me know that we were going to Manikpur. Trains were booked out, so we would have to take a Friday morning flight to Bagdogra, which was the nearest airhead. A car would be waiting for us at Bagdogra airport; Manikpur was a little over 150 km from there—a distance that we hoped to cover in about three and a half hours.

'The winters can get really chilly in those parts,' Maity said on the call. 'But it will be pleasant now. Pack light, because our accommodation has not been arranged yet.'

We met directly at Dum Dum Airport on Friday morning and learnt that our flight was on time. Mrs Sengupta had come to the airport to see us off. Before she bade us farewell, she walked up to Maity and said, 'I can't thank you enough for doing this, Mr Maity. And I'm sure you will appreciate why I didn't want to go to the police with this. I hope you will keep it that way, for my sake.'

'Rest assured, madam,' Maity said, 'I will handle the matter with the discretion it deserves.'

Mrs Sengupta handed over a sealed envelope to Maity and said, 'Please keep this with you. I have written down the names of the other three men that I spoke of last night, along with all the details I could remember about them from my conversations with my husband. I have also kept a photograph of my husband in the envelope. I . . . I'm sorry, but I don't know how else to help you in the matter.'

'Don't worry, this should be enough for now.' Maity kept the envelope in his pocket and said, 'Oh, by the way, what is your husband's name, Mrs Sengupta?'

'Prabhat,' said Mrs Sengupta, 'Dr Prabhat Sengupta.'

Maity stared at the lady's helpless face and said in a soft, gentle voice, 'Prabhat! What a beautiful name!'

Mrs Sengupta's eyes welled up in an instant, and she lowered her head to hide her tears. Maity placed a soft, reassuring hand on her shoulder and promised that he would bring her husband back to her safe and sound. Then we bade her goodbye, made our way through security and boarded our flight. It was a short flight—just a little over an hour—and Maity spent the entire duration scrutinizing the contents of the envelope. Although I was sitting two seats away from him, with the middle seat empty, I could barely read the notes Mrs Sengupta had made, but I did manage to take a close look at her husband's photograph, when Maity handed it over to me. Dr Prabhat Sengupta seemed like a calm and reserved gentleman, with broad shoulders, a square jaw and an upright posture, along with neatly parted hair and a soft smile on his lips. There was something very remarkable about his eyes: they had a twinkle of intelligence in them and lent a certain dignity to his personality. Maity himself stared at the photograph for a long time, until the captain announced that we were about to begin our descent.

'What made you change your mind, Maity?' I asked, as we buckled ourselves in. 'Why did you decide to take the case after all?'

'Two reasons, Prakash. One, from everything that Mohan Sharma had told us, there was no way to tell if there was indeed any credible threat to his employer's life. But now, things have changed, and we must—'

'Wait, I don't understand,' I interrupted him. 'Someone did break into the old man's bedroom in the bungalow, right?'

'Yes, but like I said, that could have been an ordinary thief.'

'But didn't Mohan Sharma say that there's nothing valuable in that room? Nor there ever was?'

'Well,' Maity folded his tray table and said, 'let's just say that Mohan Sharma's logical faculties aren't the best in the business. Granted, there were never any valuables kept in that room—now or in the past. But an ordinary thief isn't supposed to know that, is he?'

I thought for a few seconds and said, 'I see your point. But . . . what about the knife?'

Maity put Mrs Sengupta's envelope into his shirt pocket and said: 'It is not unlikely for a thief to carry a knife. Especially when he is entering a house where there is a guard patrolling the compound.'

'So, you are sure that the intruder hadn't come in with the intention of getting to Chowdhury?'

'No, I'm not sure about that at all. What I am sure of, though, is that one should not reject the possibility that it could have been a thief too, and that he had no intention to harm the old man. That's a possibility that Sharma and his boss seem to be in a hurry to rule out. And there can be only two reasons for doing so: either they are downright daft, which is highly unlikely, or . . .'

'Or,' I chipped in, 'they really believe that the intruder wanted to harm Chowdhury.'

'Correct!' Maity said. 'And under what circumstances do you think they would believe so?'

'If they are afraid?'

'Exactly!' Maity nodded his head. 'Fear! The lifelong companion of a man who has blood on his hands.'

I frowned, 'But Maity, how do we know that Mitali Sengupta is telling us the truth?'

'Excellent point, Prakash. Right now, we don't. Mitali Sengupta could be lying, or her husband could have lied to her, or maybe they were right, and it was Sharma who painted a rather saintly picture of Jagat Narayan Chowdhury before us—there is simply no way to know for sure. We'll get more clarity on this when we get there, on ground zero, and dig into the past. But what is important to note is that up until Mitali Sengupta spoke to us about her husband and his three friends, I wasn't sure if there was a genuine threat to Chowdhury's life. But now, we know for sure that his life is in danger. That's a fact that is beyond any doubt, as of now. And sitting at home doing nothing about it is out of the question.'

'Agreed,' I nodded. 'And the second reason? What else made you change your mind and take up the case?'

Maity was seated next to the window. He stared out of it at the white carpet of clouds beneath us and murmured his next few words: 'There's something very unique about this case, Prakash. On the face of it, it looks like an ordinary series of events, and not without good reason. In all our adventures so far, a crime was committed and we had no idea who the culprit was, and we had to solve a complicated puzzle and make a number of deductions to get to the murderer. Here, we already know who the potential perpetrators are, and all we need to do is to stop them from committing the crime. That's all there is to it, really. It is—what one might call—a straightforward problem. And therein lies the challenge.'

'But aren't straightforward crimes the easiest to solve?' I asked.

Maity shook his head and said, 'Easiest to *solve*, perhaps, but not necessarily the easiest to *prevent*. Think about it for a second: how would we go about preventing Jagat Narayan Chowdhury's murder?'

'Well, it shouldn't be too difficult now, right? All we need to do is to speak to the four potential murderers and warn them that we know of their intentions and that we would be watching them.'

Maity turned to me and smiled. 'So, for instance, if we walk up to Dr Sengupta and tell him that we know everything about him, and that we have our eyes on him, will that dissuade him from committing the crime that his beloved wife of five years has not been able to talk him out of?'

I didn't have a suitable response to Maity's question.

'No, Prakash,' Maity shook his head slowly, 'doing such a thing can only delay the catastrophe, it cannot prevent it. It is not merely difficult, it is nearly impossible to talk him out of it, let alone the other three men—about whom we know hardly anything so far.'

I considered the situation for a minute or so. Then I said, 'What if we try to approach the problem from the other side? What if we try to protect Chowdhury from these men? You know, keep him from harm's way? In a safe place?'

'How long do you intend to do that?' Maity asked. Once again, I didn't have a suitable response to his question, and I began to see the real difficulty of the situation.

'There is no expiration date to the vow these four men have taken, my friend,' Maity sounded concerned. 'You see, revenge is a strange thing. Let's say you're walking down the road and a cyclist comes and hits you from behind. Your first reaction is to hit back at him, right? But let's say you can't get to him at that moment, let's say he runs away. What do you do then? You still keep fuming, and in your mind, you still harbour ill-will against him. But as the days go by, and then the weeks and the months, your thirst for vengeance slowly begins to die down, as more important things in your life begin to take precedence and priority. Time heals your wounds—those to your body, as well as those to your mind. But you must understand that what these four friends have gone through is no ordinary misery. If we assume everything that Mitali Sengupta has told us to be true, then what these four men are harbouring in their hearts is not just vengeance—it is something far more dangerous than that. It is an obsession: an utterly unhealthy one. One that is destroying them—all four of them—from the inside, bit by bit. Twenty years, Prakash! Not a joking matter! If those little boys have not forgotten in twenty years, then no matter how much you and I try to dissuade them, they are not going to listen to us. Nor can the police do anything, because they haven't really committed a crime yet.'

'But isn't the intent to commit murder a punishable crime in itself? I asked.

'It is, but only if that intent can be proved beyond reasonable doubt. There is no way to establish such intent in this case, unless the murderer or murderers are caught red-handed in the act.'

'Yes, of course.'

'So, you see the problem? Introducing ourselves to these four men as someone who is aware of their intentions is not going to help us in any way—this way or the other. It is merely going to make them put off their plans, or—worse still—put them on their guard. And we cannot wait around indefinitely. Whereas they can.'

'Gosh!' I exclaimed. 'I hadn't really thought of all this so far. On the face of it, it seemed like a simple problem. But now, it almost seems like our hands and feet are tied behind our backs and our eyes are blindfolded! What are we going to do, Maity?'

Maity remained silent for some time, and then said, 'That's an interesting simile you've used there, my friend.' He smiled and said, 'And we are going to do exactly what we *could* do if our hands and feet were indeed tied behind our backs, and our eyes were blindfolded.'

'And what is that?'

Maity stared out of the window and said, 'We are going to *think*!'

And at that exact moment, Air India's flight AI-721 touched down on the runway with an awkward jolt, and I realized we had reached Bagdogra.

[4]

Maity had arranged for a car, and it was waiting for us at the airport. The driver was a dapper young lad, probably from the hills, clad in a Stanford University sweatshirt, denim jeans and a greaser cap. Every time he smiled, his eyelids almost shut in on themselves, and there was a toothpick constantly dancing between his lips. He said his name was Pele, and when asked where he was from, he simply said, 'Darj'. We later learnt that he had left his home in the hills several years ago and now lived in a town bordering the Manikpur Tea Estate itself. Maity had this habit of striking up conversations with local people to get a general idea of the place. From Pele, we learnt that the faint blue zigzag outlines in the northern horizon were nothing but the Himalayas— the hills of Kurseong, to be precise. I looked at the majestic mountains and marvelled at their mind-numbing stature. Even from such a great distance, it seemed to me that those hills were grand and regal—standing like silent but watchful sentries, towering over the fertile plains below since the dawn of time. I had never been to this part of the country and I soon realized what I had missed. Bagdogra Airport was just outside the city of Siliguri, and soon after we had left the cacophony of urban traffic behind, a soothing effect began to descend upon me. The road ran through vast empty fields that rolled away towards the horizon on both sides. I turned around once to realize that we were leaving the hills behind and moving away from them. There were signs of rural Bengal spread all around us—the abundance of plantain, papaya and betel nut trees, dense bamboo groves next to green algae-filled ponds, large stacks of hay, thatched-roof and clay-wall houses, and amidst all these, the incongruous presence of tall microwave towers standing in a row. Maity was right. The open fields and the fresh air had already begun to calm my nerves, lending clarity to my mind and invigorating me with a renewed sense of purpose. But the real surprise was still to come.

We travelled for several hours; the sun was setting behind the woods towards the west and my eyelids had begun to droop. I must have dozed off, when suddenly, a soft nudge from Maity's elbow woke me up. I opened my eyes and looked outside, and it almost felt like I was hit by a sudden rush of green. As far as my eyes could see, there was a lush green carpet spread all the way to the dense treeline towards the west. The carpet was not on the ground though, it was a few feet above it, and there were tall trees popping out of it here and there. I realized we had reached the tea gardens. The sight was so beautiful, so comforting, that I simply couldn't take my eyes off it, nor could I say anything by way of an explanation. Maity told me that the tea plant was actually a shrub, and that it needed two extremely important things to flourish. The first was shade—that's what the taller trees were for, in fact they were called 'shade trees'. And the second was water—running water—that would not stand or collect at the shrubs' bases. Which was why, Maity pointed out, there were ridges dug out between the beds of the shrubs, so that rainwater could flow out of the garden without stagnating.

'Two leaves and a bud,' Maity said, as he pointed towards a group of local women whom I now saw moving around in the middle of the gardens. 'That's what constitutes the perfect pluck. That's what the pluckers aim for.'

'Two leaves and a bud!' I muttered, as I watched the women pluck the leaves and buds with their nimble fingers and fling them over their shoulders into the bags on their backs in a swift, rhythmic motion. 'How beautiful! Isn't there a song by that name?'

'Yes,' Maity replied, 'by Bhupen Hazarika. And not just a song, there's also a novel by that name by Mulk Raj Anand.'

I looked out of the window towards the other side of the road. This was the east—this side had become dark by now, the sky over the shade trees had turned slate-grey. The sky towards the west still had hints of pink remaining. The women on the eastern side of the road had stopped plucking and were now busy tying up their bags securely. Maity explained that they would now hike back to the trucks parked nearby, where their bags would be weighed and payments made. I was marvelling at the beauty of the scenery all around me when our car took a right turn and entered through a large unmanned iron gate with the name 'Manikpur Tea Estate' written on the rusty archway.

Maity instructed the driver to head straight towards the owner's bungalow. The young chap seemed to know the place like the back of his hand. We kept a small white single-storeyed building (which seemed like the local school, because there was a large field with goalposts just in front of it) towards our left and moved forward. After around ten minutes or so, we reached the estate's factory. It was a massive building, albeit old, and there was a steady mechanical hum emanating from within its compound. The hum was quite loud because we could hear it even over the sound of our car's engine, and there were thin clouds of smoke billowing out of the twin chimneys towering above the factory. There were at least a dozen small trucks and vans parked along the walls of the factory, and their netted carriages were all full of tea leaves. Maity glanced at these trucks and said: 'We seem to have come in the middle of the plucking season, isn't it, Pele?'

'Yes, sir,' came the reply, 'mid-March to early December is when the plucking happens. And maintenance is done from December to March. But production is low this time.'

'Why?' Maity asked.

Pele's response came a trifle late. It seemed like he was hesitating to answer that specific question. 'The owner has grown old. There's no one to look after the business. The gardens are not in good condition.'

'Isn't there a manager?'

'There is one. Rafiq sahib. Good man. Lives in the manager's bungalow over there, with his family. Rafiq sahib works very hard, tries his best. But . . . '

'But what?'

'I don't know, sir. Things are in bad shape. There are rumours in the village that the owner hasn't given manager sahib enough freedom to take care of the gardens in his own way. Too much interference. Rafiq sahib is a good man. Kind, gentle. Very loyal. Had it been anyone else, he would have run away long ago. Not him.'

'What's the owner Mr Chowdhury like? Is he a kind man too?'

Once again, the response came after some delay. We had left the tarred road behind, and the unpaved path ahead was rather bumpy. Having successfully dodged a basketball-sized rock lying nonchalantly in the middle of the path, Pele said: 'No one becomes rich and powerful by being kind, sir. Many rumours in the gardens. You are city people, intelligent people, you know how things are. I just drive this taxi, ferry passengers. Manikpur to airport, airport to Manikpur. I do my job, keep my mouth shut and eyes on the road.'

'Has anyone come from the airport to Manikpur in the last week or so?' Maity asked. 'Any gentleman in his mid-thirties or so?'

'Lot of people come and go, sir. I myself have to drive to airport at least three to four times a week. Lot of forests nearby. Chilapata, Gorumara, Jaldapara. Lot of tourists. Sometimes people come to the gardens too. To relax. Or click photos.'

'How about this man?' Maity raised his hand and held up the photograph of Dr Sengupta in a straight line from the rear-view mirror. Pele glanced at the mirror and said, 'Oh, this gentleman? Yes, he came six or seven days ago. He came via Bagdogra, but I did not drive him here. He must have taken a taxi from the airport itself. Gopal's Innova—eighty-four twenty-seven. I saw them on my way to the airport, they had stopped for tea.'

'Was there anyone else with him?' Maity asked.

'No, just him.'

'Did you stop there for tea yourself?'

'No, I was passing by. Had a passenger with me. Had to catch the 6.30 p.m. flight to Delhi.'

Maity smiled and said, 'Then how did you know that this man in the photograph was alone? Someone could have been with him.'

'No, not possible.'

'How can you be so sure?'

'Because I saw him board the cab and leave. No one was with him. Except the driver.'

Maity glanced at me and smiled. 'I see! You seem like an intelligent young man. In fact, I have an offer for you.'

The toothpick in Pele's lips stopped dancing for a second or two. He eyed Maity in the rear-view mirror and said, 'Offer?'

Maity pointed towards me and said: 'You see this gentleman here? He is a famous writer. He writes novels, his name is Prakash Sir. He wants to write his next novel based on a tea garden. So, he and I have come here to Manikpur; we'll stay here for a few days. He wants to see the place, understand the setting, interact with the locals, make notes. We'll probably do quite a bit of walking, but it would help to have a car around as well. Would you be willing to stay with us for these few days? Prakash Sir will pay you, of course.'

As Pele inspected me with narrowed eyes in the rear-view mirror, I cleared my throat and tried to summon a writerly look to my face. It was a decidedly uncomfortable situation, but thankfully, the moment passed sooner than I had expected.

'Will cost you quite a bit,' Pele finally said. 'I drive to airport, four times, sometimes five times a week. It's 165 km, each way. Diesel is—'

'Don't worry about money,' Maity interrupted him with a smile, 'Prakash Sir is a very successful author.'

I sighed, and before Maity could say anything else to embarrass me any further, Pele shot his next question without taking his eyes off the road, 'The man in the photo is a character in your novel?'

Smart guy!

Maity was unperturbed. 'You could say that, yes,' he said calmly.

Pele didn't say anything further. We drove on. It was almost dark by now, but Pele had still not switched on the headlights. Having lived in the city all my life, I was not accustomed to this kind of eerie darkness. It was a moonless night. There were fireflies glowing in the shrubs and bushes, and some of them seemed to have made their way up to the sky and permanently lodged themselves into the jet-black firmament. As far as my eyes could see, the narrow, unpaved path stretched out—bifurcating the garden into two. The hum of the factory had died down, and far towards the left, there were one or two lights twinkling in the dark. Pele pointed in that direction and remarked that the original village of Manikpur was where the lights were coming from. The garden, apparently, had been named after the village, not the other way around.

We reached Jagat Narayan Chowdhury's bungalow in a few more minutes. It was a massive two-storeyed British manor–type building, standing in a large compound that had been fenced by a thick and tall hedge on all sides. I looked around and reached the conclusion that it would be an exceedingly simple affair for someone to make their way either through or over the hedge in order to reach the compound. Maity gave our names to the chowkidar at the gate and asked him to inform Mohan Sharma that we were here.

In less than two minutes, the chowkidar opened the teakwood gates and our taxi rolled in. We drove over a narrow. cobblestoned path running through what seemed like a large lawn and moved towards the main bungalow. Mohan Sharma had himself come down to the portico to receive us. Clearly, he was not expecting us; that was obvious as much from the look of pleasant surprise on his face as from the scarlet dressing gown he was wearing over his cotton pyjamas.

'Oh, Mr Maity!' he said, beaming as he shook Maity's hand, 'I can't tell you how relieved I am to see you!'

'Mr Sharma, I'll be quick,' Maity said in a direct, matter-of-fact manner. 'I have reason to believe that your employer's life may indeed be in danger after all. I want you to step up his security without any delay, and I want you to ensure that no outsiders are allowed to visit him, under any circumstances whatsoever.'

'What's the matter, Mr Maity?' Sharma looked worried. 'Is everything all right?'

'So far, yes, everything *is* all right,' Maity said. 'But I'm not sure how long things will remain that way. Please do not ask me how I know this. If you want me to help him, then you will have to listen to what I say. Where is he right now?'

'He is in his cabin, by the pond. Why?'

'I would advise you to go to him right this instant, and ensure that he remains indoors. I recall your mentioning that he has a personal butler who lives with him?'

'Yes.'

'Can this man be trusted?'

'Oh yes, very much so. Charan has been with Mr Chowdhury for more than thirty years now.'

'All right, good. Tell the butler that he is not to let anyone into the cabin under any circumstances. Certainly not without speaking to you. I can see that the cellular networks can't be trusted around here. Is there a medium of communication between the cabin and the bungalow?'

'Yes, there's a phone—a landline.'

'That'll be useful,' Maity nodded. 'Please keep in touch with the cabin at regular intervals. In fact, it would be best to shift Mr Chowdhury to the bungalow for a few days.'

'He wouldn't come, Mr Maity, we've tried. Perhaps you could persuade him?'

Maity hesitated for a few seconds and then said, 'In the beginning, it is best not to tell Mr Chowdhury that I'm in Manikpur. In fact, it would be best not to reveal the purpose of my visit to anyone in Manikpur at the moment, not even to the local police.'

'Very well. But where would you be staying?'

'I'll figure something out. The driver was mentioning a lodge outside the estate.'

'A decidedly run-down place,' Mohan Sharma said firmly. 'Nothing doing. You've come so far to help us, you will stay at our guest house.'

'But Mr Sharma . . .' Maity protested.

'Mr Maity,' Mohan Sharma took a step closer to us and lowered his voice. 'Do not, for one moment, believe that I am not aware of my employer's flaws. I didn't get a chance to do so the other night, but I apologize to you now—for whatever happened. It is my sincere request to you; please stay at the estate's guest house. It is a beautiful little cottage, built during the days of the Raj, and recently renovated, and it's not too far from here either. I'll send my man with you. He'll take care of everything.'

Maity and I glanced at each other. 'All right, since you insist,' Maity said, 'but we have our own car with us, so you needn't worry about sending anyone. And please ensure that Mr Chowdhury's safety is taken care of. I cannot stress the importance of this enough.'

Having said this much, Maity and I went back to the car. Pele knew where the guest house was, and Mohan Sharma said that he would ring up the caretaker right away and make all necessary arrangements. After bidding Mohan Sharma goodnight and promising to meet him at 9 the next morning, we set off for the guest house. On the way, Maity asked Pele if he could find out where the gentleman in the photograph was staying.

'Only one place to stay for outsiders,' Pele said, 'Green View Lodge. Not a comfortable place to stay, as the gentleman was saying. Food not good. Bed full of bugs. Water problem. But in daytime, you open window and look out of room— view very green.'

'Aren't there any hotels nearby?'

'Of course! Just 95 km away.'

I was wondering how long we would have to stay in Manikpur and put up with our driver's sarcastic sense of humour, but from the smile on Maity's face, it seemed he had found the fellow quite interesting and was enjoying the conversations with him.

In three of the four directions around us, everything was just a black mass of darkness. Up ahead, the headlight beams of our car had managed to illuminate only a scant portion of the unpaved, pebble-covered path. Maity explained to me that the pebbles had been strewn so that the path would not become muddy during the rains. Thanks to the pebbles, which were constantly slipping under the tyres, we could not go too fast.

But despite the slow speed, the ride lasted for less than fifteen minutes. When our car stopped in the compound of the guest house, a shiver ran through my spine only to imagine that we would have to stay *here* for as long as we were in Manikpur. Not that the cottage was old or dilapidated. On the contrary, as Mohan Sharma had rightly claimed, the pretty little building did seem to have gone through a recent bout of renovation. The compound too was quite large and there was a lovely little lawn in one corner, complete with a swing and a flower garden. But the surroundings of the cottage were so desolate, so dark, that it gave me the chills to think that we would have to spend our nights here.

'What godforsaken place have we come to, Maity?' I remarked, as I stared at the guest house, from which the caretaker had come running to carry our luggage in. 'Are we in the middle of the forest or something? There's not a single speck of light anywhere around.'

'Are you sure?'

On hearing Maity's words, I turned around to look at him, and found him staring in a certain direction. Following his gaze, I looked into the dark, and after a few seconds of searching, much to my surprise, saw a few unsteady glimmers of light in the distance.

'Is that the . . .?'

'Yes, it is.'

By now, my eyes had adjusted a bit more to the all-enveloping darkness around me. And I saw a barbed-wire fence on the boundary of the guest house's compound. Beyond the fence, for several hundred yards, there was total darkness. But once I squinted my eyes and looked a bit farther, I could see a two-storey building standing next to a large tree. Unlike Jagat Narayan Chowdhury's bungalow, or this guest house, there was nothing British about the building. Even from a distance, one could clearly see that it had been built several years after our former rulers had left this country.

Pele raised his hand, pointed towards the building and said, 'Green View Lodge.'

He needn't have said it. On the roof of the building was a tacky, cheaply drawn signboard, announcing the name of the establishment under the ever-shifting glow of a solitary, inadequate, soot-covered tube light that was constantly flickering. And beneath the signboard, there was a row of windows with low-power electric lights burning inside them. It didn't take me much time to realize that they were the rooms of the lodge, and that they were all occupied.

All four of them.

[5]

The next morning, much to my surprise, I woke up quite late. And that too only when Maity shook me by my shoulder.

'Get up, Prakash,' he said, 'we need to go meet Mohan Sharma.'

I sat up on my bed and took a minute or so to find my bearings. The guest house had all of two bedrooms, with an interconnecting door between them. Maity had offered me the large one, and taken the smaller one for himself. It was an old rest-house-style cottage—small but tidy—with high ceilings, carved doorways and a lovely little fireplace in the hall. Even the furniture seemed quite ancient, and perhaps bore memories of many visits by erstwhile British merchants who had come to this beautiful land wanting to make a fortune out of one of the most-loved beverages in the world.

Sitting by the edge of the bed, I recalled last night's dinner. It had been served in the sparsely decorated and dimly lit dining room of the guest house, and had been a rather simple affair—thanks perhaps to the fact that we were not exactly expected. Maity had eaten to his heart's content, and remarked that because of the sweet groundwater and the fresh oxygen all around, our appetite was bound to have gone up by several notches. I too had found the meal decidedly delicious, although it had constituted simply of rice, dal, spring onion fry and a thinly running curry of green papaya.

I have often noticed that those living in rural or sparsely populated areas prefer to use very dim lighting at nights. This is perhaps because they are used to the darkness around them and cannot stand bright lights. We city folks, on the other hand, are habituated to living amidst glaring lights, and our eyes are attuned to them, which is why, when we come to places such as Manikpur, everything looks poorly lit and mysterious after nightfall. Last night too, I could barely find my way around the bedroom. As I looked around me now, I caught a better glimpse of the room and its surroundings. There were birds chirping right outside my window—I heard a cuckoo, a mynah and even a *koel*. A slanting beam of sunlight had found its way into the room through the open window and fallen on a portion of the mosaic floor. There was no cacophony of traffic, no din of people rushing to work, no yelling or jostling in public transportation or any other clamour of any kind. Just a sweet and soothing silence—wondrous in its permanence—interspersed only by the occasional chirping of my avian neighbours. If I were to be perfectly honest, I had an intense urge to immediately lie down on the comfortable bed, pull the soft comforter over my ears and go back to sleep. But I knew there was work to be done, and that we were not on holiday. Maity's bed was visible through the interconnecting door, and from the neatness of the manner in which it had been arranged, I realized he must have stuck to his habit of rising early even here, in the middle of this blissful ambience. I dragged myself out of bed, and after a quick shave and a refreshing shower, joined Maity in the veranda outside, where he was busy folding the morning's newspaper back to its original state. He responded to my 'good morning' with a bright smile, pointed towards an empty cup on the table next to him and remarked, 'I don't think I will be able to have my regular tea ever again, Prakash.'

Unlike dinner, breakfast was a fairly elaborate affair, and as Maity had correctly pointed out, the tea was absolutely heavenly. But Maity seemed in a hurry and I had no other choice but to rush through my meal too. Pele had arrived on time, just as planned, and without any more delay, we set out for Jagat Narayan Chowdhury's bungalow.

The autumn morning air was fresh and crisp, and although the sun was shining brightly, it wasn't too hot, thanks perhaps to the abundance of trees all around us. Once again, we had to drive at a slow speed, for there was a distinct risk of the tyres skidding over the loose pebbles. The green tea shrubs spread out on both sides of the road for as far as we could see. To the west, they were stopped only by a distant line of trees which looked like pine, but weren't. I knew that beyond those trees was the highway, and on the other side of the highway was the lodge we had seen last night. To the east, the tea garden seemed to stretch out for miles, unhindered, and marked only by the various shade trees rising from here and there: siris, sal, chhatim, horse neem and even the occasional palash and gulmohar.

In daylight, the drive from the guest house to the bungalow didn't seem too long, and we reached in just over ten minutes. Last night, I hadn't had a chance to assess the grandness of the bungalow, but now as the chowkidar saw our car and pulled the gates open, we realized what a majestic piece of architecture stood before us. Such regal buildings were seldom seen these days, and I kept staring at it for the longest time.

But even as I did, a sombre thought crept into my mind and my heart sank. If Mitali Sengupta's words were to be trusted, then all this grandeur, all this opulence, was built on the hopes, dreams and corpses of helpless and innocent people. What stood before me was not just a grandiose building, it was also a symbol of tyranny and oppression.

Mohan Sharma was waiting for us under the portico, and he welcomed us into the bungalow. There was a grim silence inside the building, one that automatically forced us to lower our voices as we spoke. Any sound louder than a murmur immediately echoed back—almost in a frightening rebuke. Although we knew that Jagat Narayan Chowdhury was not living in the bungalow any more, his distinct signature was evident everywhere we looked. For one, the décor of the place was just like Chowdhury—jagged, sparse, unwelcoming, and decidedly joyless and devoid of any warmth whatsoever. Room after room stood like silent silos—their floors bare and hostile, their walls unadorned and their doors too heavy to budge. There was a clear sign of parsimony everywhere, and I wondered: of what use was all the wealth that the owner of the house had amassed all his life, if it hadn't been put to the noble use of bringing joy and happiness to his own abode? A few flower vases were placed here and there, but no flowers were in them. There were no portraits or paintings or wall-hangings of any kind anywhere. The drapes—although heavy and opaque—had clearly not been changed or dusted in a long time. There was a dank gravity inside the place, and everyone—even Mohan Sharma and the rest of the staff—seemed to whisper to each other at all times. What were all these people so frightened of? And how could they live like this for days, weeks, months and years on end? I myself had never seen a home so uninviting and inhospitable as this, one that lacked even the slightest sign of warmth, and I felt stifled and uncomfortable just being in it. And the fact that it was so distasteful despite the owner and resident of the house being one of the most affluent people in this part of the country made it all the more unbearable.

We were ushered into a large sitting room that contained exactly two pieces of furniture: a double sofa and a grandfather-style armchair, both very distant from each other for some unfathomable reason. Offering us the sofa, Mohan Sharma walked across the length of the room and sat on the edge of the armchair with visible difficulty. Even on a bright and beautiful morning such as this, there was an unsettling darkness in the room, and Sharma being at a distance from us, we were having to strain our eyes just to see his face. Maity declined his offer for tea and went straight to the point.

'Have you met Mr Chowdhury this morning?' he asked Mohan Sharma.

'Yes,' replied Sharma. 'His breakfast had been served by the pond, and I met him at the table to get his signature on a few important papers.'

'How is he doing?' Maity probed. 'Is his health all right?'

'Well, he is seventy-nine, you know? He gets by and doesn't complain too much—even if something is bothering him. He considers it a weakness—doing so. He can be extremely difficult that way. Quite arrogant, even. Arrogant, but childlike. Last night, before you arrived, I had gone to see him—to ask if he needed me for anything else or if I could retire for the day. He seemed quite restless at that time; he was finding it difficult to sit at one place and was pacing up and down the room. He was muttering to himself constantly. "Never trust anyone, Mohan," he kept saying, "not even your own shadow. You won't see the arrow before it hits you." He seemed to be in a rather foul mood, to be honest. He was throwing a fuss and yelling at everyone.'

'But you must be used to that, no?'

Maity's habit of asking completely unexpected, extremely abrupt and ruthlessly hard-hitting questions was not unknown to me. But for someone like Mohan Sharma, it must have been quite startling. A long and uncomfortable silence followed, in the duration of which a half-smile denoting both embarrassment and professional dignity floated over Sharma's face. When he finally spoke, his voice was lined with cautious reserve.

'As I have told you before, Mr Maity, my employer is seventy-nine. And men of such age can get a little—'

'Rude?'

Mohan Sharma smiled gently and said in a calm voice, 'Cranky.'

Maity stared at him for some time with his piercing eyes and said, 'When you met me in Kolkata, you mentioned that you have been with Mr Chowdhury for the last six years.'

'That's right.'

'May I ask where were you before you took up this job?'

'Certainly,' said Sharma. 'I was in the employ of Duke Singhania. He was an industrialist. Various businesses, mainly textile.'

'Was?'

'Yes, he passed away towards the end of 2011—suffered a massive stroke while playing golf. I was with him that day, but not on the links. I had a few phone calls to make, so I had stayed back in the club's business centre. By the time we could rush him to the hospital, it was all over.'

'Where did this happen?'

'In the city,' Sharma said, 'Kolkata.'

'I see,' Maity said. 'His sudden death may have caused you a bit of . . . inconvenience?'

'Well, I did fall out of employment, if that's what you mean. And it took me some time to find my next job. But Mr Singhania had always been a careful man—a man of foresight, if one may say so. He had had his will made, and he left me a small sum of money too. When I say "small", I mean small by *his* standards. For me, it was enough to live a comfortable life for several years.'

'But not enough for the rest of your life?' Maity's eyes were watching every gesture Sharma was making, and every emotion that his face struggled to conceal.

'No,' Sharma shook his head with a smile. 'Certainly not. Why else would I take up this job?'

'Why indeed?'

Once again, there was a brief and uncomfortable silence in the room.

'Moreover,' Sharma was the one to break the silence, 'one should never live an idle life, no matter the circumstances. It's never a good idea.'

'An admirable point of view,' Maity remarked. 'One might even argue that like your previous employer, you too are a man of considerable foresight.'

Mohan Sharma remained unperturbed and nodded his head. He smiled lightly and said, 'I see what you are hinting at, Mr Maity. And it's not just you, anyone in their right mind would think the same way. After all, I was in the house on the night the intruder came in. I could have had an accomplice on the outside. And I have been here for just six years.'

Maity didn't say anything.

'But,' Sharma continued, 'think about it for a minute. If I had to steal from Mr Chowdhury, there were far safer options available to me. The rich do not exactly keep their riches stashed under their mattresses, do they, Mr Maity? I didn't have to invite someone to climb the rainwater pipes to get into a room that is practically vacant. That too with a knife in hand.'

'And if you wanted to harm your employer, you would have instructed your accomplice to go to the cabin by the pond, not the house, right?'

Mohan Sharma nodded.

Maity remained silent for some time and said, 'What do you know about your employer's past?'

Mohan Sharma's casual smile seemed to waver, just for the tiniest fraction of a second. After a brief pause, he said, 'I see you've already started making your inquiries. And I must say I am quite impressed. You've only been in Manikpur a little more than twelve hours, after all!'

'The tongue is a slippery serpent, Mr Sharma,' Maity remarked.

Mohan Sharma watched Maity for some time and then said in a calm voice, 'What have you heard?'

Maity stared right back at him and said in an equally calm voice, 'What have you?'

Sharma shook his head, shrugged his shoulders and said, 'One cannot run a business as vast as this without taking some tough decisions, Mr Maity. Sixteen thousand hectares of plantation—not a joking matter! And that's

just Manikpur. There are other gardens too, several of
them. The leprosy may have been a myth, but there are
other, more serious problems facing us every single day.
Pest infestations, leopard attacks, bison attacks, bear
attacks, snakebites, malaria, cholera, fire, sabotage—how
many shall I name? Fifty years ago, the climate in Dooars
was conducive to the cultivation and production of tea.
It isn't any more. Imbeciles in the city are burning holes
through the skies and the planet is all but responding.
But what can we do about it, tell me? Nothing. Do you
know how difficult it has become simply to keep our
books in the green? There is no dearth of demand, mind
you. But how do we keep up our production? How do we
protect the reputation that our brands have earned over
the decades? Which is why, sometimes, one needs to take
some harsh decisions. For the greater good. And can I tell
you something, Mr Maity? If you allow me to be perfectly
honest with you? More than all the problems I mentioned
earlier, there is one problem that has been plaguing not
only the gardens of Manikpur, but all tea plantations,
anywhere in the subcontinent, at all times.'

Maity and I listened to Sharma's impassioned speech.
Although the smile hadn't left his face, it was no longer one
of serenity. There was a twisted disdain in it, one that often
came from a position of privilege.

'Alcohol!' he exclaimed, his voice rising a little. 'Illiteracy
and alcohol have always been a dangerous combination, Mr
Maity. A perfect recipe for vested interests to instil in the
labourers of the garden the fear of an oppression that does
not exist. You'd be surprised to know the lengths to which
my employer has gone to ensure the welfare and well-being

of his labourers. He started as an ordinary employee of this very estate. He was a tea-taster. His job was to taste and grade tea that came from various kinds of leaves, various gardens, that's all, nothing more. But it was his hard work and his knowledge of the local people's needs and aspirations that resulted in his astronomical rise. He was soon promoted to the position of manager—of the entire estate. And when the British left, he bought the estate from them. He built hospitals for the labourers, and schools for their children. He gave them fair wages, a secure future.

'Legend has it that in the 1970s, when the raging waters of the Torsha wreaked havoc in the region, Mr Chowdhury opened the doors of the very bungalow you now sit in and cast insinuations at him—just so that the poor and homeless could take shelter and save their lives. On countless occasions, he has personally picked up his Winchester, jumped into his Jeep and vanished into the depths of the Chilapata forest to go after man-eating leopards and tigers, just to protect the villagers. To this day, villagers sing ballads of the time he had gone all the way into the hills of Bhutan to hunt down a tigress—a Bengal tigress, ten feet from nose to tail—tracking and pursuing her for three days on foot, finally hunting her down and bringing her back to the village of Manikpur, all by himself. People used to worship him, revere him; they would do anything for him. And not without reason—he was their benefactor. He loved them like his own, worked day and night to see that their rights were protected, and that they were taken care of.'

Having said this much, Mohan Sharma stopped, slightly panting to catch his breath. I looked at Maity and found him still observing Sharma.

'As you yourself said, Mr Maity,' Sharma said, after calming down, 'the tongue is indeed a slippery serpent. Which is exactly why it is not to be trusted. An intelligent man like you ought to remember that.'

Even if there was something going on inside Maity's head, it was impossible to know what it was from his facial expressions. He sat up on the sofa and made an effort to change the topic of the discussion: 'You mentioned earlier that Mr Chowdhury had been feeling rather uneasy last night. How is he doing now?'

With some effort, Mohan Sharma brushed his former annoyance aside and forced a smile back on his lips to resume normality. 'He is somewhat better now. He had a very light breakfast, said he didn't have an appetite at all and would rather go back to bed. This was perhaps because of the sedative that was given to him.'

'Sedative?' Maity frowned. 'What sedative?'

'I'm not quite sure what it was. Dr Kishore is the resident physician here at the hospital at Manikpur Estate. He is also Mr Chowdhury's personal physician. He has been—'

'Where can we find him?' Maity interrupted. 'We need to know what's wrong with Mr Chowdhury. And we need to find out right now.'

'Oh, but you can't,' remarked Sharma.

'What do you mean?' the frown on Maity's forehead deepened.

'Dr Kishore had to leave for his home in Bhagalpur to attend to a family matter. He has been gone for almost a week now. Early this morning, when Mr Chowdhury was still feeling sick and we were wondering what to do, we suddenly remembered that there is a doctor who has come from Kolkata for a holiday in the forest. I sent someone to fetch him. He came and checked Mr Chowdhury and said that he needed to rest. It was he who gave Mr Chowdhury the sedative.'

I looked at Maity and saw that his face had turned grave. As my heart began to thump inside my chest, Maity said, 'Where is this doctor now?'

'The doctor?' Mohan Sharma asked. 'Why, he must have gone back to the lodge, of course. The Green View Lodge. He has been staying there for a week now. What was his name, now? Ah yes, one Dr Sengupta.'

[6]

What went on in my mind for the next few minutes—I would never be able to describe. Maity immediately asked if he could do an inspection of Mr Chowdhury's cabin, although I knew he was, in fact, keen to rush to the old man himself, and that too as soon as possible. From the externally calm expression that he wore, it was quite evident that he did not want to tell Mohan Sharma anything about Dr Sengupta's true identity. But having known Maity for some years, I could also tell that he was feeling very restless, because if Dr Sengupta had indeed injected Jagat Narayan Chowdhury with something, there wasn't a single moment to be wasted.

Unfortunately, though, Mohan Sharma knew nothing of this urgency, and was taking his own sweet time to lead us to the cabin, talking about the affairs of the garden instead. Maity could not rush him because doing so would arouse Sharma's suspicions, nor could he sit back and relax in small talk. It was a decidedly tense and nerve-racking moment. Finally, after wasting a lot of time, we stepped out of the house on to the lawns and started walking east. The lawns themselves were beautifully kept, with pretty flowering plants and picturesque trees in abundance all around. But the state

of my mind was such that I could hardly spare a look at
all the flora flourishing around me. Only one question was
hammering inside my head: Had Prabhat Sengupta done
what he had come here to do? Had his mission been
accomplished? There was no way to know until we got to
the cabin. I knew Maity had promised Mitali Sengupta that
he would bring her husband back to her safe and sound. His
grave face was an indicator of the dilemma in his mind. He
had to protect both the victim as well as the killer, and the only
way he could do so was by preventing the murder. I couldn't
think of even one instance in the past when Janardan Maity
had been faced with such a strange and bizarre challenge.

It was a huge compound, and the lawns were vast. Which
made the long walk even more tense. After walking for almost
ten anxious minutes towards the eastern side of the house,
I saw a cabin at a distance, built on the side of a lovely little
pond. Despite my state of mind, I could not help but marvel
at how pretty the cabin looked. This was exactly the kind
of place where one would want to retire, in one's old age.
It was a wooden cabin, slightly raised from the ground on
wooden pillars, and it stood surrounded by several tall trees
that had created a lovely canopy of green over it. This shade,
however, was not uniform, because the foliage was anything
but dense. This resulted in a mesmerizing play of light and
shade on the cabin and its vicinity—an intricate tapestry of
a million designs that were in a constant state of flux as the
branches of the trees swayed in the morning breeze. The
waters of the pond were full of lilies, lotuses and a couple of
other ornamental aquatic plants whose names I did not know.
There were a couple of cane chairs and a cane table placed

on the banks of the pond, with a small cane stool placed next to one of the chairs. Maity shot a glance at the pond and the chairs, and we quickly stepped into the cabin.

A fifty-five-to-sixty-year-old man almost collided with us as we entered what seemed like the hall of the cabin, and from the serving tray in the man's hand, it seemed to me that he was Mr Chowdhury's butler. But there was another, much younger, man standing in the corner of the hall and staring out of the window, and we had no idea who this was.

'Where is he, Charan?' Mohan Sharma asked the butler.

The butler pointed towards the door at the far end of the hall and then made a gesture with his hand and his head which indicated that his master was fast asleep.

'Mr Maity, please meet Mr Rafiq Ali, our estate's most treasured . . .' Mohan Sharma had just begun introducing Maity to the other gentleman in the room, but he was forced to stop short. Because without paying any heed to his words, Maity had already entered the bedroom through the doorway.

My heart racing away, I slowly stepped into the bedroom myself. It was a reasonably large-sized room, with an armchair in one corner, a couple of wardrobes and chests along one of the walls and a large four-poster bed near the window that overlooked the pond. There was a silk mosquito net covering the bed, and the first thing I saw through the fine mesh of the net was Maity's grave face on the other side of the bed. He had hunched down over Jagat Narayan Chowdhury's body, and held his index and middle fingers next to the man's nostrils. Chowdhury looked a far cry from the arrogant and obscenely rude old man who had visited us back in Kolkata. He looked feeble and helpless now. Maity later told me that slumber had the power to make even the deadliest person in the world look like a gentle baby. But my feet were still trembling. Because Chowdhury's body looked too still—too still for comfort. His face was haggard and his mouth was wide open. His long silvery grey hair was unkempt and the locks fell backwards from his wrinkled forehead, because his chin had risen up in the air. The rest of his body was not visible.

Maity's hand came down from his nostrils and grabbed something from the bed. I realized that the eerie, bony thing that Maity had picked up from the bed was Mr Chowdhury's right arm. Maity's fingers were now placed at a specific point on the old man's wrist.

'The breathing's weak,' Maity said in a soft voice. 'So is the pulse. But he is alive.'

I let out a sigh of relief and placed a hand on the doorway to support myself. By now, even Mohan Sharma and the other gentleman had stepped into the room and were watching us. Maity looked at Jagat Narayan Chowdhury's face through the net for some time and then said in a grave voice, 'As of this instant, Mr Sharma, I want you to put this cabin under constant vigil. No one in or out without my permission. I remember your saying that this log cabin was originally meant to be a quarantine. That is exactly what it is going to be from now on. I want total seclusion for Mr Chowdhury. No exceptions.'

'Certainly, Mr Maity,' said Sharma, with a bewildered look on his face. 'As you wish.'

Maity now looked at the other gentleman who had stepped into the room and said, 'You must be the manager of the estate, Mr Rafiq?'

Rafiq gave a slight nod and said, 'Yes, and you must be Mr Janardan Maity.'

Without responding to Rafiq's question, Maity walked up to me and said in a low voice: 'We need to meet Prabhat Sengupta right now. I don't know what he injected the old man with. If necessary, we may have to move Chowdhury to the hospital.'

'Will he be safe there?' I asked.

'Exactly my thought. Let's see, we will take that call as the day progresses. But the first job is to meet Prabhat Sengupta.'

'And the rest of his friends?'

'Yes, yes—them too. One by one. All of them.'

'Is he . . . is he going to . . .' I gestured towards the sleeping old man.

Maity shot a quick glance at the other two men standing at a distance and said in a low voice, 'He is fine for now, but we have to be on our toes from now on.'

'What do we do, Maity?' I said in a voice marked with hopelessness. 'How can we—'

'This is not the time for weakness, Prakash. Now that we are here, things will be under control, at least to some extent. But we must look for Dr Sengupta right away. Circumstances have changed. We have no other option but to confront him.'

I nodded in support. Maity turned around to face Mohan Sharma and said, 'I'd request you to stay here, Mr Sharma. Please do not leave the cabin. Ask Charan to be always by his master's bedside. If there is any trouble—anything at all— give me a call. Prakash and I are leaving for some time, but we will be in touch with you. Mr Rafiq, would you mind coming with us? I would like to have a word with you.'

Before Mohan Sharma could say anything, Maity had stormed out of the cabin, almost dragging Rafiq by the elbow. I followed them, and we headed towards our car as quickly as we could.

'How long have you been in the employ of Mr Chowdhury?' Maity asked Rafiq Ali as we walked across the lawns.

'Well, it would be seven years come November,' said the gentleman, even as he struggled to catch his breath.

'Well then, probably you will be able to help me. If I want to know more about Manikpur and its history, who would be the best person to ask?'

'What kind of information are you looking for, exactly?' Rafiq asked after a brief pause. 'About the estate?'

'About the estate, yes, certainly. But I am also interested in the history of Manikpur, the village. The village and the villagers. Perhaps someone could help me?'

I looked at Rafiq Ali and saw him steal a quick glance at Maity, even as he kept pace with Maity's massive strides. Then he said, 'I can think of only one man who can help you in this regard.'

'And who might that be?'

'Ashu Sir. His full name is Ashutosh Mukherjee. Everyone calls him Ashu Babu or Ashu Sir. He used to teach at the local school here in Manikpur. He's retired now, is almost seventy-five. Keeps ill too—used to be a chain-smoker in his youth. Doesn't step out of his house any more, unless it is absolutely essential. He should be able to tell you everything you want to know.'

Maity exchanged glances with me and said, 'This school that you mentioned—is this the only school in Manikpur?'

Rafiq Ali said, 'Yes. There's another one in Sonarpur, but that's almost 20 km away. It was built around three years ago. The children of Manikpur go to the estate's own school.'

On seeing us rushing towards him, Pele had jumped into action and quickly brought the car around. Before stepping in, Maity turned towards Rafiq Ali and said, 'I can't thank you enough for your help, Mr Ali. I would like to sit down with you sometime to have a word. There are several questions that are bothering me, and I have a feeling you are just the man who could help me with the answers.'

Rafiq Ali shook the hand that Maity had extended towards him and said with a pleasant smile, 'Certainly, Mr Maity. I'll be glad to help in any way I can.'

Maity nodded and got into the car. Just before Pele stepped on the pedal and the car sped away, I heard Rafiq Ali's voice once again over the sound of the engine: 'But be careful, Mr Maity. The gardens only *look* quiet and tranquil. It's easy to lose your way around them. Lots of wild animals too. Be careful.' I looked at Maity. Had he heard the man? Of course, he had. A frown had appeared on his forehead, and I had never seen his face so grave.

Our car was now making its way towards the gates of the Chowdhury compound. I turned around to see Rafiq Ali still standing there, watching us leave. What did he mean by those last words? There was no way to know. We would have to wait to find out. But one thing was clear. Something very sinister was going on in Manikpur. And we were already in the thick of it.

[7]

To reach Green View Lodge, one had to get out of the estate and reach the highway first. This could be done in one of two ways, Pele explained. The first was to go back the way we came in last night—past the factory, then the school and finally out of the rusty iron gates with the estate's name written on the grillwork. The other was to take a slightly winding but scenic route, through the gardens, past an old temple and then through the Sunday market, opening up on to the highway. Maity asked Pele to take the second.

'We must try and get familiar with the lay of the land here,' Maity said to me as we sat back. 'It will be useful later on.'

'What are you going to tell the doctor?' I asked.

Maity shook his head and said: 'I didn't realize that he would be able to get to the old man so easily. The advantages he has thanks to his profession never quite occurred to me—I thought we'd have more time. But things have changed; in fact, things are constantly changing, even as we speak.'

'What do you think the manager, Rafiq Ali, meant by those last few words? Were they supposed to warn us?'

'I don't know,' Maity said, as he looked out of the window. 'But they sure as hell won't stop Janardan Maity.'

I smiled. Maity was not the sort of man who would get scared and cower down, no matter what the circumstances. Having spent the last few years by his side, I knew him well enough to know that these warnings would only strengthen his resolve further. But nevertheless, the question remained unanswered. Why did the manager warn Maity? What was he trying to say, really?

In a bid to take my mind off the dangers looming large, I looked out of the window too, hoping to find some solace in the verdant scenery outside. That such a strange and bizarre episode of hatred and vengeance was being played out in the middle of such enchanting and breathtakingly beautiful locales was quite unimaginable to me. Everywhere I looked, there were various hues of green, and hovering over them, the clear blue sky smiled at us with great benevolence, peeping from within the spaces between the canopies formed by the sprawling branches of the shade trees.

A few minutes later, we crossed the garden's temple, to our right. As it turned out, it was not just one temple, but more like a small complex of five or six tiny temples dedicated to a number of deities. The entire compound was no more than a hundred feet wide and a couple of hundred feet deep into the tea plantation, and a large portion of the complex stood under the shade of a massive peepal tree on one side and an equally mammoth banyan on the other. It wasn't too difficult to infer that the trees predated the temple, and that the compound was built in the conveniently auspicious spot offered by the two. A couple of bicycles were parked outside the complex next to a water tap where visitors were supposed to wash their hands and feet before stepping into the compound. One or two local people were tying red threads around the many offshoots of the banyan and the peepal, which they considered sacred. Others were ringing the temple bells and bowing in deep reverence in front of their gods. Still others were carrying water in brass vessels to pour into a tiny concrete pool bang in the middle of the compound. I looked towards the far end of the open area and on seeing a pretty little well standing in one corner, gave a shudder. The memories of one of our previous adventures came rushing back to me. Maity and I had been on a number of strange and perilous adventures in the past. But never before had I found him so helpless.

Half a mile or so after the temple came the market. Pele explained that the market functioned only on Sundays, when labourers found time from their daily work to take home necessary supplies. Wages in the gardens, he explained, were paid on a weekly basis, and hence the market remained closed for the rest of the week. As we drove past, I looked out of the window. Spread across a large, squarish area—at least a quarter of a mile on each side—were a number of slightly raised platforms of varying sizes, all made of hardened clay. From the four corners of each such rectangular platform rose four wooden posts, evidently to support a canopy of tarpaulin, if required. The window of commerce was small, and could not be disturbed by either heat or rain—hence the need for shade and shelter. But for a couple of dogs basking in the sun, the platforms now lay barren in anticipation of the upcoming weekend, when this very place would liven up with the soaring calls of hawkers, peddlers and sellers of wares. Although vacant at the moment, I had never seen such a beautiful site of human congregation—a vibrant spot where people would gather, trade, barter, argue, haggle—

all for the universal purpose of sustenance. Everywhere I
looked, there were platforms and pillars, with small walkways
meandering through them. For a few seconds, I shut my eyes
to contemplate the nature of mankind, and the beautiful
ways in which we humans had set ourselves up on the planet.
There was life, and family, and work, and the struggle to keep
oneself alive. There was the constant bond with nature—
strong or weak—no matter where one went. There was joy
and sorrow, and love and betrayal—all on this orb of blue
and green. Man interacting with man, day in and day out—in
various capacities, with varying objectives and intentions—to
fulfil a wide array of purposes. That was all. That was all there
was to it. But lying deep within the complexities of the various
emotions that came along with these deceptively simple and
straightforward transactions were the dark motives of man.
Greed, fear, envy, hatred.

And vengeance!

As I breathed a sigh and opened my eyes, I realized we
had reached the highway. Finding room amidst a stream of
speeding lorries carrying timber, Pele took a cautious right
turn, and after a couple of minutes of driving, he swerved
left to enter the compound of the Green View Lodge. The
two-storeyed building itself was a relatively new one, not
more than seven or eight years old. There were four rooms
on the first floor, and the ground floor seemed to house
the office, a small canteen of sorts and what seemed like
a tiny storeroom in the corner—we could see a few rolled
mattresses, a large iron bucket, brooms and broken chairs
inside through the open window. There were a couple of
cows happily devouring the marigold flowers that had grown
in a garden in one corner of the compound, and paying no

heed to the intruding cattle whatsoever, a forty-to-forty-five-year-old pot-bellied man clad in a chequered lungi and a Guns N' Roses T-shirt walked out of the office, relieved his mouth of the scarlet pool of betel juice that had accumulated in it, smiled with great pride and contentment, and said with a shake of his head, 'Completely full, sir.'

'Oh no, no, no, no, NO!' Maity's face portrayed an intense sense of despair and dejection, as he said in an uncharacteristically loud voice, 'That's too bad! I was hoping to stay for a few nights. I've come all the way from Kolkata.'

The man carved up a bit of lime from a tiny scrap of newspaper in his hand, stuck it into his mouth, frowned in deep contemplation as if to arrive at a solution to the distressed party's troubles, and then turned towards Pele to offer counsel: 'Have you tried the forest bungalow in Mendabari? They always have a spare room. For VIPs and such. Just slip the caretaker a couple of—'

'Oh, no, no, how preposterous! That simply won't do,' Maity interjected as forcefully as he could. 'We have heard so much about your lodge back in Kolkata. The view from the rear windows is captivating, we're told. Our friends in Kolkata said to us—and in no uncertain terms, mind you—that if there is *any* place we should choose for our stay in Manikpur, it simply has to be the Green View Lodge.'

I looked up at the rooms and thought that no matter how green the view at the back may be, if I had to sleep in the middle of this constant noise of speeding vehicles passing by, I wouldn't be able to shut my eyes for even a second.

The man, however, seemed to be as oblivious to the clamour as to the other disaster that was going on ten feet away from where he stood. Half the bed of flowers had already disappeared, the bovine duo was steadily advancing towards the other half with surgical precision. Instead, the manager flashed a red-stained grin and said, 'Very sorry, sir. You should have called in advance. Do take down the number though, for next time. It's on the board up there.'

I looked up and my heart stopped for a second. A man had stepped out on the balcony, perhaps on hearing the conversation that was taking place down below. I now realized why Maity was speaking at the top of his voice. I knew this face. I had seen it just yesterday. In a photograph.

'Good heavens, isn't that Dr Sengupta?' Maity exclaimed. 'What a pleasant surprise! What on earth are *you* doing here?'

The doctor's face did not spare any emotion. The manager looked up and down a couple of times and then asked Maity, 'You know this gentleman?'

'Of course, I do!' Maity spread his arms dramatically and flashed his most brilliant smile, 'I am a friend of his wife Mitali!'

'What a pity!' Pele suddenly said. 'Such lovely flowers!'

The manager now looked in the direction pointed out by our driver, let out a deafening scream and ran towards the cows to save whatever remained of his beloved garden. Maity patted our driver's back a couple of times, muttered a soft 'Thanks, Pele', and quickly moved towards the stairs leading up to the first floor. By the time the manager could shoo the cows away and return to the compound, Maity and I had already made our way up to Dr Sengupta.

'May I have a word with you, doctor?' Maity said, his face now grim and serious once again, his voice calm and Maity-like. 'Perhaps we could step into your room, if you don't mind?'

The doctor stared at Maity with a mix of suspicion and disbelief on his face. I glanced at the situation down below and found that the manager's initial apprehensions about letting two unknown men into his property had been skilfully abated by the lure of a shining new filter-tipped cigarette from our newly acquired and extremely intelligent friend. Presently, we found ourselves being ushered into the doctor's room.

As expected, Dr Sengupta's room was a small one, and although everything about it was evidently basic, it was quite clean and tidy. There was a cot against the wall, and a small wooden table with a tin chair in the remaining space. There was no cupboard or wardrobe of any kind, although a red plastic hanger hung from a nail in the wall on top of a calendar that showed dates from three years ago. The room had two windows—one against the balcony, the other that opened towards the back. Without wasting any time in taking in the titular green view through the latter, Maity went straight to the point after the doctor had offered us seats.

'You do realize that you are being rather foolish, don't you, Dr Sengupta?'

Now that I was seeing him up close and in flesh and blood, I realized that the doctor was taller than he appeared in the photograph, and just a tad bit weathered and exhausted. Maity had once told me that murder was a very taxing crime; it always took a heavy toll on the one about to commit it, no matter how evil their intentions were, no matter how diseased their psyche. Dr Sengupta had clearly not slept well in the past few days, if at all. His eyes were bloodshot, there were bags under them, his hair was unkempt, and he was well past the time for his morning shave. Despite the fact that he was a strapping young man, his shoulders had drooped, and his movements were slow and weary. On hearing Maity's direct and unexpected question, he swallowed hard a couple of times, but did not respond.

'Your wife Mitali came to me, for my help. She's told me all about you and this . . . this obsession of yours. I have come all the way from Kolkata to stop you from doing what is not only going to ruin your life but your wife's too—forever. And I can see now that I was right in coming here because it is quite evident that you have neither the ability nor perhaps the intention to cover your tracks. Why else would you come out here and give out your real name and profession to everyone?'

Dr Sengupta still did not respond.

Maity tried once again: 'What would it take for me to stop you from spelling your own doom, doctor? You tell me. Because I don't see you escaping from this situation once you have committed the crime. They will get to you, you know? Jagat Narayan Chowdhury is one of the most influential people in the region. Do you think you can simply pack your bags and take a flight back to Kolkata after murdering him? What were you thinking, if you were thinking at all?'

'Stop.'

This was the first time we had heard Dr Sengupta speak, and I realized his voice matched his personality.

'Please,' he said, his voice firm and resolute, 'stop. I have no idea what you are talking about.'

Maity took the doctor's photograph out of his pocket and held it up 'Ramchandra had given Hanuman his ring so that Hanuman could show it to Sita when she was trapped in Lanka. This is the ring. Can we talk now?'

After a brief pause during which his lips trembled a couple of times, the doctor seemed to shake off his hesitation and said, 'So you have a photograph of mine in your possession. That doesn't prove anything.'

Maity shook his head in frustration and said, 'This is so unlike you, doctor . . .'

'What do you know about me?' Dr Sengupta's patience had run out, his voice was now laced with disgust and irritation. 'You think you can come in here and—'

'I know you well enough to tell you that you are in grave danger,' Maity's voice was not hesitant either, and he spoke with the surety of a man who knew what he was doing. 'And that's all that matters to me right now. As it should to you. Your wife is concerned about you, and rightfully so. And I am amazed to see how naïve you can be in the whole matter. What exactly is your plan, might I ask? What do you intend to do? You think you can waltz into the old man's bedroom, jab a needle into his vein and walk away with no consequences at all? Is that how you plan to avenge your father?'

I knew Maity had intentionally hit a raw nerve, and it worked. Dr Sengupta's entire personality underwent a devilish change. He began to breathe heavily, his face contorted and it seemed to me that for a few seconds, he could not believe that a stranger could come into his room and speak to him in such a manner. We knew very little of the man, no doubt. But if Maity had to stop him, he would have to work with whatever little he had.

'That injection contained a mild sedative, nothing else,' said the doctor, fuming. 'A high dose could have been fatal, but I gave him just enough to fall asleep.'

'See, there you go again,' said Maity, exasperated. 'You give away too many things about yourself, without anyone even having to ask.'

Dr Sengupta immediately saw his mistake, but was at a loss for words. He broke eye contact with Maity and looked out of the window.

'And do you know why you tend to do that?' Maity continued. 'Because inherently, you are a good man, an honest man. One who has nothing to hide. You are fundamentally incapable of committing murder. Or even planning one to perfection.'

'Am I?' The man rose from the bed and walked past Maity and me to go and stand next to the window. 'You don't know me. And you are wasting your time, Mister . . . whatever your name is. I don't know why my wife sent you to me, but what I do know is that she made a grave error in judgement.'

'Maity! My name is Janardan Maity. And I am here to tell you that your wife has committed no error. I know you are hurt by the fact that she has shared your deepest, darkest secrets with another man—an outsider. Under normal circumstances, that may very well be the definition of a breach of marital trust. But the current circumstances are far from normal. She's done it out of love and concern. For you. You, on the other hand, seem to have nothing but hatred and vengeance in your heart, doctor. And I assure you today that this is not going to end well for you.'

'Janardan Maity?' Dr Sengupta frowned as he turned around to face us. 'The famous detective?'

Maity shut his eyes in great agony and said, 'Ohhhh, now you've gone ahead and given me another reason to be furious with you.'

Dr Sengupta looked perplexed; he had perhaps never imagined that he would find himself in this decidedly odd situation.

Maity went and stood next to him: 'Look, doctor. Why don't we both take a step back, okay? Let's sit down and have a civil discussion about this. Man to man. With the courtesy that we both deserve.'

'Very well. What do you want to say? Other than what I think you want to say?'

'Good. For a very brief period of time, I would like to forget everything about you and your vengeance.'

'That would be my advice to you too, yes.'

'For a brief period of time, mind you,' Maity raised a finger. 'But pray, tell me about these three other friends of yours, who seem to have converged upon this ecstatically beautiful place with motives as vile and foolish as yours.'

Dr Sengupta thought for a few seconds and said, 'Why should I tell you?'

'Because if you don't, then I shall ask my excellent driver waiting downstairs to take me to the nearest police station—post-haste—so that I can personally hand you over to the law.'

After a short pause, during which Dr Sengupta locked eyes with Maity, the former said in a calm voice, 'Are you threatening me?'

'My good friend Prakash here is a brilliant author, and is hence exquisitely skilled with words. But even he could not have described my intentions any better than you just did.'

Several uncomfortable seconds passed by and none of us spoke. Finally, Maity's patience got the better of the doctor, who let out a deep sigh of resignation and buried his head in his hands. After a few seconds, he pulled himself up and said, 'Abhi is mad. Mad is an understatement, really. He's insane. He thinks it's all a big adventure, an expedition, a picnic in the tea gardens! Sometimes I worry about him. What sick mind thinks of murder as a break from work?'

'Abhi, as in your friend Abhijit Lahiri, the banker?' Maity asked.

Dr Sengupta nodded, 'I see my wife has told you everything. Perhaps I had underestimated her. Yes—Abhijit Lahiri. Investment banker. A cool customer, so to speak. Can own any room that he enters. King charmer, smooth talker, great personality. But a child at heart, even today. Which is exactly why the crime against him is so horrendous, so vile.'

'There was an incident with his sister—'

'Raped, right in front of his eyes. By Chowdhury. Then by his men.'

A minute or so ago, Maity was in one of his notoriously sarcastic moods, but now, his face looked like it had turned into stone. His hawk eyes were still fixed on the doctor's face.

'Poor little Abhi did not speak for a whole month. We . . . those who knew . . . him . . . we felt so bad for him, so helpless. He was a great kid. A kind, gentle young lad. And then . . . and then . . . something strange happened . . .'

Maity and I looked on as Dr Sengupta stared into the void, as if trying to retrieve some dark and sinister piece of memory from his past.

'He came to school one day, and he seemed perfectly normal! As if . . . as if nothing had happened at all! It was incredible, impossible for me to describe! He was once again the same old Abhi we knew so well from before the incident. Talking, smiling, cracking jokes and playing pranks. The entire school was shocked, as were the teachers. But we who were his close friends . . . we were happy to have our old friend back. But no matter how normally he behaved, we knew. We knew that something had changed deep within him.'

A pair of sparrows came and landed on the windowsill. Dr Sengupta watched them in silence, as they pecked at something on the wood and looked here and there before flying away.

'It was Abhi who proposed the idea to us. He was quite close to us, despite being a year junior to us. It was Abhi who suggested that we take the vow. That twenty years later, we would all return to Manikpur and avenge the crimes committed against our families. And the manner in which he did it all was so . . . sinister. We had met in the school building, in one of the empty classrooms. While the rest of us were angry, fuming, trembling with fury, Abhi had a strange calmness on his face, to the point that we were . . . frightened of him. Never once did we hear him say anything against Chowdhury to anyone. All he told us was that he would kill the man. And that he didn't care if we were in it with him or not. He said he would be happy to do it on his own.'

Maity asked, 'You were in touch with him after Manikpur?'

'Yes, Abhi went to live with his grandparents in Asansol, whereas I was raised by a distant aunt in Kolkata. We kept in touch, or rather, it would be fair to say that I kept in touch with him. I later heard that he had gone to Delhi for his studies and then on to the US for his MBA. Apparently, he gave up several plush job offers in the US so that he could return to India. I think I now know why.'

Maity was about to respond, when suddenly, something whizzed past my right ear, crashed against the wall and smashed a mirror hanging from it into several pieces.

Before I could even understand what had happened, I heard Maity curse under his breath, as he rushed to the wall on the opposite side of the room and looked out of the rear window.

'No use giving chase,' he growled, shaking his head. 'It's a jungle out there. Are you all right, Prakash?'

Although I nodded to say yes, my heart almost felt like it would explode, and I was dazed. What on earth was happening? Did someone just throw a rock at me?

'Mr Maity!'

We turned around to find that Dr Sengupta had picked up the rock from the floor and removed the paper that was wrapped around it.

'I . . . I think . . . you should see this!' The doctor's voice had been steady all this while. This was the first time that I caught a hint of anxiety in it.

Maity snatched the piece of paper from the doctor's hand and held it out so that he and I could read it together. Despite the creases from the crumpling, the words written on it in crooked handwriting were quite legible:

I know who you are.
I know why you are here.
If you value your life, get out.
Now.

'Deliberately written with the non-dominant hand,' Maity commented. 'Same letter written in different ways in different places.'

'I . . . I think . . . I think someone knows!' exclaimed the doctor. 'I think someone's trying to warn me!'

'We certainly shouldn't rule that out, Dr Sengupta,' Maity said gravely, as he folded the sheet of paper and put it in his pocket. 'Nor should we rule out the other possibility.'

'And what is that?' asked Dr Sengupta, with a look of fear and surprise on his face.

Maity looked out of the window at the thick, lush bushes swaying in the midday breeze and said, 'That someone's trying to warn *me*.'

[8]

Presently, there was heavy knocking on the door accompanied by what sounded like an anxious voice. Dr Sengupta opened the door to let a strange-looking man in. The man probably suffered from dwarfism, so he could easily slip into the room from under the doctor's arms. He was not more than four feet in height, had small shoulders, almost no neck, and even his arms and legs were tiny. He had a swarthy complexion, the hair on his head was crisply set in a gaudy style and he wore a pair of terylene trousers and a half-sleeve shirt that were probably custom-made for him, for although they were short in length, they had significant girth.

'I heard a noise,' the man said. 'Something crashing. You all right?'

What struck me most about the man were his expressions. Normally, when people talk in day-to-day life, they use their expressions only to the point where they don't look 'dramatic'. With this gentleman, things were completely different. Every single word was pronounced with theatrical emphasis, and duly accompanied with a gesture or a facial expression that looked comical at times and plain exaggerated at others. For instance, there was a sense of supreme urgency and loud alarm in his manner while uttering two-thirds of what he said to the doctor, and an expression of great concern in the final third.

'Yes, yes, I'm fine,' Dr Sengupta replied. 'This is Mr Janardan Maity. He is from Kolkata. And this is his friend . . . er . . .'

'Prakash,' I said. 'Prakash Ray.'

'Would it be an accurate assessment to say that you two gentlemen were responsible for this unfortunate mishap?' With a Chaplinesque motion of his hands, the man pointed towards whatever remained of the mirror on the wall.

Maity had clearly found the man to be very interesting. He nodded with a smile and said, 'Yes, milord.'

The man immediately rapped Maity on his wrist with the air of a schoolmaster and said in a dramatically grim voice of admonishment, 'Seven years of bad luck for you!'

'You will have to forgive Shibu,' the doctor said, 'He has the habit of making the most of his life—a habit that can take a bit of getting used to. Mr Maity, this is my friend Shibnath Sarkhel.'

Sarkhel gave us a bow that would put even the most courteous French artist in the world to shame. 'Very pleased to make your acquaintances, gentlemen.'

'Very pleased to make yours,' said Maity. 'Might I ask, what is it that you do, Mr Sarkhel?'

'Oh, there's a broken piece of glass on your shoulder here,' came the reply, and having said these words, the man startled me by darting out his right hand towards my ear, only to draw it back quickly and produce a red ball—slightly larger than a ping-pong ball. The entire thing happened so quickly, that I was quite taken aback, but Maity said, 'Ah, you are a magician!'

'Precisely!' Sarkhel bowed again.

Dr Sengupta said, as he began picking up the broken pieces from the floor, 'Magician, escape artist, juggler, acrobat—Shibu has many talents.'

Shibnath Sarkhel smiled genially and said, 'Life decided to make me small, sir. So, I decided to live my life large.'

Maity was visibly impressed by the man. I knew how much he admired the dying arts of magic and acrobatics. He was a regular visitor to the circus even today, and often lamented the fact that technology was steadily ruining our ability to be awed by the human miracle. He looked at Shibnath Sarkhel with great reverence, so much so that I was concerned that he might forget what we were here for. But his very next words proved how wrong I was:

'Knife-throwing?' he asked, with a genial smile floating on his lips, 'Do you do knife-throwing as well?'

In all the years that I have been with Maity, I had seen even hardened criminals crumble under the pressure of his intense gaze and pointed questions. Shibnath Sarkhel's smile wavered a little, and for a very brief moment, I caught the glimpse of a dark and violent heart hiding behind the jolly façade. But he quickly managed to regain his composure and nodded his head.

'Have done that too, Mr Maity, have done that too. And blindfolded, mind you. What can one do, sir? The struggle for survival makes you do things that you would never imagine you were capable of doing. I was sixteen when I found myself wandering the streets of Kolkata all by myself, with nowhere to go and not a single penny in my pocket. It wasn't too bad, really, I don't have any complaints. What most people don't seem to realize is that there is more kindness, more friendship, more love on the footpaths than one can ever hope to find in the comforts of safety and affluence. When night falls on the street, people look after each other, they share a fire, or a piece of bread they had picked up from the dump. They protect you from barking dogs and screaming policemen. But most of all, they listen to you. They listen to what you have to say. They have all the time in the world after all, you see?'

Maity smiled and uttered his next few words in a calm and gentle voice, 'I am listening too, Mr Sarkhel.'

Without breaking eye contact with Maity, Shibnath Sarkhel smiled a little and gave a small nod of gratitude and respect. Then he said: 'Another advantage of living off the streets is that you get to meet dozens of artists every day. True artists. Art that will astound you, leave you speechless. Art born out of hunger and pain, out of the sheer will to live. How else does a mother gather the courage to stand her little girl up against a board and throw knives at her, tell me? That too, blindfolded?'

Maity was listening to the man with rapt attention, his gaze fixed on Shibnath Sarkhel's funny little eyes, his own eyes like a sponge—showing less and soaking in significantly more.

'I learnt knife-throwing from her. Her name was Bhanvri. She was from a small, obscure village in Jharkhand. She was hardly in her thirties at that time. But a true artist. A fighter! She was my guru, and that was how I began.'

Had I not met Shibnath Sarkhel, I would never have believed that a man's face could seem both funny and tragic at the same time. Sarkhel was clearly overcome with nostalgia.

'From there on,' he continued, reminiscently, 'I learnt a number of things. Contortionism, card tricks, making things disappear and reappear, tightrope walking, juggling, jumping through hoops of fire—I could go on and on. Started to earn some money, didn't have to sleep on a hungry tummy any more. And then, one day, I was showing card tricks on the pavement outside the post office on Park Street; my friend Heera was shining shoes a few feet away, when I noticed a man shove a coin into his palm and come and stand in the crowd that had gathered around me. I knew right then that something was about to happen, that my life was going to change.

'And that's exactly what did happen. After my tricks were over, when I was collecting the coins from my mat, the man gave me a ten-rupee note and asked me if I would like a job. I asked him what job he was talking about. He said he owned a restaurant in Park Circus nearby, and that I would have to be the doorman. I would have to stand on the pavement and show my tricks and practically "lure" people off the streets into his restaurant with my magic tricks. He would offer me three meals a day and a place to sleep, but no salary.

'I didn't think twice, Mr Maity, nor did I rue the fact that there was no salary. Because I knew that just like this man had seen my magic on the streets and given me a roof over my head, someday, someone would walk in through the doors of that restaurant and open new doors for me, give me an even better life. And once again, that's exactly what happened. I now have my own show, my own troupe. "Sarkhel ka Khel"— one of the papers called my show, and the name stuck! I tour the suburbs widely and have even done shows outside the state. I am "settled" now, as you gentlemen often say, and it all began with a ragged woman in ragged clothes with a ragged urchin on her lap teaching me how to throw knives with a blindfold on.'

Maity did not speak for a long time. The atmosphere inside the room had become quite heavy, and had it not been for the fact that along with the rear window, even the door was now open, I would have felt quite stifled and out of breath in here. Maity let out a deep sigh and finally broke the silence.

'Do you know why I am here, Mr Sarkhel?'

Shibnath Sarkhel shook his head and gave a clown-like shrug.

'I am here to stop you and your friends from ruining what seems to be a life that all of you have had to struggle to achieve. I am here to tell you that very few people are as fortunate as you have been, and that you should do your best to treasure what you have. I am not unaware of what has happened to your mother in Manikpur, Mr Sarkhel. I know it must have been difficult for you. But you simply cannot commit one crime to avenge another.'

Shibnath Sarkhel's face turned red in an instant. He turned around to give Dr Sengupta a betrayed glance, 'You told him everything?'

'No!' The doctor shook his head vehemently. 'Trust me, I didn't.'

'Then how does he know?' The hurt in Shibnath Sarkhel's voice was not one bit exaggerated. 'How could you, Prabhat?'

'I didn't,' the doctor took a step forward. 'I swear I didn't. Mitu must have—'

'How I know is of no consequence, Mr Sarkhel,' Maity's voice was stern, and it helped him regain control of a conversation that was getting away from him. 'What matters is what you are going to do now. What matters is the future. Jagat Narayan Chowdhury is seventy-nine years old. The man is already standing on the edge of his grave. Why shove him into it? It's just a matter of time before—'

'Before what?' Shibnath Sarkhel interrupted, 'Before he passes away? In his sleep? Peacefully?'

Maity did not respond.

'Fourth-degree burns in over 80 per cent of her body, Mr Maity,' Sarkhel's face was now dripping with pain and fury. 'I was twelve years old then, didn't even know what a fourth-degree burn is. So, I asked everyone I came across—nurses, doctors, neighbours, even strangers outside the hospital—running from one to another. But no one would tell me. No one wanted to tell a twelve-year-old boy how painful his mother's death was. They didn't even let me see her.'

I looked at Dr Sengupta to find his hands trembling. Maity was still staring at the magician whose eyes had started glistening.

'*But the stench?*' Shibnath Sarkhel stood up and yelled out so loud that it seemed the tiny room would explode. 'That horrid, ghastly stench that ran through the corridors of the hospital and made me puke my guts out? How do I forget that smell, Mr Maity? The smell of my mother's molten flesh?'

Maity had nothing to say in response. I knew no words of his would make any sense at the moment.

'No, Mr Maity,' Sarkhel said. 'I can't forget that. I don't know who you are, nor do I want to know what your intentions are. I don't know how you know about my mother, or what your relationship with Manikpur is. But know this, once and for all, that the man who was responsible for my mother's slow, gruesome, agonizing death will himself not die peacefully in his sleep.'

Having said these words, Shibnath Sarkhel stormed out of the room, entered his own room and slammed the door shut.

Maity sighed and hung his head. His whole disposition was one of abject failure. I had never seen him so helpless. No matter how much he threatened these people that he would call the cops on them, I knew that he would never do such a thing. Not only because of the promise he had made to Mitali Sengupta but also because the police could only provide a temporary solution to the problem. And to be perfectly honest, somewhere in the deepest recesses of my mind, I too did not want him to call the cops. No matter how ashamed I was to admit it, it was true that having listened to everything that had happened in Manikpur all those years ago, one part of me felt that perhaps Jagat Narayan Chowdhury deserved the fate that was awaiting him.

'Do you see now, Mr Maity?' Dr Sengupta said. 'Do you see how futile your efforts are? You've come all this way for nothing. I know you mean well. But you are not going to stop any of us.'

Maity rose from his seat with an exhausted look on his face and said, 'I have to try, doctor. Just like you are bound by your principles, I am bound by mine.'

The doctor and Maity exchanged smiling and respectful glances—a respect that two warring opponents in sport usually feel for each other. Both wanted to win, but not at the cost of the other's dignity.

'Will you go to the police?' Dr Sengupta asked.

Maity let out an exhausted sigh and said, 'You know very well that I won't.'

The doctor nodded and said: 'Yes, I do. I know my wife well. If she has chosen to tell you everything, she must also know that you won't do anything to harm her husband.'

'But I *will* continue to desist you,' Maity said. 'You're not seeing the last of me, doctor. I assure you.'

The doctor smiled and said: 'I respect you for that. Your position, as I understand it, is a difficult one. One part of me admires you for what you are doing. But as a person, as a human being and as a son, I am more than that part, Mr Maity.'

The two men stared at each other for some time, till Maity nodded and broke eye contact.

'Well, I might as well have a word with your banker friend then, Abhijit Lahiri. Is he in his room right now?'

'No, I don't think so,' said the doctor. 'Abhi left in the morning, said he had a few things to take care of.'

No sooner had he said these words, than we heard the door at the far end of the passage open, accompanied by the sound of someone stepping out.

'And that must be your third friend?' said Maity, as we looked out of the open door on to the passage, waiting for the said individual to walk down it and come into our view, the footsteps now growing louder. 'The one who was sexually abused by Chowdhury?'

'Good morning! I figured I'd go out and get some shots after all. Would you like to join me, perhaps?'

I looked at Maity, the frown had returned to his forehead. I myself was dumbstruck. The man standing at the doorway was a burly, fair-skinned, blonde-haired foreigner, clad in a Hawaiian holiday shirt, white shorts and a safari hat. There was an expensive-looking Canon camera hanging from his neck, and from the twang and nasality in his accent, it seemed to me that he was, in all probability, an American tourist.

After Dr Sengupta had expressed his inability to join him, and the man had bid us all goodbye before walking down the stairs, Maity asked the doctor in a grave voice, 'Where is your third friend?'

'Who, Arjun?' said the doctor. 'Why, I thought you knew. He didn't come!'

'Didn't come?' Maity was clearly not expecting this. 'But . . . but why?'

'That I don't know,' said the doctor. 'He was supposed to—in fact he said he would. The rest of us don't seem to know much about him, to be honest. He sort of . . . disappeared after we left Manikpur. Never kept in touch. Just a few days ago, I got a call from him. In fact, all of us did. I asked him how he got my number, but he didn't say. It was he who reminded the rest of us that the time to honour our vows had come. And that we should all return to Manikpur. We all came, but Arjun didn't turn up.'

Maity frowned hard and stared at the floor, as if in deep thought, his right hand clutched into a fist, his left tugging on his lips, as I heard him mutter under his breath, almost in a whisper, 'Why? Why? Why? Why didn't he come?'

[9]

It was quite late in the afternoon, so we decided to head back to the guest house for lunch. Maity had fallen silent, although this was nothing new to me. I knew he was now processing every single fact, every bit of information, everything he had heard and seen and felt so far, arranging them in a neat order in his mind, to be recalled and reused at some future point in time as per his need and convenience. Which is also why he did not make a single comment on the lunch itself, which was nothing sort of lavish. Mohan Sharma had obviously decided to compensate for last night's simple dinner, and although, at first glance, I was absolutely sanguine that I would not be able to eat even a third of what was spread out before me on the table, I was surprised to find that by the end of it, I had had significant helpings of everything on the menu. Part of this astonishing phenomenon I attributed to the general climate of the garden and its rich-in-minerals drinking water, while the other part was perhaps because of the chat I had with Maity during the meal, which was engrossing, to say the least.

'The doctor seemed quite obstinate,' I remarked.

'He is making a big mistake,' Maity said. 'I had not expected him to be so unprepared.'

'But that's good, don't you think?' I asked. 'For us? I mean, it would help us stop him.'

'No, Prakash. There is nothing more dangerous than a foolish man. Because you can't predict what his next move will be. Especially when along with being foolish, he is obsessed and vengeful at the same time.'

I thought for a few seconds and said, 'What did you think of the magician—Sarkhel?'

'He is a tricky one,' Maity said. 'The man's probably had to face ridicule throughout his life. Has seen some hard times too. The incident with his mother is not the only burden he has been carrying on his shoulders. I would not be surprised if he decides to pour all his accumulated anguish on to Chowdhury. Nor would I be surprised if he were to hold Chowdhury responsible for *all* the troubles in his life.'

'Even his dwarfism?' I asked.

Maity stopped eating. He looked out of the window of the dining room and said: 'The human mind is a strange thing, Prakash. Especially if it is a bruised mind. It is in a constant search for things to latch on to. It isolates each emotion, each thought, and attempts to attribute it to something. Or someone. You must have noticed that a child is always very quick to brand people around him—this man is fun because he gives me toffees and cookies; that woman is not so good because she always scolds me and asks me to sit in one place. As we grow up, we change. We learn not to be in a rush to assign blame, we learn how to take our time in judging people. But buried somewhere in our psyche is the same child who didn't think twice before making gods and monsters out of people he came across. And no matter how grown up, how mature we are, it is this child who comes to the forefront when we face trauma. That is exactly what I fear has happened with Shibnath Sarkhel as well.'

'But how can you be so sure, Maity?' I asked. 'Isn't all this mere conjecture at this point in time?'

Maity resumed eating and said, 'Of course, it is. But a conjecture based on facts. An informed deduction. A derivation, not mere guesswork.'

'Facts?' I asked, 'What facts?'

Maity looked at me and said, 'What was the crime committed by Chowdhury against Dr Sengupta?'

'Well,' I began, 'his father is suspected to have been murdered by Chowdhury and his men, and the murder was made to look like suicide.'

'Correct,' said Maity. 'And what was the crime committed against the banker, Abhijit Lahiri?'

'His sister was raped.'

Maity nodded. 'And the fourth man, Arjun Banerjee. He is known to have been molested by Chowdhury, as a child. He was the youngest . . . youngest . . . youngest . . .'

Maity's voice trailed off. I looked up at him to find him staring out of the window once again, lost in his thoughts. I chose not to disturb him and waited.

After almost half a minute or so, Maity shook himself out of his trance and said: 'He was the youngest of the four—barely eleven years old—and one can only imagine what a child of that age must have gone through.'

I suddenly felt disgusted by the fact that for all practical purposes, we were trying to help a murderer, a rapist and a paedophile—and enjoying his hospitality at the same time. Why did Maity have to take up the case? What on earth were we doing in Manikpur, after all?

This change in my behaviour was not lost on Maity. He cast a sideways glance at me and said, 'But remember, if we have to solve this mystery and prevent this crime from happening, we must try and be as objective as we possibly can. We must see everything for the way it really is. And we cannot let our emotions get the better of us. For instance, I'm going to say something that you will not like to hear, but the fact remains that what I am saying is true.'

'What is it?' I asked, feeling wretched and miserable.

Maity paused for a moment and said, 'The crime committed against Shibnath Sarkhel is the least of the four.'

I was confused, so I said, 'How do you mean?'

'All that Chowdhury had done was to accuse Sarkhel's mother of theft and throw her out of her job. Compared to some of the other things that he is known to have done, this is a much—shall we say—lesser crime. Heinous, unjust—but relatively lesser. There is no doubt about that. Why then did she commit suicide? Why could she not take the shame and ignominy of being called a thief? In a village where the oppression of Jagat Narayan Chowdhury was not unknown to anyone, I find it hard to believe that people would have accepted his word over hers and slandered her of thievery. Why did she set herself on fire then? What exactly happened?'

I had no answer. And I also saw the difficulty we were in. How could we possibly know what happened all those years ago? I asked him the same.

'We will get to that in good time,' he said. 'But the fact remains that Sarkhel does not have as strong a reason to murder Chowdhury as the rest of his friends. In other words, it may not be a wild assumption to claim that the magician perhaps has the weakest motive to commit the crime that we are trying to prevent.'

'Does this mean that he would be the easiest to stop, relatively speaking?' I asked.

Maity shrugged his shoulders and nodded, 'In one way, yes, you could say that.'

'And who do you think would be the most difficult to stop?'

Maity had just finished drinking a glass of water to conclude his meal. He stared at the empty glass for a long time and said, 'The one who promised to come, but didn't.'

After this, despite my repeatedly asking him what he meant, he refused to say anything further.

After lunch, Maity announced that he wanted to stay alone for some time.

'Get some rest, Prakash,' he said. 'I'll take a quick stroll and come back in half an hour or so. Just need to clear my head.'

I lay down in my bed as Maity walked out, and began to think of all the people who were involved in this incredibly complicated affair. Whom had we met first? Jagat Narayan Chowdhury, along with Mohan Sharma. Then came Mitali Sengupta. Next, we met her husband Dr Prabhat Sengupta and his friend Shibnath Sarkhel. Then another friend—what was his name—ah yes, Lahiri . . . Abhijit Lahiri. He was out since morning, so we didn't get to meet him. And the fourth man, Arjun—his surname I couldn't remember—had promised to come to Manikpur, but hadn't. Oh, and I had forgotten about one more person: Rafiq Ali, the manager of Manikpur Tea Estate, whom we had met very briefly, and who had said some really strange things to us.

All these people seemed to be connected with each other through a fine network of threads, with their own motives, intentions and characteristics. And at the centre of this intricate web was one man. His crimes had finally caught up with him, and although I knew Maity was trying his best, I had serious doubts if Chowdhury would be able to escape his nemeses.

As these thoughts were crowding my head, my eyes had begun to close. But Maity returned soon after, and added yet one more name to my list as he announced that we should pay a visit to Ashutosh Mukherjee, the village schoolmaster.

'If we are to stop these men from doing what they intend to do, we need to know more about them, understand them better. We also need to know what exactly happened in Manikpur twenty years ago. And if there is anyone who can help us in this regard, it is that man—their teacher.'

Maity summoned Pele and asked him if he knew where Ashu Babu lived. Pele said he did, and that he would be able to take us to the man's home in the village. The sun was about to disappear behind the treetops towards the west, and once it did, it wouldn't take too much time for darkness to engulf the gardens. Without wasting any more time, Maity and I set out for Manikpur village.

Coming out of the guest house, we reached the pebbled road bifurcating the garden, crossed the temple and reached the fork from which we had taken a right to get to the market in the morning. This time, we took the left instead. We were now moving away from the highway, towards the east. Pele was constantly driving at a cautious speed, which gave me enough time to admire the pristine beauty of the place. Far away, towards our left, I could see the two chimneys of the factory rising against the skyline from over a row of trees. I realized that had it not been for the abundance of trees surrounding its compound, we would have been able to see the twin giants from our guest house too.

Everywhere I looked, all my eyes could see was green. I drew Maity's attention to the various hues of greenery all around us and said with a smile that people living in the gardens would probably never need to wear spectacles all their lives, to which he simply gave a dismissive shake of his head, remarked that the health of the human eye depended on several other factors than merely what colours it was receiving, and turned away to look out of his window before drowning in his thoughts again. I was quite miffed at this cut-throat scientific rebuttal of my poetic imagination and decided to return to my own engagement with nature. The orange disc of the sun had dipped behind the shade trees and begun playing hide-and-seek and a wailing siren had sounded from the direction of the chimneys. Maity glanced at his wristwatch and muttered something inaudible, and Pele pointed towards the north and said that the dense treeline on the horizon beyond the sprawling carpet of green was the notorious Chilapata forest range. I suddenly saw a number of houses and huts up ahead by the side of the road and realized that we had reached Manikpur village.

This was not the first time I had noticed that unlike in cities, houses and huts in the villages of India were scattered over a large area, with a great deal of distance between them. Manikpur, too, was no exception. Not a single house was within a hundred yards of another, and with dusk slowly falling upon the village and the light from the sky rapidly disappearing, I wondered how scary it would be to live like this. Small flames had begun to light up in various lamps within the households, the sound of conches being blown reached our ears, a little girl came running out of her house to collect a shirt drying on a clothesline, a shrivelled old man with a head full of grey hair stepped out on his veranda with a hookah in his hand and a vest on his body that must have had at least a hundred holes in it, and a middle-aged woman paused the prayer she was offering to the tulsi growing in one corner of her yard to look up at us with innocent curiosity. All in all, the perfect scene of an Indian village at dusk.

Dusk! My favourite time of the day. My mind danced at such simple yet beautiful sights, but Maity seemed too engrossed in his thoughts to notice any of them. Well, his loss!

'Is there no electricity in the village?' I asked Pele.

'Electricity is there,' came the response, 'but the number of power cuts is shockingly high.'

I smiled and said, 'The forest is quite close by, isn't it?'

'Couple of miles. Sometimes, wild animals wander out of the forest and enter the village.'

'Tigers?'

'Leopards, bears, elephants.'

I passed my tongue over my dry lips and said, 'Does this happen quite . . . frequently?'

'No, no,' Pele shook his head and said reassuringly, 'but when it does, there's big trouble.'

After passing a large overflowing water tank to our left, we took a right turn and stopped next to a tiny railway-quarter type house, only this one had a tin roof over it. There was a hedge fence around the house, consisting entirely of garden crotons, or what was commonly known in these parts as the paatabahar shrub. The leaves were about the length of one's palm, and spotted with different hues—as if someone had dipped a paintbrush in a mix of different colours and shaken it over the leaves. We stepped in through a small gate made of wood and sheets of tin and Maity called out Ashu Babu's name. For several minutes, there was no response, so Maity called again. Why was it so dark inside the house? Was the gentleman not at home?

A few more minutes passed; nothing was stirring within the residence. We were looking around, wondering what to do, when a young lad—around fifteen or sixteen years old—came out of the house and stood on the veranda.

'Is Ashu Babu at home?' Maity inquired.

'He is unwell,' the boy replied. It was quite obvious from his expression that he had no intention of ushering a couple of strangers into the house.

'Yes,' Maity said, 'so we have heard. But it is very important that we see him. We have come all the way from Kolkata.'

The boy was still staring at us, probably trying to ascertain our intentions, when there was a faint murmur from inside the house. The boy immediately rushed back in, leaving us outside the veranda. It was almost dark by now, and we could hear the chittering of the crickets. Perhaps because it was right on the bend of the road, there was no other house around Ashu Babu's. Which was also why there was no sign of a lamp or a light anywhere. There were large trees all around the house, and a sweet floral smell wafted about in the air.

'Come in.'

The boy had reappeared at the door, and was now welcoming us in, not of his own will and accord, I imagined.

We stepped through the door and found ourselves in a tiny sitting room. Maity's eyes saw much more than anyone else's in the dark, so he was scanning through the room. I, on the other hand, could barely make out the faint outline of furniture.

'In here.'

We stepped into the adjacent room through another door to our left and immediately realized that this was a bedroom. There was a small kerosene lamp burning near a bed against the wall, and its weak but steady flame illuminated only a part of the man lying on the bed, wrapped in a heavy blanket. Everything outside the periphery of the light was steeped in darkness. There was a faint blue square in the topmost section of the mass of darkness to my left, and I realized it was nothing but a ventilator on the wall that opened to the sky outside. The man's face was turned towards the wall, and on hearing us enter, he tried to sit up on the bed.

'Please, sir,' Maity took a step forward, 'you don't have to get up.'

The man had either not heard what Maity had said or not paid heed. As he struggled to sit up, I noticed his shadow on the patchy lime-washed wall behind him, cast by the light of the lamp. Where had I seen that shadow very recently?

'You are from Kolkata?'

The boy had brought us the same chairs I had seen in the previous room. Having taken his seat, and having asked me to do the same with a gesture of his hand, Maity answered the old man's question, 'Yes, sir.'

'Have some sweets,' the old man's voice was hoarse and raspy, and his words came in laboured instalments, as if he was having difficulty speaking. 'Very delicious. Swapan Moira owns a sweetmeats shop. In Sonarpur. Tiny little store. But Swapan has magic in his fingers. I knew his father too. The apple hasn't fallen far from the tree, it seems.'

That shadow, that shadow! Where had I seen that shadow on the wall before?

The boy brought us our plates, a couple of steel glasses and a green plastic jug with a white lid on top. Maity was never one to say no to food, and certainly not to sweets.

'Charlotte Stuart!'

Ashu Babu was now sitting cross-legged by the edge of the bed. His breathing had normalized to some extent. The boy helped him wrap the blanket around his shoulders, although it was not cold at all. Why the old man had uttered the strange name, hung his head and fallen silent was also a matter of great mystery to me. I looked at Maity to find that he had already dug into the sweets.

'In the year 1817,' Ashu Babu's head was still hanging, his eyes shut, his chin stuck to his chest, 'the same year Raja Ram Mohan Roy and Scottish watchmaker and philanthropist David Hare founded the Hindu College in your city, on the other side of the world, the then British ambassador to France, Sir Charles Stuart's wife Lady Elizabeth Yorke gave birth to a lovely little baby in the British embassy in Paris—a girl who was later baptized Charlotte. Charlotte grew up to be a beautiful young woman, acquiring such fine skills as painting, singing, riding and holding learned discourses on any subject under the sun. For young Charlotte was a voracious reader. In fact, it was the life of an aristocrat that she abhorred. One could always find her in the gardens, studying a fig leaf or a cherry blossom. The ways of the nobility were not for her to enjoy, and she spent her time in the soothing lap of nature.'

I glanced at the young boy standing a few feet away from us in the near darkness. His eyes were watching the old man as he himself leaned against the wall, his hands patiently folded behind his back.

'And then, one day, Charlotte fell in love! With the son of a former Prime Minister of Britain, no less! A strapping young man named Charles, with a great future in diplomacy. But oh, Charlotte's father had great ideological and political differences with Charles's father, so he was severely opposed to the relationship. But Charlotte was a spirited young woman. Going against the wishes of her family, she married Charles, and soon, the couple came to this part of the world, where Charles Canning was posted as the Governor-General of the Indian provinces. Sadly though, Charlotte's marriage to Charles was not a happy one. For one, it yielded no child. And while she would have expected her husband to stay by her and attempt to assuage her grief, Lord Canning was too busy quelling the Sepoy Mutiny and with every other duty that a man in his official capacity was expected to perform. Poor Charlotte was heartbroken and left to fend for herself. Her husband's attempts to bring her out into the world remained unsuccessful. Why, she even found the city of Kolkata too crowded. She would wander around the gardens in her country house in Barrackpore and draw pictures of trees, plants, leaves, roots and flowers. Such creations were her own way of coping with the emptiness in her life. Not that her husband wasn't aware of her state of mind, you know. But just like most men in the world, Charles Canning thought that he would be able to win his wife's heart over with material gifts, not realizing that the greatest gift a lonely wife craves for is the simple and yet loving company of her husband. Anyway, Canning decided to do something special for Charlotte's fortieth birthday. So he hired one of the most renowned confectioners of Kolkata—Bhim Chandra Nag—

to prepare a special sweetmeat in his wife's honour. It was then that Bhim Nag made a new sweet—deep fried sweet balls soaked in sugar syrup—the one that you are relishing right now.'

Having said this much, Ashu Babu looked up. Maity simply put the last piece of sweet into his mouth and stared back at the man.

'Ledikeni!' said Ashu Babu, a soft smile hovering on his lips. 'Polluted through decades of mispronunciation and aberrated from its original name: Lady Canning!'

'It's delicious,' said Maity, after putting the plate down on the floor beside his chair. 'And more so when one gets to know such an interesting story behind its origins.'

Ashu Babu slowly nodded his head and said: 'Not that you did not know the story before I told it to you, isn't that true, Mr Maity? So please accept my gratitude for letting a sick old man twice your age bask in a few moments of futile glory.'

I looked at Maity. His face had a soft smile, and a sure sign of deep reverence was in his eyes. Ashu Babu's eyes—old and exhausted and sickly as they may be—were presently twinkling with intelligence and wisdom. Although they were staring right at Maity, and had evidently seen right through him, Maity was calm, and was staring right back without even the slightest sign of hesitation. I, on the other hand, was quite startled and taken aback. For one simple reason.

We had not told the old man our names yet!

How did Ashutosh Mukherjee know who we were? Did he also know why we were here, then? Those eyes, those piercing, all-knowing eyes. I didn't know how Maity was doing it, but it was impossible for me to stare at them for too long. As soon as I took my eyes off him and looked at the shadow on the wall again, my heart stopped.

In a sudden flash of recollection, I remembered where I had seen that shadow before. Just a few days ago. At the movie that Maity had taken me to!

Nosferatu!

The wizened, shrivelled old vampire—who could read people's minds and see through their souls!

[10]

'Since you already know my name,' Maity said in a calm voice, 'I am sure you will appreciate why I am sitting here before you today.'

'Perhaps,' said Ashu Babu, 'but even if I do, I would like to hear it from you. You will have to come to the library, Mr Maity. The library won't walk up to you. It never does.'

Maity paused for a while, perhaps to choose his next words. Then he said, 'I am here to learn more about a few of your students.'

The light from the lamp wasn't very strong. Did Ashu Babu's face suddenly become grim just for a second? Or was I seeing things? The blue square on the wall was no longer there.

'Is that so?' the teacher asked. 'Which students?'

'Well, to begin with, Dr Prabhat Sengupta.'

'What do you want to know about him?'

'Well,' Maity was treading cautiously, 'it's actually his father that I am keen to know about. There was an incident here in Manikpur . . .'

Ashu Babu stared at Maity for a long time. Finally, he spoke, his voice feeble but clearly audible: 'Radhanath Sengupta. A fine young man, a head full of ideas and ideals.

He was my student too. Got his father's job in the estate's office; the family had moved here from a small town in Hooghly district. Radhanath was a brilliant student, had a sharp mind and an unmistakable sense of right and wrong. When his father passed away merely a year before he was supposed to retire, Radhanath got his job. Everything was going well for him, everyone in the village loved him, respected him. He was always nice to people, helped them in their times of need, gave them counsel when they came to him for guidance, encouraged everyone to send their children to school. People looked up to him, really. He had a happy and contented life here in the gardens.

'But then he lost his wife to childbirth. Radhanath was shattered. He loved his wife more than anything else in the world. Her death broke him and left him dejected. For several months, it was the neighbours who took care of little Prabhat, nursing him, raising him. Radhanath had submerged himself in his work. But time—they say—heals all wounds, no matter how deep they are. Radhanath took his son in his arms one day, and there was no looking back from there on. His son became his life, just as his wife once was. He showered all his love on his son. Father and son became almost inseparable since then.

'But then, something happened. Radhanath was in charge of the wages and payments of the labourers of the garden. And the labourers had been pleading with the owner of the garden, Jagat Narayan Chowdhury, to increase their wages—something that had not happened in a long time. When Chowdhury turned a deaf ear to their ardent appeals, the labourers met Radhanath—who they knew would at least listen to them. They welcomed him to their slums on the northern fringes of the gardens, and what Radhanath saw there must have shaken him. Because upon his return, he walked straight into Chowdhury's office and asked him to consider the labourers' demands for increased wages. Chowdhury was not the least bit pleased by the fact that Radhanath had visited the slums. He threw Radhanath out of his office, but not before insulting him for his audacity and his father for raising an arrogant spawn, telling him in as many words that servants should never forget their place. This infuriated the young, educated and principled Radhanath so much that he decided to stand up for the labourers' rights. He soon led an agitation, and thanks to the popularity he commanded amongst the labourers, not a single leaf of tea was plucked in Manikpur that year. In all the years that the British ran the estate, never had this happened, never had the wheels of the factory stopped turning.

'As expected, Chowdhury suffered huge losses. And he took this very personally. But the shrewd man he was—he did not retaliate at that point in time. On the contrary, he met the labourers and promised them that he would revise their wages. The labourers were simple, gullible people, they believed what he said and went back to work. But a few days later, Radhanath Sengupta's body was found hanging by the neck behind his own house in the village. The police came and claimed that he had committed suicide, even a note was found in his pocket. But everyone in the garden knew what had really happened.'

Maity was listening quietly so far. He now asked, 'How old was Prabhat Sengupta when his father died?'

Ashu Babu narrowed his eyes in an effort of recollection: 'How old could he have been? Hardly thirteen or fourteen.'

Maity paused for a few seconds and said, 'How did he take it?'

Ashu Babu gave a sad smile and said: 'How does a thirteen-year-old take his father's death, Mr Maity? Especially if he has never seen his mother? His father was all he had. Naturally, he was devastated. He fell ill and remained in delirium for several days. The neighbours who had helped raise him nursed him back to health and sent him to school as quickly as possible, thinking it would help him take his mind off everything that had happened. But young Prabhat was visibly affected. He used to sit aloof in class, his back to the wall, his face blank. He would stare out of the window for hours on end. Didn't respond even when called by his name. I was quite worried about him, to be honest. I tried speaking to him, comforting him, engaging him, giving him books and tasks. But nothing seemed to work. He used to be . . . he used to be a happy child, you know? He was one of my favourite students, had a very keen mind, always eager to learn. A smiling, laughing, playful child. Could be quite naughty at times too. Why, he had played so many pranks on me, that little imp. He and his friends. They thought I never knew who it was, but I did. We teachers . . . you see, we always do. But we love them so much, it is such an undefinable pleasure to see these young children learn and grow up and have fun, that more often than not, we pretend not to know.'

Ashu Babu paused to catch his breath, his face lined with a strange mix of joyful reminiscence and the grief of recollection.

'But ever since he saw his father hanging and swaying from the branch of that tree, Prabhat changed forever. He was never the same old naughty boy again. Oh, how often I wished he would play the same pranks on me again. But . . . he never did. Never again.'

My own heart had become quite heavy. Especially when I remembered what a devious man we were having to protect. Maity was silent for almost a minute. I knew he had more questions, but was giving the old man some time to rein in his emotions. Other than the steady chittering of the crickets, there was only one other sound that reached my ears now—the faint and faraway beating of drums. The labourers were playing their *madals*, perhaps. The sound was coming from the north. That's where their slums were, by the edge of the forest. Perhaps they were dancing around a fire after a hard day's work. Were they singing too? It was impossible to tell from so far away.

'There was another student of yours, perhaps in the same class as Prabhat,' Maity said. 'A boy named Shibnath Sarkhel.'

'Who, Shibu?' Ashu Babu smiled, nodding fondly. 'Yes, yes, a piece of work! Wasn't interested in studies at all, but was very good with the football. One day, I was in class teaching *Julius Caesar*, we were deep into the lesson, when all of a sudden, there was a racket towards the back of the classroom. Upon investigation, it was revealed that Shibu had fallen off his bench on to the floor, his body was shaking violently and his mouth was frothing. I immediately called my colleague who was teaching in the next room. He held some smelling salts under the boy's nostrils and the shaking seemed to ease out over the next few minutes. After some time, Shibu sat up, although in a daze, his jaws still twitching from the fit. He didn't seem to remember anything at all. My colleague told me that it would be best for the boy to rest for the day, so I sent him home. I continued to teach, and once the period was over, I decided to pay Shibu's home a visit, just to see how he was doing. He used to live on the other side of the village, towards the forest. Walking to his place, I reached Harinarayan Majumdar's orchard on the way and decided to take a shortcut through it. I must have gone no more than 50 metres into the orchard, when I saw Shibu Sarkhel sitting on the high branch of a mango tree, still in his school uniform, happily sucking away at a recently plucked mango with great contentment. I tiptoed to a spot under the tree and kept watching him for a long time. Meanwhile, Sarkhel Babu sucked the seed of the mango dry to the point where it had turned completely white, flung it away, and was just about to pluck another ripe one, when he saw me standing on the ground and watching him. The moment he saw me there, he started to shake his limbs violently once again, mumbling and groaning, eyes rolling, even as he was sitting on the branch!

'Naturally, I was not to be fooled this time. So, I calmly asked him to come down from his perch. To this, the boy immediately stopped shaking, pinched his ears, pulled a sad face and begged me to forgive him. I, on the other hand, was finding it exceedingly difficult to suppress my laughter, but I somehow managed to pull a grave face and asked him why he had to put up such an act in class. The response that came was vintage Shibu. He said: "Sir, all I had been hearing throughout the morning was Caesar did this, Caesar did that. So I thought, let me show the class what a real seizure could do!"'

Maity and I laughed out loud, and so did Ashu Babu, but Maity's next question changed the mood of the room in an instant.

'Is it true that his mother set herself on fire?'

Outside, the wind was probably blowing in this direction now, because the sound of the madals just grew louder. I thought I could hear the faint sound of singing too. It was just one tune, a rustic one, being repeated over and over again.

'It's true, all right,' Ashu Babu sighed, 'A most tragic affair, if there ever was one. Her only son was stunted in height. People used to laugh at him all the time. The boy never seemed to mind it too much, though. He lived his life on his own terms—had a very good friend in Prabhat, was a happy-go-lucky sort of a chap, couldn't care less about people's jeers and sneers. But his mother—poor woman—she got deeply affected by it.'

'It was because of this bullying and ridiculing that her son had to face that she took her life, isn't it?' Maity asked.

'Yes, you could say that,' said Ashu Babu. 'That, and the poverty. The family was quite poor. Shibu's father was an alcoholic, and he used to beat his wife every day. I had tried to talk some sense into him on several occasions. He would apologize to me, wail his heart out, swear he would never touch alcohol again, but after a few days, would repeat the same mistakes. Shibu's mother used to work in the Chowdhury household, washing utensils, mopping floors. Her income was the only source of sustenance for the family.'

'So you are saying that Shibnath Sarkhel's mother's death had nothing to do with Jagat Narayan Chowdhury?'

'*I am not saying that!*' Ashu Babu snapped and yelled out with such ferocity, that I was quite startled. He must have been a strong man in his heyday, but this sudden outburst immediately sent him into a bout of wheezing and violent coughing. The young boy standing in the corner quickly walked up to him and rubbed his back, trying to stabilize him, but failing hopelessly. I felt we should do something too, but when I turned towards Maity to say as much, I found him sitting still and staring at the old man with a steady gaze.

'I am not saying that,' said Ashu Babu again, once he had settled down a bit, this time in a softer voice. 'Ask anyone in the village, Chowdhury was a tyrant. Still is. Had it not been for that new manager who has taken on the reins of the estate, people would have shredded him to pieces. Everything that has been done for the welfare of the people of Manikpur and its adjoining areas is all because of that manager fellow.'

As the boy was giving the old man a backrub, the blanket had fallen off his body. With the boy's help, Ashu Babu now picked up the blanket and wrapped it around his shoulders once again.

'I . . . I tend to digress these days,' he said. 'What was your question again?'

'There was an incident with Shibnath's mother . . . '

'Yes, yes. They said she stole a wristwatch—an expensive one. It was never found.'

'Who said that?' Maity asked.

'Chowdhury, of course, who else?' Ashu Babu was still wheezing and finding it difficult to speak. 'People of the village did not believe him, but the poor woman couldn't take the shame and dishonour that came with the accusations. Chowdhury has committed some unspeakable crimes in his lifetime. I . . . I know. I have been around, you know? The things I have seen, the horrors . . . I . . . I just . . . '

The old man shut his eyes tight, his face had contorted in pain and disgust.

'So, it's all true, then?' Maity pushed on. 'What they say about him?'

'Every word of it.' Ashu Babu was still fuming: 'Oh, the injustice of it all! It's . . . it's too difficult to bear, sometimes. You lead a good life, an honest life, try to make the most of it, despite all the constraints of fate and fortune. And then comes a man like Chowdhury, ruining everything that you have built. Destroying homes, ravaging families, crushing anyone who dares to protest or cry foul.'

The boy in the corner suddenly said, 'You should rest now. I'll show these gentlemen out.'

Maity stared at the boy for a long time. Since he was standing at a distance from us, outside the reach of the light, his face was not quite visible. All I could see was that there was a calm expression on it.

'What is your name, son?' Maity asked.

The boy looked at Ashu Babu, and with a gentle nod of his head, the latter encouraged him to respond.

'Kanai,' the boy said.

Maity smiled at the boy and turned towards Ashu Babu once again, 'Would you mind asking Kanai to step outside for a few minutes, sir? I don't think he should be around to hear what we are about to discuss next.'

Maity's words were simple and direct, spoken with such composed authority that despite the visible unwillingness of young Kanai to oblige, Ashu Babu asked him to wait outside.

'There was another student in your school,' Maity waited for the boy to leave before continuing, 'perhaps not in the same class as Prabhat and Shibnath, probably in a lower class. His name was Abhijit Lahiri.'

Ashu Babu nodded, his expression grave and sombre, 'I remember him all right. he was one of the brightest boys I have taught.'

Having said this much, the old man paused. Maity seemed in no mood to prod him any further. He simply waited for Ashu Babu to start speaking again.

'But,' he resumed, 'he was also one of the most dangerous minds I have seen in any child in all my years as a teacher. I . . . well . . . it would not be an exaggeration to say that I was afraid of him, at times. Both of him, and for him.'

'Afraid?' Maity seemed curious, 'Why?'

'The boy . . . he was far too mature for his age. His grasp on concepts far beyond his age was pleasantly surprising, let down only by his knowledge of the ways of the world . . . knowledge far too inappropriate for his age. As a child, there was no sweetness in him—his manner was far from being childlike. I don't know if this came from the fact that he had no parent, or from something else, but one could easily see back then that this boy would grow up to be a quiet, reserved and calculating young man—the sort of man who even the most dangerous people would like to steer clear of, you know?'

'Did you ever fear that he could do something . . . bad? Something criminal?'

'Certainly not,' said Ashu Babu. 'How shall I explain this to you? It was just that he was completely different from the other children. There never seemed to be any childlike joy in him.'

Maity asked, 'Did you notice this behaviour in him when he joined your school? Or did something spark this change in him?'

Ashu Babu eyed Maity once and said, 'I knew you would ask about him when you sent Kanai out. Because it is clear that you have heard things. Things about Manikpur and about everything that has happened here over the years. No, it wasn't the incident with his sister that caused this most undesirable change in him. Abhijit had always been like that. A little too quiet, a little too cautious. He was just . . . different. Not just in terms of intellect, but in terms of awareness too. I . . . I am not quite sure if I am being . . . able to . . . '

'Of course, you are,' Maity's soft voice of assurance seemed to put Ashu Babu's mind at ease. 'What must have been his age when the incident happened?'

'He must have been no more than twelve years old, as far as I can remember. The scar of a lifetime for a child—to witness something like that. The two siblings had lost their parents a long time ago. Their uncle used to work as an overseer in Chowdhury's factory. Abhi and his sister used to live with him and his wife. It was the day of the Vishwakarma Puja that the incident happened. The poor, poor girl. The entire village was shaken by the incident, and as always, the police came. But Chowdhury had deep pockets, and his influence throughout the region was the stuff of legend. Nothing happened to him. One of his own men admitted to the crime, was taken into custody and was produced in Alipurduar court. The judge sentenced him to five years in prison; he walked out in one. For good conduct. Runs a government-approved ration shop in Sonarpur now. The things money can do!'

Ashu Babu was visibly distressed, even Kanai was not around to calm him down, so Maity gave him some time. Then he said, 'What happened to Abhijit's sister?'

A proud smile appeared on the old man's face, even as his voice trembled with emotion. 'She went on to become a professor! Teaches in a college in Delhi, it seems. A few years ago, she came to see me. I knew it must have been hard for her, you know? Coming back here? But she came . . . to see me . . . '

Ashu Babu's voice choked, 'Has a little boy and a girl of her own now, and a husband. Fine young man—teaches in the same university. They came into this very room and touched my feet, took my blessings. I pulled her kids to my bosom. Feels good, you know? Seeing them all grown up, going about their own ways, making an honest living. I . . . I feel . . . '

The flame of the lamp was now being reflected in Ashu Babu's glistening eyes, as he said one last word before hanging his head out of exhaustion,

' . . . content!'

A gentle smile hovered on Maity's face. In as soft a voice as possible, he asked, 'Did she say anything about her brother?'

'Yes.' Ashu Babu raised his glasses and wiped his eyes with the corner of his shawl. 'She said he had gone abroad for studies. Earned a masters in something, I don't quite remember. He is doing well for himself too, I presume. Although he never came to see me—none of the boys did.'

Ashu Babu seemed lost in his thoughts. Maity was watching him patiently. It had been quite some time since Kanai had left the room. It must be pitch dark inside, but Maity was taking his time. His eyes were still trained on the veteran teacher's face, which now seemed to give way to a new emotion.

Anger!

My observations were proved accurate by the man's response to Maity's next question.

'I have one final question about a student of yours, sir. After this, I promise I won't bother you any more. There was a student named Arjun in your school. Arjun Banerjee.'

Ashu Babu flared up in an instant, 'I think you should leave now, Mr Maity. And please send Kanai back in as you go. The forests are less than a mile from here; it's not safe to remain outside after dark.'

'Certainly, sir . . . but this boy, Arjun Banerjee . . . '

'I have nothing more to say to you, Mr Maity,' Ashu Babu growled with all the might left in his sick, feeble body. 'There was no one by that name in my school. Never ever. I am too old, I am too sick, I am dying. Please . . . leave me to myself. Please . . . just . . . just leave.'

[11]

Ever since we had reached Manikpur, no matter where we had
gone after sundown, there was at least some source of light
visible to us, however feeble or distant it might have been.
After stepping out of Ashu Babu's house, I truly understood
what the term pitch dark meant. No matter which direction
I looked, it all seemed the same to me, because it was like
staring into a wall of ebony on a moonless night. Maity
always saw more than anyone else in the dark, but now even
he seemed to have trouble finding his bearings.

'Let's give it a minute,' I heard him mutter.

We stood there waiting for our eyes to adjust to the
darkness. Kanai had shut the door behind us—quite
emphatically at that—plunging us in a deep and dark pit of
blackness. The sound of the madals still reached my ears,
although the tempo had picked up. There was a soft breeze
blowing, and somewhere nearby—perhaps towards my
left—I could hear the rustling of leaves.

Very, very gradually, I began to see things around me—
mostly trees. These were relatively easier to see because their
branches were swaying in the breeze against the background
of the night sky. Also, because they were the only things that
were there for us to see. As I had mentioned before, there

115

was not even a single house in sight, other than the one we had been thrown out of.

But the car? Where had the car gone?

We tried looking around, wondering how our trusted driver could have done something so irresponsible as leaving us here in the middle of the night, when suddenly, we heard a low grunt towards our far right. We followed the source of the sound to reach the corner of the road, on turning which, we saw a strange sight.

Just under the water tank that we had crossed on our way here stood our car. And squatting on the ground right next to it was Pele himself. On hearing our footsteps approaching, he stood up and threw his hands up in the air.

'What happened?' Maity asked.

'Swine!' Pele cussed. 'Scoundrels! Filthy dogs!'

'Puncture?' Maity asked. 'Did you drive over a nail or something by accident?'

'One tyre, I can understand. Maybe I made a mistake. But four?! That's no accident.'

'All four of them?' I asked, my voice laced with a mix of fear and incredulity.

'The tank was overflowing,' Pele pointed towards the huge rectangular water tank rising up in the sky. 'I thought you were going to take some time inside. So, I gave the car a nice wash. Then I went towards the woods over there. I had run out of cigarettes. The woods over there have some nice kunia trees, the dry leaves can be smoked. Came back here to find all four tyres completely flat.'

My heart had already started galloping away. Someone had done this on purpose! How on earth were we supposed to return to the guest house now? It would easily be a couple of miles away, if not more. Through the gardens. And I could barely see my own palm.

Maity did not seem too bothered, though. He said in a calm voice, 'Where's the nearest garage?'

'On the highway. Towards Sonarpur.'

'Perhaps we could call them?' I asked.

'We're in the estate's subdivision right now, far from the factory,' Pele said. 'No network here.'

Maity seemed unwilling to waste any more time. It was decided that Pele would lock the car and head towards the garage, to get help. And we would have to find our way back to the guest house on our own. All of this, of course, had to be done on foot. Once the car was brought back to a usable state, Pele could bring it to the guest house, just in case we needed him later tonight.

We quickly sprang into action. Pele opened the trunk of the car and brought out a small iron rod, roughly the size of a baton used in a relay race. He gave the rod to Maity and said: 'This is not much. But better than nothing if you come face to face with a wild animal.'

Maity handed the rod over to me and said, 'What about you, Pele?'

'I don't need anything,' Pele said, as he slammed the trunk shut and locked the doors. 'I grew up here. I know what to do.'

Having shot a quick prayer to our stars, we started walking. Pele would have to walk along with us till we reached the fork in the road. From there, we would have to take a right towards the temple and reach the guest house, whereas Pele would continue walking straight, towards the market, reach the highway and try to see if the garage was still open.

If not, he would have to catch a bus or hitch a ride all the way to Sonarpur to find help.

We were going back the same way we had come. For the first fifteen minutes or so, the path meandered through the village. I was astonished to see that there was absolutely no sign of anyone—neither a voice, nor even a remote sight of a lamp or light anywhere. It seemed like the entire village had just upped and left, leaving the dark, ghostly houses behind. Where had all the people gone? On asking Maity, he said: 'This is a common characteristic of villages in India. Especially the ones situated near forests. After dark, you hardly see anyone. But rest assured, they are all in their respective homes. Over there, for instance, is the veranda where the old man with the hookah was sitting and having a smoke. And to your left is the courtyard where the woman was offering her evening prayers. Up ahead, we will cross the household from which the little girl had run out to fetch her father's lime-green shirt. They're all in there.'

I was so surprised that I couldn't say anything by way of a response. Maity had noticed everything on our way to Ashu Babu's house! I thought he hadn't, but he had. He had seemed lost in his thoughts then. In fact, he wasn't even looking. But the man had seen it all! And not only had he remembered everything, he was able to identify the houses in this pitch dark too, when I was having to take every step with caution. Hats off to the man's eyes, really!

Pele was walking ahead of us; Maity and I were following a couple of yards behind. From up ahead in the dark, I could still hear unprintable curses being thrown at the unknown miscreants who had damaged our beloved driver's car. Right next to me, Maity was whistling 'Lara's Theme'. We were gradually leaving the village behind. On both sides, there were gardens; the smell of tender tea buds wafting in the air, the leaves rustling in the breeze. Even the temperature seemed to have dropped a notch or two out here. I shrunk my shoulders, put the iron rod under my armpit and rubbed my arms, hesitating to put my hands in my trouser pockets, lest I stumbled and had to break my fall.

I looked up at the sky but couldn't see a single star; must be overcast, I thought. Last night was moonless too. Perhaps there was a crescent moon up there somewhere, behind the clouds. The sound of the madals was getting fainter. Far away towards my left, I could see the frame of my view split into two different shades of black, one on top of the other, the top one slightly lighter than the one below. I realized one was the treeline of the Chilapata forest range, and the other was the sky. I looked behind me a couple of times. The chances of our stumbling upon a wild animal might be slim, but whoever sabotaged our car must have done it with some evil purpose. An encounter could not be ruled out.

Maity was whistling away without a care in the world, though. He had moved from Mozart to Mohammad Rafi by now. Pele was trying to see if he could get a bar or two of network on his cell phone. Something moved in the tea shrubs to my left. Maity didn't stop whistling. Pele put his phone back in his pocket, plunging us all into darkness once again. My heart was almost in my mouth.

'M-Maity?' I somehow managed to utter his name, although my mouth had turned completely dry.

'Can I ask you a question, Pele?' Maity completely ignored me and addressed our driver. Had neither of them heard the movements in the shrubs? In the dark it was impossible to know in which direction Maity was looking, or what his expressions were.

'On our way from the airport,' Maity continued, his voice casual, 'you told us that you were from Darjeeling, right?'

The cussing stopped. The silence that followed was long and uncomfortable, accompanied only by the crushing of pebbles by three sets of footwear. The sound of the madals was no longer there. We had come a long way from the car. We were literally in the middle of nowhere.

After a few more anxious seconds, I heard Pele's voice in the dark, and got the distinct feeling that it had changed somehow. 'I said I was born in Darjeeling. But I grew up here.'

'Ah, I see!' quipped Maity. 'Very interesting!'

Everyone fell silent again. We walked on. I tightened my grip on the rod. What was going on in Maity's mind? Why did he ask Pele that specific question? Did he feel that our driver was hiding something from us? What did we know of him, really? We had met him just yesterday, after all. And now, he was guiding us through the dark in the middle of unfamiliar terrain.

We continued to walk. Everything was silent, a bit too silent for my comfort. I wish Maity would start whistling again. But he didn't. Something was definitely playing on his mind.

'You go right from here,' Pele suddenly said. 'I go straight. Do you want me to come with you?'

I was so preoccupied with my thoughts that I hadn't noticed the fact that we had reached the fork in the road.

'No, that won't be necessary,' said Maity, 'we'll find our way. I suggest you focus on getting the tyres mended. Once you are done, please come and see us at the guest house. If, for some reason, you do not find us there, check with the chowkidar of the bungalow if we are inside. If not, try the Green View Lodge.'

'And if I don't find you there either?' Pele asked.

The answer came after a brief pause, but when it did, the message was loud and clear: 'Call the police.'

In the dark, I could not see if Pele understood Maity's instructions or not. He simply turned around and walked away without saying another word. In less than five seconds, he had vanished into the darkness. Maity watched after him for some time. Then he said, 'What a lovely night for a stroll, don't you think, Prakash?'

'Very funny, Maity.'

'Oh, come now!' Maity said. 'We've seen worse.'

Which was probably true. Maity's words gave me a bit of courage, although for the life of me, I couldn't understand how he was able to be so casual about the situation we were in.

'Why did he lie to us?' I asked, as I struggled to keep up with him.

'Who?'

'What do you mean, who?' I said with some amount of irritation. 'Pele, of course.'

'I have my reasons for asking, my friend,' said Maity. 'I have my reasons. And as for Pele, didn't you hear what he said? He offered a perfectly reasonable explanation, didn't he?'

'And you believed him?'

'Do you see any reason not to?'

I realized Maity was in one of his notoriously non-committal moods, and that asking him anything further would be absolutely futile. We continued to walk on the path, the pebbles continuously shifting under our feet. To avoid slipping over them and falling face down, Maity suggested a strategy. The path itself was around ten feet wide, but only five to six feet or so of it was covered with pebbles—and this segment was right in the centre of the path. The rest of it, towards the edges, was covered in ankle-deep grass.

'Stick to the grass,' Maity advised, 'but be careful not to go too much towards your left. You don't want to end up in the ditch.'

'I can't see a thing, Maity,' I said. 'Can you?'

'Just a thing or two,' he said. 'You walk ahead, I'll be right behind you. That way, if you stray from the path, I'll be able to guide you back in. Literally speaking, that is.'

The man's peculiar habit of resorting to humour in the most inapt of situations was a matter of intense irritation to me. Anyway, I tried to focus my mind on the march instead. We were making good progress, thanks to Maity's suggestion, but even at this pace, it would still take us around twenty more minutes to reach the guest house, in the best scenario. The wind had picked up, blowing from the north to the south. The distant hooting of an owl added to the eeriness of the atmosphere. Once the call of the bird died down, a heavy silence seemed to hang over the gardens. Even the crickets weren't chittering any more—Maity said it was because of the pesticides sprayed around the shrubs.

I was just about to ask him if those pesticides would keep snakes away as well, but before I could, a loud metallic clang rang out from my left, scaring the wits out of me, making me jump and sending my heart right to my mouth. It took me all of five seconds to realize that the strange ghostly noise was nothing but the tolling of bells swaying in the breeze, and that we had reached the temple. But by the time I had realized this, I had dropped the iron rod from my hand.

'Let it go,' Maity said, his voice grave now. 'It's fallen into the ditch, which is quite deep. It's too dark to look for it now.'

'I . . . I'm sorry,' I said, 'the bells . . .'

'Don't worry about it. Let me lead the way now. Stay behind me and tread softly.'

Maity moved ahead, and I followed his lead. Even in the dark, I could sense a sudden and distinct change in his behaviour. He had stopped whistling long ago, but now even his gait carried a certain amount of caution and alertness. His head had stooped forward a bit, and the sprightly steps that he was taking thus far were now replaced by sure footings that resulted in as little noise as possible.

A section of the sky seemed to clear out, leaving a gaping hole in the clouds from within which a few stars peeked down at us. After a few more minutes of walking—or shall I call it tiptoeing—we reached the T-junction from where we would have to take a left turn to reach the guest house. The road up ahead ran for a mile and a half to reach Jagat Narayan Chowdhury's bungalow, and upon crossing it, would lead to the estate's factory.

'Come with me,' Maity's whisper reached my ears, 'and don't make a sound.'

Why was he whispering?

To my utter surprise, in the faint light coming from the stars, I saw him completely ignore the left turn and push ahead, his back hunched, his hands stretched out a tad to give him the much-needed balance of walking almost on the edge of the ditch. It was clear that Maity wanted to avoid walking on the pebbles. In all likelihood because he did not want our footsteps to be heard.

I felt an irrepressible urge to ask him where on earth we were going, but I clenched my teeth to contain my query within me. Instead, I found myself following his footsteps to walk softly on the grass, until the junction was left behind us and we had reached a small building of sorts, made of bricks and tiles. It was completely dark.

'This way.' Had my senses not been working overtime, I would have missed Maity's low whisper altogether.

The clouds parted a bit more, letting a few more stars out. Had Maity's hand not reached out and gently steered me around it, I would have walked right into a large circular iron structure of sorts, placed bang in the centre of the courtyard that we had now entered. As I passed it by, I realized it was a post box—the old red ones that we normally used to see on street corners, and which—like many other beautiful memories of the good old days—were now rapidly disappearing, being replaced by the obnoxious-looking, flat-faced squarish ones.

Had we reached the estate's post office, then?

I remembered having crossed the post office while we were driving down to the lodge this morning. From the outside, it had looked like a small two-room affair. What were we doing in the post office in the middle of the night?

I was about to ask Maity, but I soon realized that there was no need for it. Because Maity had no intention of going anywhere near the post office. His destination, in fact, was the small building that was situated a few yards behind it, right at the edge of the steel fence that separated it from the tea garden.

What was this building? I didn't even know that it existed. All I had seen was the post office. I had never had a chance to see what lay behind it. But as usual, Maity had noticed it, and was now creeping towards it in the dark with an intention that was known only to him.

There was a large open area just outside the second building. Once Maity reached this clearing, he stopped and looked around, as if to gauge the layout of the surroundings. Then he quietly gestured for me to follow him and stepped on to the veranda of the building. It was a single-storeyed building, with a slanting roof at the top, and a wide veranda running along its entire length. With impeccable stealth, Maity quickly moved towards one of the many doors lining the veranda and pulled the panes ajar. The door opened without a creak, and I quickly made my way to Maity who told me to follow him inside.

As I entered the building, two things happened at the same time. A strange, unpleasant smell hit my nose and made me cringe. And my outstretched hand touched something slithering and made me jump back with a start. By now, Maity had moved to the other side of the room and opened a window, letting some natural light inside. And it was in this light that I slowly began to see the strange curtain-like things hanging from the roof of the room.

'Come and settle down in this corner, Prakash,' Maity whispered into my ears. 'Unlike outside, here we have an advantage over them.'

Them?

Before I could say anything further, Maity had moved away from me. I followed his instructions and crouched down in one particularly dark corner of the room, wondering all the while what those strange things hanging from the ceiling could be. They looked like curtains, but they were everywhere, except where they should have been—on the doors and the windows. They seemed to come down from hooks or clamps fixed to the beams on the ceilings, widening as they descended, and then rising up again to reach another clamp on the overhead beam. In a sudden flash of realization I figured out what those curtain-like things were.

Hammocks!

Dozens of them! What were they doing in this room here? Who had hung them here?

'What is this place, Maity?' I whispered.

'Oh, haven't you realized it yet?' Maity's voice was laced with genuine surprise. 'It's a creche. For the children of the labourers. The mothers leave their children here before entering the garden to pluck tea leaves, or do other work such as pruning, clearing weeds or spraying fertilizer.'

It was a sight to be seen, really! Never had I thought that I would witness something so unique and haunting. Dozens of makeshift hammocks, now empty, hanging from the roof of a ghostly building, swaying gently in the cool breeze on a moonless night. But what advantage was Maity talking about? Advantage over whom?

I was about to ask him, but he shot a forefinger up to his lips and shook his head. I had no other option but to refrain from speaking any further. The suspense was killing me, but I knew Maity wouldn't divulge anything else and that I would have to find out myself. Maity's penchant for theatricality was not unknown to me, and in all these years, I had sort of gotten used to it. I decided to wait, although in my mind, I was not sure for what or whom.

We sat in the dark corner, the hammocks gently swaying in front of us. I noticed that Maity had left the door of the room half open—one of the panes was shut, the other ajar. The window that he had opened was on the wall against which we now sat. We could not see out of this window because it was above our heads and behind us, but the faint light that came through it helped us see a section of the room.

I looked down at my watch in the dark. The radium dial gave me the time—just a few minutes past nine. It wasn't too late, but in a place like this, it seemed like the dead of the night. I took a deep breath and tried to steady my nerves. The foul smell hit me again. It reminded me of poorly maintained hospitals. Probably came from some sort of disinfectant. Not a very soothing smell for babies in a creche, I thought. I wondered if the corner that we were sitting in was clean enough. Well, at least there were no mosquitoes. I remembered Maity had told me in the morning that ample doses of DDT were sprayed in the gardens, but even that couldn't prevent instances of malaria and dengue among the labourers. What was it that he had said the acronym stood for? Dichloro . . . diphenyl . . .

What was that?

The room had suddenly become a bit darker. Because something in the doorway was blocking whatever little light was coming in from outside.

A man!

When had he come and stood there? I couldn't tell. He wasn't there a moment ago. Had Maity seen him? Although Maity was sitting just beside me, the corner was too dark for me to see him. Moreover, it was impossible for me to take my eyes off the door. I swallowed hard but was afraid to breathe. The man just stood there, without doing or saying anything.

To my right, Maity's heavy breathing was bothering me. If I could hear it, so could the man. In fact, the man did seem to look in our direction a couple of times, although he probably couldn't see us. Why on earth was Maity being so careless? Very slowly, I raised my hand to tap him on his arm in a bid to warn him that we were in the grave and immediate danger of being discovered, when a sudden realization froze my hand in mid-air and numbed me from head to toe.

It wasn't Maity who was breathing heavily!

Right over my head was the window. There was someone standing at it, looking into the room from outside. A strong smell of cheap tobacco cut through the pungent smell inside the room and hit my nostrils.

'Are you sure they came in here?'

The voice was gruff and harsh, the dialect local but comprehensible, the speaker literally inches away from my head.

The man at the doorway moved the pane a couple of times and said in a soft voice, 'The door's missing a bolt.'

The two men were clearly together. In all likelihood, they were the ones who had sabotaged our car. As I tried my best to keep my hands from trembling, I wondered how Maity knew of this building. Or why he had come in here. More importantly, how did he know that the bolt on this specific door would be missing? I suddenly remembered that he had asked me to take a bit of rest in the guest house after lunch and had himself stepped out for a while. Was it here that he had come on the pretext of taking a walk? Was it he who had removed the bolt? Had he anticipated the ambush then?

'Check the corners,' the man at the window said. 'I'm coming around.'

I desperately extended my hand to clutch Maity's, but my fingers touched nothing but the cold, bare wall. My heart almost jumped up to my mouth. He was sitting right next to me a moment ago! Where had the man gone? And how did he manage to leave my side without my noticing? I realized I would have to look for him.

Too late!

The first man had stepped into the room by now. He had a torch in his hand which he now switched on. I realized I was done for. I curled myself up and shrunk as deep into the corner as possible. The beam from the torch was not thick, but was moving systematically around the room, sweeping the nooks and corners, halting over dark recesses, steadily moving closer and closer towards me.

Where in the blasted hell was Maity? Why had he left my side when I needed him the most?

I shut my eyes. I was forced to, in fact. The light was now shining on me and it was too bright for me to stare into it. I heard a soft chuckle in the dark behind the glare of the light.

'Found one!' the man yelled.

Footsteps!

One, two, three.

The light was now right on my face. The man had probably squatted on the floor to take a better look at me. I brought my knees up to my forehead and prepared myself for the inevitable.

'You look just like a stray dog, you know?' said the voice, laced with contempt. 'Cornered, with its back to the wall. Do you know what we do to stray dogs out here?'

What was that sound?

The light shifted from over my face. I opened my eyes to find the man—one whom I had never seen before—staring at the wall to my left. The terror on his face meant he had seen it too, but was too late to react. With a loud creak, a heavy teakwood cabinet full of medicine, utensils, baby food, etc., came crashing down on him, sending broken shards of glass all over the floor of the creche.

'Pick up the torch, Prakash!' I heard Maity growl in the dark, even as the second man rushed through the door. Before I could do as instructed, before the man writhing on the floor could yell out in pain, or even before the second man had a chance to realize what had happened, Maity had pounced on him, wrapping one of the hammocks around his face.

Once, twice, thrice.

The room was now filled with the blood-curdling shrieks of the first man, at least one of whose legs had been smashed to bits. The second man struggled to free his face from the hammock's cloth, but the more he tried, the more he entangled himself. I picked up the torch from the floor and pointed it towards the middle of the room. Maity was calmly standing at a little distance, quietly watching the second man, who was burying himself deeper and deeper into increasingly complicated knots of fabric that he had no hope to free himself of. The man was now gasping for breath; his hands had given up any hope to free himself from the deadly cover on his face and were instead looking for help and mercy, which Maity was clearly unwilling to grant him.

'You have roughly two minutes before the last bubble of air is sucked out of your lungs.' I had never heard Maity speak in such a menacing voice. His shadow on the wall was shaking violently, not because he himself was trembling, but because the torch in my hand was. Maity was rock steady. As always.

The shrieks of the first man had become deafening by now. But Maity's baritone voice rang over it, as he continued to address the man entangled in the hammock: 'Had you not panicked, you probably could have squeezed an extra couple of minutes in there somewhere. Which would have given you enough time to work out the knots. But it's a bit too late for that now, isn't it? So why don't you forget all about that and tell me who sent you?'

With a deadly war cry, the man on the floor somehow managed to free his leg from under the heavy wooden cabinet, grab the wall and rise on his other foot. I looked at the fractured leg, and it was immediately clear to me that he would never be able to walk on it again. The man quickly pulled out a tomahawk-style axe from under his shirt and held it up to face Maity.

'No, no, not like that!' Maity took three quick steps towards the man, shaking his head all the while. 'Hold the handle here, son. Not here. And put your other palm over here. Firmly. If you hold it like this, you'll get a better swing.'

The man was so surprised to hear the words from Maity that for a brief moment or two, he didn't know how to react. It was a very short period of time, but that was enough for Maity to casually step on the man's fractured ankle. The man sent a piercing cry out into the night sky and swung the hatchet blindly. Maity calmly sidestepped it and moved out of its radius. The man kept swinging away at him, limping all the while, frothing and bleeding from the mouth, even as the other man's limbs were slowly wilting away.

'Save a life,' Maity pointed towards the hammock, 'rather than taking one. Do the right thing.'

The limping man hesitated for a second or two, but then quickly made his way to his friend and slashed at the cloth of the hammock, sending the other man crashing to the floor. The fallen man began to cough and wheeze violently, even as his friend freed his head from the cloth and tried to drag him out of the room.

'Who sent you?' Maity asked again, as he helped the coughing man up and wrapped his wilting arm around the shoulder of the limping man, who was clearly finding it impossible to believe that the old man he and his friend had come to kill had gotten the better of them with a hammock and a cupboard.

'Be strong,' Maity said, as he led the two men out of the door. 'You will have to carry him for some time. Five minutes, or so. After which, you will faint, thanks to that ankle of yours. Then, it will be his turn to carry you. Who sent you, though?'

The man simply cast a furious glance at Maity and walked out of the door, limping laboriously, struggling to hold his friend upright. Maity watched them go, sighed deeply and shook his head a couple of times. Then he walked back into the room and said, 'Are you all right, Prakash?'

'Y-yes,' I somehow managed to say.

'Excellent! Come on then,' he said. 'Let's get back to the guest house. I'm hungry.'

'Mr Maity?'

The torch in my hand almost involuntarily swivelled towards the doorway once again. There was a man standing there. I had never seen him before.

'Yes?' Maity said in a composed voice.

'I was heading to the guest house, looking for you,' the stranger said. 'And I heard someone yelling. What happened in here?'

'Oh, nothing much,' Maity said with a dismissive gesture of his hand. 'Just a couple of kids looking for stray dogs. And who might you be, sir?'

'I'm Lahiri,' the man said. 'Abhijit Lahiri.'

[12]

As soon as we reached the guest house, Abhijit Lahiri asked the caretaker to take him to the kitchen while Maity and I settled down in the living room. We had been through a nasty experience, and although Maity was the personification of calm and was now sitting on a sofa and staring at the floor, I was shaken to my core.

'Who were those men, Maity?' I somehow managed to ask.

'I wish I knew, Prakash,' Maity said, his eyes still fixed on the ground. 'There are layers and layers of mysteries here in Manikpur. One on top of the other. Some are in the past, some in the present. People are not who they seem to be, everyone is hiding something or the other. Motives, intentions, beliefs—it's all jumbled up in one big mess. Our job now is to single out the individual threads and see how each thread is interacting with the others. See them for what they truly are.'

Before I could say anything in response, Abhijit Lahiri entered the living room with the caretaker in tow.

'Have this,' he said, 'it'll strengthen your nerves and give you a quick boost of energy.'

On our way to the guest house, Maity had described to Abhijit Lahiri what had happened back there in the creche, and how the two men were waiting for us on the turn of the road in ambush, and how he knew something of this sort would happen and was prepared for it all. He now looked at the thick, dark, viscous liquid in the cup that the caretaker had placed before him and said, 'What is this?'

'It's tea,' said Lahiri. 'A highly concentrated one, with some additional spices thrown in. It'll give you a kick, so take short, gentle sips.'

Maity and I exchanged glances and took our first sip. Indeed, it was a strong solution—more of a paste than a liquid--and it hit the back of my head and sent a shiver through my body. It didn't taste very good, but after three or four sips, I felt remarkably better. Maity looked inside the cup and said,

'This is really helpful. You seem to know quite a bit about tea, Mr Lahiri.'

Abhijit Lahiri sat down on a sofa and said, 'Yes, I grew up here, as you very well know.'

Maity looked up. Abhijit Lahiri went on with a casual smile:

'I know who you are, Mr Maity. So neither of us needs to put up a charade. Prabhat and Shibu have told me everything. I had some work in Sonarpur, so I was out all day. When I returned to the lodge, they spoke to me and told me everything about you and your friend. So I decided to come and meet you in person. I was on my way here, when I heard the scuffle.'

Maity took one last sip from the cup, placed it neatly on the centre table and said, 'How did you know where we were staying?'

Abhijit Lahiri shrugged his shoulders and said: 'I didn't. But I figured that if you have indeed come to Manikpur with the purpose you claim, then you might want to stay somewhere close by, not too far from the lodge. I also figured that your first reaction might be to warn Chowdhury, and that he might want to keep you close to him. So, I took my chances.'

'An astute, logical deduction,' Maity nodded. 'Your reputation seems to precede you. We have heard that you have a very clear mind, and we now know that to be true.'

Abhijit Lahiri simply gave a slight nod. He was a tall, suave-looking man, with a well-groomed and polished appearance. His attire was smart and evidently expensive. Those patent leather shoes, by themselves, must have cost a fortune. The French beard gave him a masculine appeal and the look in his eyes was of cautious and meticulous contemplation. It seemed to me that he was the sort of man who was always careful about and responsible for every single word that came out of his mouth.

Maity was watching him closely too. He now said: 'Which is exactly why I am surprised to see that an intelligent man such as you could do something so foolish. Teaming up with a bunch of unprepared, emotionally-charged men in trying to pull off a crime such as murder, which requires such an immense amount of planning. You know you are going to be caught, don't you?'

'I don't think so,' Lahiri shook his head. 'If I were to indeed commit murder, I wouldn't leave any tracks behind. None that would lead to me anyway. But if it means anything to you, I have decided not to do it.'

I am not sure about Maity, but I was absolutely unprepared for that response. Maity was frowning too.

'I'm sorry?' he said, 'What do you mean?'

'It's simple,' Lahiri said in a calm voice. 'I've decided to drop the entire thing. It's not worth it.'

I glanced at Maity. The look on his face betrayed the same emotion that was going through my mind as well—one of strong suspicion and doubt. Surprisingly though, Abhijit Lahiri made no attempt to address the suspicion in our minds.

After some time, Maity said, 'You do admit that you were, in fact, planning to murder Jagat Narayan Chowdhury?'

'I do,' came the calm and brief response. There was no hesitation in Abhijit Lahiri's manner. He was sitting quite comfortably in his seat, left leg crossed over the right one, a cigarette burning between his fingers, a thin swirl of smoke making its way up from the fiery tip.

'You are saying that you have forgiven Chowdhury?'

'Certainly not,' Lahiri said, 'but I don't want my revenge any more. As I said, it's not worth it.'

'Have you spoken to your friends about your decision?'

'Yes, I have.'

'And what did they have to say?'

Lahiri took a long puff, dropped the ash in the tray on the table and said: 'They weren't too happy about it, naturally. In fact, they tried to dissuade me. And when that didn't work, they said some . . . well . . . some not so nice things to me.'

Maity watched him keenly, 'They called you a coward?'

'Among other things.'

'Indulge me with specifics, please.'

'Well, they said a lot of things, really. They said I was abandoning them. They said I was scared, that I had developed cold feet because our other friend Arjun hadn't turned up. They said a life of affluence and comfort had erased the pain and the anguish from my heart. But there was one thing they said that . . . hurt me the most . . . '

As Lahiri fell silent, Maity waited for some time and said, 'That your heart wasn't in it right from the beginning?'

Lahiri nodded gently. Maity and I looked on in silence. It was clear that there was a battle of emotions raging on within the man. After some time, the next few words he spoke clearly showed who'd won.

'But I have made up my mind, Mr Maity,' he said, 'and that's exactly what I told them. My pain is by no means less than any of theirs. And I have burnt in the same fire as they have, to the same extent as they have. My sister was brutally raped. Nothing is going to change that fact. For years, I have lived under an oath of vengeance. I was the one who had proposed the idea of the reunion in Manikpur. I was the one who had said we should kill Chowdhury. But when I look at my sister now, I find her happy! She has a loving husband, two beautiful children, friends who love her, students who respect her, colleagues who admire her. And that made me wonder: Who am I fighting this battle for, really? Who am I avenging? Is it her? Or is it me? And then everything became crystal-clear to me. There is no greater vengeance than success. To rise, to pick up the pieces, to learn to be truly happy is what life is all about. There is no greater revenge than to move on, Mr Maity.'

Maity was silent for some time. Then he slowly nodded his head and said: 'I am happy to hear that you have found your peace, Mr Lahiri. I am happy for you. I only wish that you could drive some sense into Dr Sengupta and Mr Sarkhel too.'

'I tried,' said Lahiri, 'but it didn't seem to work. I'm going to try and speak to them again before I leave, though.'

'You are leaving?' Maity asked, his tone marked with a clear sense of surprise. I myself was not able to believe what I was hearing. Things were moving at a fast pace, and I was finding it difficult to keep up.

'Yes, now that I have made up my mind, there's no point staying here any more. I would rather distance myself from Manikpur as much as possible, and get on with my life. I have made quite a few sacrifices in the pursuit of revenge, neglected several things that required my attention. I need to see to them now. But there's one thing that I would like to make amply clear to you.'

'What is that?'

A steely look had come upon Abhijit Lahiri's face as he replied: 'That I have *not* forgiven Chowdhury. I will never be able to do that, as long as I live. I still believe that he deserves what's coming to him. I may be sparing his life, but if I were to find out in the newspapers tomorrow that someone has indeed murdered him, I would neither be surprised nor unhappy.'

Maity made no comment.

Abhijit Lahiri snubbed the cigarette out in the ashtray, rose from his seat and extended his hand towards Maity. 'There's an early morning flight from Bagdogra to Delhi tomorrow. I managed to get a seat on it somehow. I plan to start in a few hours. The roads will be relatively free after midnight, and I will reach the airport by dawn. It was wonderful meeting you, Mr Maity, and I appreciate your coming out here. My mind was seeking closure, so I thought I'd come see you. I wish you and your friend well, and I can only hope that you do not judge my friends too harshly. Thank you, and goodbye.'

Having said this much and shaking Maity's hand, Abhijit Lahiri walked out of the living room, stepped down the stairs of the veranda and disappeared into the dark, leaving us speechless for several minutes.

'What just happened, Maity?' I finally asked.

'An extraordinary turn of events, no doubt!' he said.

'But . . .' I was still unable to believe everything I had just witnessed, 'this is excellent news, isn't it? Two out of the four friends aren't going to be our problem any more! Half the battle is already won!'

Maity did not respond and the conversation ended there. We made our way back to our rooms, freshened up and then sat in my room, trying to fully comprehend this new development. Maity left for a few minutes in between, and I heard him speak over the telephone placed in the drawing room. I sat on my bed, exhausted, thinking about everything that had happened so far. The incident in the creche had left me rattled, but now I began to organize my thoughts clearly. In particular, I began to wonder how easily Maity could get rid of two of his biggest problems—Abhijit Lahiri and Arjun Banerjee. One realized, in the nick of time no less, that he was making a big mistake. The other never turned up. This left us with the other two men—the doctor and the magician. Somehow—and I don't know why I felt that way—it seemed to me that Maity would be able to talk at least the doctor out of it. Perhaps I felt this way because despite his external appearance and determination, the man seemed not only too unprepared to commit a crime such as murder, but too upright for it too. Or perhaps I felt this way because Abhijit Lahiri and Arjun Banerjee had stopped just short of the actual crime. Murder—as Maity had explained to me on several occasions in the past—was never an easy thing to do. Murderous intent might be common in many people, but when it came to the actual act of taking a life, even the strongest of hands shuddered in hesitation. As far as I could see, Maity would have one and only one tough task—stopping Shibnath Sarkhel. That man was a slippery customer. Behind his comic appearance and dramatic mannerisms, I had seen glimpses of a very disturbed mind. Had Maity seen it too? He must have. If there was one thing that I had learnt about Maity in all these years, it was that he saw everything.

Caretaker Gangadhar came in and announced that dinner had been served. I met Maity directly at the dining table. He looked worried and exhausted. I knew he loved good food, and Gangadhar's wife was an excellent cook. But Maity was lost in his thoughts, eating carelessly and unmindfully—as if his heart and mind were elsewhere.

'Whom did you call, Maity?' I asked.

'Hmm?' He seemed to come out of a trance.

I repeated my question, to which he said, 'Mohan Sharma.'

'What did he say?'

'Chowdhury is all right. He had woken up a couple of times in between; he spoke to Charan as well. He is sleeping again now. I have asked Mohan Sharma to ensure that no one is allowed inside the cabin.'

'I see,' I said. 'And the other call?'

'The other one was—'

Maity suddenly stopped eating and looked up at me, 'Wait a second. Did you overhear my conversations?'

I was baffled by this sudden change in his behaviour. I stammered, 'N-no . . . I was in my room . . .'

'Then how did you know I made two calls?'

'I don't know,' I said. 'I just . . .'

'Think, think, think . . .' Maity raised his voice, an intense grimace of impatience spreading across his face.

'I . . . I don't know, Maity . . . perhaps because I heard you speak at two different volume levels . . . in the beginning, I could hardly hear your voice, but a couple of minutes later, you were speaking at the top of your voice. So I thought . . .'

Maity stared at me blankly for a long time. Then he said, 'Yes, yes, I . . . I see what you mean . . . When I made the second call, the line wasn't clear . . .'

I was wondering why Maity was taking such a trivial thing so seriously, and even his next words did not offer any explanation at all. He said in an unmindful manner: 'It's fascinating how we perceive these little things around us, isn't it? Without actually knowing that we do?'

I didn't know what to say. Maity shook himself out of his thoughts. He resumed eating and answered my earlier question: 'I have a contact in Air India, back in Kolkata, an old friend. That's whom I had called. If Abhijit Lahiri catches the six o'clock flight from Bagdogra tomorrow morning, or if he doesn't, either way, we will get to know.'

'Are you saying Lahiri could have lied to us?'

'No one is to be trusted in this case, Prakash. We must suspect everyone.'

'Everyone?'

'Everyone.'

After dinner, Maity and I went straight to our respective rooms. The door between our rooms was always kept open.

It had been a long, exhausting day, and within minutes after he had wished me goodnight and stepped into his room, I heard Maity's heavy breathing. I realized he had fallen asleep.

I, on the other hand, was feeling restless. Dozens of questions were bothering me: Why did Ashu Babu say that he didn't know Arjun Banerjee? And how did he know our names? Why did Pele lie to us about where he was from? Who was the man who had tried to get into Chowdhury's room in the bungalow? What did Rafiq Ali mean by those mysterious words of his? Who threw the rock at us with the warning message? Why did Arjun Banerjee never turn up in Manikpur? Did he have a change of heart, just like Abhijit Lahiri did? If he did, then why did he call up the other three men and remind them of their vows? And finally, who sent the thugs to attack us?

I realized if I continued thinking about all these mysteries, I wouldn't be able to get a wink of sleep all night. Meanwhile, Maity's breathing had turned into a snore. And it was irritating the hell out of me. I was just wondering if I should go up to his bed and ask him to turn sideways so that the snoring stopped, when I suddenly heard a soft sound in the dark.

What was that? I held my breath and perked up my ears to listen carefully.

A car!

I realized Pele must have been able to repair the tyres after all. He must have brought the car to the guest house to see if we needed him tonight. I glanced at my watch. It was almost one o'clock. I rose from the bed and walked up to Maity to wake him up. But he was fast asleep, and I decided against it. If it was simply a matter of telling Pele that he could go home now and ask him to pick us up tomorrow morning, then I did not need Maity to do that. I could do it myself.

I put on my slippers and unlatched the door as softly as I could. Then I stepped out on the veranda. The night wasn't exactly chilly, but there was a cool breeze blowing. Perhaps that was why I had heard the sound from a distance because there was no sign of the car yet. I decided to wait. To my left was the door to the living room. To my right was the door to Maity's bedroom. Both these doors were now shut. There was a tiny bulb glowing in the middle of the veranda, just outside the dining hall. The light from it did not reach the far end of the veranda, and I had never been to that side. I felt a strong urge to explore the other side but didn't want to stray too far from the bedroom, given the fact that there had been an attack on us merely a few hours ago, and also because of everything that Pele had told us about wild animals. If a fox or something entered the room and hid under the bed, I would be in trouble later in the night.

Where on earth was the car? It should have reached by now. Had I made a mistake then? Perhaps I had heard something else?

My eyes went to the other side of the veranda once again. It was merely 30 feet away, but thanks to the bulb's position and the glare from it, I could not see anything beyond it.

Dash it all!

My curiosity got the better of me, and I made my way towards the dining hall. Step by step. The light was now above me, I was standing directly below it. The far end of the veranda was now dimly visible to me. What was that room over there? I had to find out.

I walked towards the end of the veranda, until I reached the room. This was probably the kitchen. There was a bag of charcoal dumped in one corner. I had read somewhere that cooking food over coal fire always gave an additional taste to it. Right next to the spot where the coal was kept, I saw a set of stairs going up. Those stairs must go all the way up to the terrace, I thought.

I had always felt a magnetic attraction towards terraces. In fact, in my Ballygunge home as well, I often spent time on the terrace. The sense of openness, the unhindered fresh air, the ability to look down on your surroundings from a vantage point, the vast sky hanging over you—all these things seemed priceless to me. Something got the better of me, and I realized I simply had to make my way up to the terrace. Almost like a man in a hypnotic trance, I took my first step on the stairs. There was a sweet smell floating around in the air—probably coming from the compound's lovely flower garden. Hasnuhana—I thought—and a hint of the smell of tender tea buds. An intoxicating cocktail. Step by step, I climbed the stairs. I had turned a corner from the veranda, so the light from the bulb no longer reached here, but there was a strange light up ahead. I realized I was in luck: the terrace door was open, and the clouds were moving away. Although there was no moon tonight, the stars were enough to light up my path.

Ahhh!

A sigh of contentment escaped my lips. Had the breeze just picked up? No. It was just that there was nothing to obstruct it any more. I had reached the terrace. I could hardly see anything around, just faint impressions. But the touch of the cool breeze on my skin was so soothing! Up above in the sky, the Milky Way was spread from one end to the other. I watched it in awe, enjoying the rare sight in all its glory. I recalled how miserable the weather was in Kolkata right now—all the heat and the sweating. Could I ever hope to see such a clear night sky from the city? Never! This was heaven, by comparison. If only I could stay here for a few more . . .

There it was!

I had heard it all right. The sound of a car's engine. Which direction was it coming from? That side, no . . . *that* side . . . over there! I quickly made my way to the edge of the terrace and looked out into the dark. This was not the front of the guest house. This was the rear. There were bushes and jungles over here. How could a car drive through all that?

The car was now somewhere closer. And it was then that I saw the signboard of the Green View Lodge, flickering in the dark at a distance. And I immediately realized that the car I had heard was not inside the estate. It was on the highway, and it wasn't trying to reach the guest house. In fact, it had stopped in front of the Green View Lodge. I could not see the car itself through the heavy foliage that blocked my view, but I knew it was there. Its headlights illuminated a portion of the lodge's compound wall. The headlights were switched off, and the sound of the engine stopped too. I still couldn't see the car. What I could see, instead, were the rooms of the lodge. Not the rooms per se, but the windows. Two of them. Which meant that the occupants of the other two rooms had either fallen asleep or weren't inside. Had the American tourist left? And Abhijit Lahiri too? Who was in the car? Was it waiting for someone? There was no way to tell.

What was that?

I tried to take a better look through the branches and leaves that were blocking my view. I had no control over their swaying because they were out of my reach and the breeze was blowing at an unsteady pace now. As they moved, I caught several short, partial glimpses of the lodge. For instance, there was now a shadow against one of the glass windows. Not a shadow, a silhouette. There was someone standing there. A man! No, wait! Not one . . . *two* men. They seemed to be talking. And from the manner in which their limbs were moving, it seemed to me that some heated words were being exchanged. I squinted and moved my head to adjust my view. Who were the two men?

I had my answer soon. Moments later, the door of the room opened. And someone stepped out.

Abhijit Lahiri!

Lahiri made his way down the stairs and stood next to the car. There was a bag hanging from his shoulder. He now threw the bag into the car through the open window and lit a cigarette. He took a couple of puffs and let out smoke that looked like a red cloud in the taillights of the car. Then he looked up towards the balcony and said something. There was a strong gust of wind blowing towards me, which is perhaps why I heard his words so clearly.

'*It's all over now.*'

If there was a response from the top, I did not hear it. Abhijit Lahiri then threw the cigarette on the ground, stomped on it with his foot and jumped into the back seat of the car. I heard the car roll up on to the dark and deserted highway and pick up speed. From the glimmer of its headlights shimmering and moving rapidly through a screen of foliage that blocked my view, all I could deduce was that it moved towards the south, in the direction of Bagdogra.

Abhijit Lahiri had probably told the truth. He had indeed left Manikpur, hopefully forever. I turned my attention towards the lodge once again, moving my head to try and catch a glimpse of the other man. But the silhouette had moved away from the window by now.

Tough luck!

But . . . wait!

There was someone else out there, at a little distance from the lodge, behind a row of bushes. I narrowed my eyes to catch a better glimpse. Someone was standing behind the bushes now. No, not standing. Crouching! In fact . . . *hiding*!

The man now looked here and there, and stood up. Then he quickly moved towards the barbed fence of the estate, climbed over it with a clean jump and disappeared from my view.

Everything fell silent again. There was no other sound except the rustling of the leaves. I stood there for a minute or two, trying to fathom what I had just heard and seen.

Then I made my way back to the bedroom. Maity was still asleep. I lay down on my bed and forced myself to think. What on earth was going on in Manikpur? Who were these mysterious people moving around in the dark? What were they up to? One of them was clearly Abhijit Lahiri, and it was obvious that he left, just like he had said he would. But who were the others? Where was Pele? Had he been able to get the tyres fixed? Or was his car still standing in the dark near Ashu Babu's house?

As my eyes slowly shut in on themselves, the last thought I remember going through my mind was whether this bizarre case could throw any more shocks and surprises at us. As it turned out, it did. Because I woke up with Maity shaking me violently by my shoulder.

'Wake up, Prakash, wake up,' he said, as I saw the morning light stream in through the windows. From the softness of the light outside, I realized it was still quite early in the morning.

'What is it?' I said, with a grimace.

'Wake up,' he said again, 'we have to go to the bungalow right now. Jagat Narayan Chowdhury has been murdered!'

[13]

There was still no sign of Pele, so without wasting any time, we set out on foot, walking as fast as we could. Out of the guest house, all the way to the T-junction, turning left, then past the post office and proceeding towards the bungalow.

Although Maity had almost dragged me out of the bed and my head was in a tizzy from what he had told me, I couldn't help but notice that the gardens had donned a fresh and beautiful appearance in the early morning. The ground, for instance, was wet, although winter was still far away and dew was uncommon. Had it rained last night then? After I had gone to bed? After walking for a couple of minutes, I realized that it probably hadn't. We had to stand aside to let a tractor pass. The vehicle was hauling a tank, from which water was being sprayed on to the path, most probably to ensure that it didn't get too dusty throughout the day. As I looked in the distance, I saw a couple of more tractors running through various parts of the garden, perhaps doing the same. The heads of the tea shrubs looked extra green, their tips now shining brightly in the soft light of the rising sun. After the sound of the passing tractor had died down, I could hear hundreds of birds chirping from the branches of the shade trees. Some of the smaller ones had even made their way down to the top of the shrubs, landing on them and hopping from one to the other. Far towards our right, the branches of a couple of large Krishnachura (gulmohar) trees seemed to be swaying a bit too much, and upon a closer look, I saw a group of black-faced langurs frolicking about within the foliage. A particularly enthusiastic langur flung itself from one treetop to the other, causing hundreds of red Krishnachura flowers to dislodge from the branches and drop on the shrubs below. From a distance, it almost seemed like the tree was shedding blood.

Indeed! Blood had been shed in Manikpur. Apparently, Jagat Narayan Chowdhury had been stabbed to death. While we were sleeping. We had failed to do the job that had been entrusted to us. There were thin billows of smoke rising from over the heads of the treetops towards the east. The village was waking up, perhaps oblivious to the news of the death of a man they all knew. News would spread though—bad news always does. Although, for some reason, it didn't seem to me that even a single tear drop would be shed in the village of Manikpur today.

As we hurried down the path, Maity said that he was awoken by the caretaker Gangadhar knocking on his door. Mohan Sharma was on the phone, and it was he who gave Maity the news. Charan had found his master lying dead on his bed, soaked in blood. There was a wound on his chest; it was obvious that he had been stabbed with a sharp weapon.

'Didn't Charan hear anything in the night?' I asked, perplexed. 'A noise or a groan or something?'

Maity shook his head and said, 'Nothing.'

'Have the police been informed?'

'Yes,' said Maity, 'I asked Sharma to call the police. This can't be kept from them any more. I called my friend in the airlines too, and asked him to inform the authorities at Bagdogra. Abhijit Lahiri was stopped from boarding a flight to Delhi a few minutes ago. He is in police custody now. They are bringing him back to Manikpur as I speak.'

'Oh my god!' I almost yelled out. 'So that's what he meant when he said those words last night!'

'What are you talking about?' Maity asked. 'What words?'

I quickly narrated to Maity everything that I had seen and heard the previous night from the terrace—including the mysterious shadowy figure I had seen in the bushes by the side of the road. Maity's frown was back on his forehead.

'Are you absolutely, positively certain that you saw Lahiri leave?' he asked.

'One hundred per cent. I didn't quite catch a proper glimpse of the other man in the bushes, nor the one at the window, who was arguing with Lahiri. But I can assure you Abhijit Lahiri got into the car and left. And just before he did, he looked up towards the balcony of the lodge and said, "It's all over now". I heard that, for sure.'

Maity was silent for a few seconds. We could now see the bungalow ahead of us. A strange sense of dread filled my heart. There was a dead man lying in there, after all.

'Did you notice anything unusual about the two men at the window?' Maity asked.

'Unusual?' I said, panting as I walked. 'I don't know what you mean. One of them was Lahiri, of course. But I'm not sure who the other man was.'

The chowkidar had seen us coming from afar. His face had turned pale, and it was quite clear that he was as worried about the tragedy as he was about his own future. He quickly opened the gates and let us through. Before rushing through the gates and walking into the lawns, Maity said only one final thing, and it sounded decidedly cryptic to me: 'We may not be sure who the other man was. But I think we can be fairly sure who it wasn't.'

There was a small group of people who had crowded at the door of the cabin. They were probably in Chowdhury's employ—the bungalow's staff. We made our way through the crowd and entered the cabin. Charan was sitting on the floor in one corner, a middle-aged lady was trying to console him. On seeing us, the poor old man burst into tears, shaking his head and blabbering something indecipherable. Maity patted him on his shoulder a couple of times and quickly moved to the other end of the room. Mohan Sharma walked up to us. It was quite evident from his face that he had received a terrible shock.

'I . . . I . . .' he began, his face looking helpless and nervous. Maity quickly held his arm and made him sit down on one of the chairs. I had an irresistible urge to step into the bedroom and take a closer look at the corpse, but Maity was busy consoling Sharma and I did not want to leave his side. Maity took a few seconds to calm Sharma down and asked, 'What happened here, Mr Sharma?'

'I . . . I checked on him last night, Mr Maity,' Mohan Sharma was still finding it difficult to speak, 'just like you asked me to. He was sleeping. He was . . . he was breathing. I know he was breathing—I saw him.'

'What time was it then?'

'Time?' Mohan Sharma stared blankly at Maity's face. 'Time . . . not sure . . . must have been . . . it was right after you called. I took your call from the bungalow, and then quickly made my way down here.'

'So, around quarter past eleven?' Maity asked.

'Yes . . . perhaps . . . I didn't . . .'

'That's all right. What did you do then?'

Mohan Sharma wiped the sweat off his face and said, 'I walked into the bedroom along with Charan, to check on Mr Chowdhury. He was fast asleep. So we stepped out without making a sound and shut the door behind us. I stayed in the living room for some more time, just outside the door. Then I asked Charan to stay here and made my way back to the bungalow. I had some paperwork to take care of, so I went to Mr Chowdhury's study. I fetched the files and walked back to the cabin—thought I'd do my work from here. Charan was still here when I got back. I asked him if he had had his dinner. He said he hadn't. So I asked him to go to the bungalow and have something to eat. He came back in around half an hour or so. I was right here in this room all throughout, no one could have entered the bedroom.'

'You didn't leave in between?' Maity asked. 'Even for a minute?'

'No, not at all! I was sitting over there on that sofa, working. If anyone would have passed me by and entered the bedroom, I would have noticed.'

Maity stared at Mohan Sharma's face for some time. The young man suddenly seemed very afraid, as a new and terrifying realization slowly began to dawn on him. 'Oh! This . . . this probably puts me in a . . . very . . .'

'I am not going to lie to you, Mr Sharma,' Maity said in a grave voice. 'It does. But I can assure you that as long as I am in Manikpur, no harm will come upon anyone who is innocent.'

Mohan Sharma didn't seem too convinced; he clutched his fingers together to keep them from trembling. Maity pressed on, 'What happened after Charan came back?'

'I continued to work late into the night. And then I suddenly woke up with a start. The file had fallen from my hands. I realized that I must have dozed off. I quickly sat up and saw that Charan had fallen asleep too. I woke him up and asked him to stay alert. Day was breaking. So I made my way back to the bungalow to freshen up. When I came back after half an hour or so, I saw Charan sitting on the floor at the doorway, his face strangely contorted, his eyes wide and terrified. I realized right that instant what had happened. I rushed into the room and found Mr Chowdhury lying there, with . . . b-blood . . . '

'*Mr Sharma!*'

Someone had called out Mohan Sharma's name from the bedroom, making us all turn our heads and look towards the bed. The silk mosquito net that I had seen yesterday was still fixed to the bed. The voice had come from within the net. It was a familiar voice. Maity stood up. Step by step, we walked towards the bedroom. Through the doorway and towards the bed itself. Behind the net, Jagat Narayan Chowdhury's lifeless body was lying on the bed. His hands outstretched, his face pale and bloodless, his eyes half-open. There were stains of blood on the bed and the blanket. There was blood on the corpse as well, creating a horrifying pattern of ill-formed concentric circles that became darker and darker in shade as they moved towards the small wound on his chest. One look at the wound was enough to tell me that the knife that was responsible for Chowdhury's death had been driven right through the man's ribcage, all the way through his heart. The weapon, however, was nowhere to be seen.

But wait a second! There was someone else inside the mosquito net!

A pair of legs had come out from inside the net and rested on the wooden floor of the cabin. I could immediately identify the shoes. I had seen them just yesterday morning. At the Green View Lodge!

'I'm ready to announce the time of death now!' The voice said again, 'Please note that a more accurate estimate would be possible only after an official post-mortem.'

'Mr Maity,' Rafiq Ali was standing in one corner, next to a glass window. He now stepped forward and gestured towards the man behind the net. 'This is Dr Sengupta. He is the one who was looking after Mr Chowdhury in the absence of his regular doctor.'

My heart was pounding away. Prabhat Sengupta now came out from behind the net and stood before Maity.

'Time of death,' the doctor said, 'between midnight and three in the morning.'

Maity stared at the doctor with a grave look in his eyes. Prabhat Sengupta stared back at him with a strange look of resignation on his face. I cast a quick sideways glance at Mohan Sharma and Rafiq Ali, as they looked on. The tension in the room was so strong that I could barely keep myself calm. What would Maity do? What would his next words be? A frown was slowly beginning to develop on Rafiq Ali's forehead as he watched Maity, and I couldn't seem to ignore it any more. Maity had now stared at the doctor for almost half a minute.

'What would you say was the cause of death, doctor?' Maity finally said.

I was not sure if Mohan Sharma noticed it, but Prabhat Sengupta seemed somewhat relieved. As was I. The tension seemed to have diffused at that moment, although Rafiq Ali was still watching the proceedings keenly.

'Perforation of one of the ventricular chambers of the heart,' the doctor said, 'most likely the right one. Leading to loss of blood. Death must have occurred in less than two minutes.'

Maity was still staring at Prabhat Sengupta.

'This is merely an estimate, though,' Dr Sengupta continued. 'The exact cause of death can only be found after a formal post-mortem is carried out.'

'Thank you for your opinion, doctor,' Maity said, before turning to Rafiq Ali.

'Has the murder weapon been found yet?' he asked.

'No,' said Rafiq Ali, 'the police are looking for it in the lawns and the adjoining areas.'

'The police?' Maity asked. 'Where are they?'

'They were here,' said Rafiq Ali. 'They must be on the other side of the pond right now. A gap has been found in the hedge fence near the southern banks. Wide enough for someone to make his way through. It was blocked by a makeshift mesh of wire till last night, but it seems someone has ripped it apart. The police are trying to see if they can find any footprints on the ground near the spot. The bushes are being checked too.'

Maity stepped out of the room. I noticed Prabhat Sengupta glancing at him from time to time. Maity picked up a file full of papers from the table in the living room and looked through it.

'The estate doesn't seem to be doing too well these days, isn't that right, Mr Ali?' Maity said, his eyes still scanning the papers.

Rafiq Ali's response came a trifle late. He said: 'There are some problems, yes. But all gardens have their own problems, Mr Maity. That's the nature of this business. One just has to deal with it in the best manner possible.'

'We've heard good things about you. The people over here seem to like you a lot. They think the gardens have survived only because of you.'

Rafiq Ali responded with a sad smile.

'Might I ask,' Maity shut the file, put it back on the table and continued, 'where were you between midnight and three o'clock this morning?'

'Mostly in my bungalow. I had a late dinner last night. There was a party at the Planter's Club in Hasimara, on the way to Bagdogra. One of our colleagues from a nearby garden was retiring, so we had thrown him a send-off. I don't drink, so I had driven myself there. I reached Manikpur a few minutes past one o'clock and went straight home. I always go on my rounds early in the morning, so I quickly went to bed. I woke up this morning when Mohan called me. Came as soon as I heard.'

'Are you a family man, Mr Ali?'

'Yes. But my wife and children are in Muzaffarpur right now.'

'So, you are alone at home these days?'

Once again, Rafiq Ali's response came a little late. He smiled and said: 'Not exactly. There's my staff—cook, maids, gardener, driver. In fact, my chowkidar will vouch for the fact that everything I have told you is correct. As will my butler.'

Maity smiled and said, 'I'm sure you realize . . .'

'I do,' Rafiq Ali nodded. 'You're just doing your job. And as I have said earlier as well, I am willing to cooperate in any way I can. In fact . . .'

Rafiq Ali looked around and lowered his voice, 'I saw someone last night, Mr Maity.'

'You did?'

'Yes. I can't say who it was, because it was too dark, but I am certain it was someone quite tall . . . roughly . . . roughly . . .'

Ali was now looking at Dr Sengupta as he stood in one corner speaking to Mohan Sharma.

'Roughly as tall as the doctor,' he said, 'give or take. The man even had a bag on his shoulder, just like the one the doctor is carrying right now. I wonder . . .'

'I would urge you to leave all the wondering to me, Mr Ali,' Maity said. 'Where did you see this mysterious figure?'

'Right next to the bungalow's compound, in the middle of the plantations. There's an entrance to the estate from the other side, towards the market; it opens on the highway. On my way back, I had come in through that entrance and was driving past the bungalow. I saw the man walk out of the shrubbery next to the hedge wall and disappear in the darkness. I couldn't make out who it was. I stopped the car at the spot where he had disappeared, but it was too dark and he was nowhere to be seen.'

'Did you happen to notice what time it was when you had seen this man?' Maity asked.

Rafiq Ali thought for a few seconds and said, 'Must have been 1.30 a.m. or so. Yes, that must have been it. As far as I can remember.'

Maity nodded his head and said, 'Very well. I may have some more questions for you, Mr Ali. But for now, I think I would like to speak to the police, if possible.'

'Certainly, I'll see if I can find Inspector Sen.' Having said this much, Rafiq Ali stepped out of the door. Maity and I turned around to find Prabhat Sengupta watching us from a distance. On finding us by ourselves, he made his way to us.

'In case you are wondering,' said the doctor in a low voice. 'I didn't do it, Mr Maity.'

I quickly glanced at the other end of the room to find Mohan Sharma sitting on the sofa trying to console Charan, who was still weeping for his deceased master. Maity, on the other hand, was looking straight at the doctor's face with a steely glance.

'I had assured your wife that I would bring you back to her safe and sound, doctor,' he now said, his voice grim, his jaw set rock hard. 'But if I find that you were in any way responsible for the death of Jagat Narayan Chowdhury—any way at all—I swear to you I will not hesitate for a second before handing you over to the law.'

Prabhat Sengupta nodded his head and said: 'I understand. But the truth is that I didn't do it. I wanted to. In fact, I can't say I am not relieved that . . . that this has happened. But the fact remains that it was not I who ended Chowdhury's life. I had come to Manikpur to kill him, I admit that, and I am willing to admit that to the police as well. But I didn't get a chance to kill him. And even if I were to kill him, I wouldn't have stabbed him. I had other means at my disposal, as you of all people are well aware. No, Mr Maity. Chowdhury was already dead when I got here last night.'

Maity's frown deepened, 'You mean when you got here this morning?'

Prabhat Sengupta hesitated for a few seconds. Then he said, 'No, Mr Maity. I came here last night. Sometime around one o'clock. And I saw a few things—strange things. Things that didn't make any sense.'

Maity asked the doctor to follow him and stepped out of the door on to the lawns. We made our way to the pond. There were birds chirping all around us. Dozens of dragonflies were floating on the calm waters of the pond, next to lotuses and lilies. The rays of the morning sun were now shimmering through the canopy of foliage over our heads. The entire place was calm and blissful, and the air I breathed was fresh and cool. Nature in one of its most alluring avatars, completely unaffected and unperturbed by the fact that a grave crime had been committed merely a few yards from the spot.

As soon as we reached the banks of the pond, Maity turned towards the doctor and said in a stern voice, 'Tell me everything, doctor.'

[14]

'Last evening,' Dr Sengupta said, 'a little after half past seven or so, when Abhi came back to the lodge, he announced that he had decided to go back to the city. Shibu and I were shocked beyond words, because we weren't expecting this at all. Among the four of us, Abhi was the one who was the most determined to get his revenge. In fact, he had once told us that he had planned everything down to the last detail, drawn up an elaborate scheme, and that each of us had a role to play in it. And then, last evening, he said he was going back, he didn't want to do it. Just like that! All of a sudden, out of the blue! Shibu and I asked him why he was backing out. Shibu, in particular, was not able to contain his displeasure. He was furious with Abhi, called him a coward. In fact, I had to stop him from going for Abhi's throat. He was fuming, so I sent him out, asked him to cool his heels. Then I tried to speak to Abhi, tried to remind him of everything Chowdhury had done. But he didn't budge from his decision. He left, said he wanted to speak to you before leaving Manikpur. I came back to my room. I was quite upset myself, was finding it difficult to come to terms with the realization that not all childhood vows and promises last the test of time. But what really saddens me now is thinking of just one thing.

Why did Abhi have to put up such a charade? Why did he lie to us? We are his friends, aren't we? Why did he tell us that he was leaving?'

'What do you mean?' Maity frowned.

'Well, haven't you realized it yet, Mr Maity? It was Abhi who murdered Chowdhury last night!'

I looked at Maity to find him staring at the doctor's face with a sharp frown on his forehead.

'Are you saying this because of what he told you last night?' Maity said. 'That it was all over?'

'How did you know that?' It was the doctor's turn to be surprised now.

'It doesn't matter how I know,' Maity shook his head. 'It was those words that made you realize that Abhijit Lahiri had already murdered Chowdhury before he left for the airport, wasn't it?'

'You are right, Mr Maity. He came back late in the night. Said that he had had a discussion with you, and that he had told you everything. Then he prepared to leave. I kept on arguing with him. But he just wouldn't listen. His final words to me were: "It's all over now." But I hadn't realized the true meaning of those words until much later. It was only when Shibu barged into my room later that night and told me that Chowdhury had been murdered that I understood the true meaning of Abhi's parting words.'

'Wait, wait, wait. Hang on a second,' Maity seemed as confused as I was. 'When did Shibnath Sarkhel tell you about the murder?'

'About half an hour after Abhi left. Must have been around half past one, approximately. I was lying in my bed, wondering what to do, now that Abhi had left, when there was a frantic knock on my door. It was Shibu. He was sweating profusely. There was a look of deathly terror on his face. I asked him what was wrong, why he looked so frightened. "Run," he said, his eyes wide in fear. "Get out of Manikpur, as quickly as you can. Abhi tricked us. I saw him. He stabbed Chowdhury!" Having said this much, he rushed out of my room. Before I could ask him anything else, he hurried down the stairs and disappeared in the darkness.'

'Strange!' Maity remarked.

Strange indeed! Was it Shibnath Sarkhel who I saw hiding in the bushes outside the lodge last night, then? What was he doing over there? And how did he know that Abhijit Lahiri had murdered Chowdhury? Had he come to the bungalow last night too? He must have—that's the only way he could have seen the murder being committed. What an extraordinary turn of events! I couldn't believe there was now an eyewitness to Jagat Narayan Chowdhury's murder!

Maity's next question brought me back to the conversation: 'But why did *you* come to the bungalow last night, Dr Sengupta?'

'I . . . I just . . . wanted to . . .' Prabhat Sengupta stammered.

Maity was watching Dr Sengupta keenly. He said: 'You wanted to see him one last time, didn't you? Dead! The man who was responsible for your father's death, the man whose heartbeat you had heard yesterday morning through that stethoscope of yours—when you were called upon by unsuspecting members of his household to treat him—the man whose pulse you must have felt. No matter how frail he was, Jagat Narayan Chowdhury was alive till yesterday. Your father wasn't! It had all seemed so . . . so unfair. Hadn't it, doctor?'

Prabhat Sengupta hung his head to shut his eyes in pain. Lips trembling, voice shaking, he somehow managed to say a few more words, between gasps and chokes: 'It . . . it felt good, Mr Maity. To see him, lying dead in his bed. Was it wrong . . . to feel good? I stood over there, by that window and peeked inside through the glass panes to see the man's blood-soaked, lifeless body lying there. And . . . and it felt good! Even from a distance, I could tell that it was all over. I am a doctor; I knew where the knife had struck. There was no coming back from there. But . . . but, Mr Maity, I am a human being too, am I not? Could I have been wrong? What if I made a mistake? What if Chowdhury was still alive? What if I could have saved his life? But . . . the truth is that I did not want to. Even if I could, I did not want to. That's the truth. No matter how bitter it is. And if he was alive, and I didn't help him, then I am responsible for his death too.

'Does that make me feel bad? As a doctor, yes it does. But as someone who has lived with the haunting memories of his father's corpse hanging from a tree, swaying in the breeze, it doesn't. It felt good. Abhi was right. It was all over! After twenty long and painful years, it was finally over! But one thing is for sure, Mr Maity. This predicament, this doubt, this guilt—this will haunt me forever. For the rest of my life!'

Maity stepped up to Prabhat Sengupta and placed a soft hand on his shoulder. In a voice as gentle as possible, he said, 'Do you realize now, doctor? Do you see now, what taking a human life can do? Bad people do bad things. In retaliation, good people cannot do bad things. That's not how the world is supposed to function. No matter how vile the man was, simply watching him dead has left you so distraught. You, who are not a stranger to seeing corpses in your line of work.

Imagine what it would have done to you if you had indeed taken his life?'

Prabhat Sengupta pinched his eyes and shook his head. He looked distraught and for good reason. In fact, I felt sorry for the man. If only he had listened to Maity!

Maity sighed and said: 'Well, it goes without saying that sooner or later, I will have to let the police know about your true intentions of coming to Manikpur. And that of your friends too. There is no other way. But don't worry, get a grip on yourself; you will not be punished for a crime you haven't committed. And speak of the devil, here comes an officer of the law.'

I suddenly noticed Rafiq Ali watching us quietly from behind a large neem tree. He was now joined by a burly, scary-looking, pot-bellied police officer, and the two of them walked up to us. Mohan Sharma had also stepped out of the cabin in the meantime. We all met at the doorstep.

'You are Mr Janardan Maity, aren't you?' the man with 'B.P. Sen' etched on a shiny tag on his khaki shirt said with a smile on his face. 'The famous detective from Kolkata?'

'Pleased to make your acquaintance, Inspector,' Maity nodded.

'Likewise, likewise,' Inspector Sen looked Maity up and down. 'Mohan Sharma here tells me that Mr Chowdhury had entrusted you with a task. There was an intrusion here, it seems, a week or so ago. And there were reasons to believe that Mr Chowdhury's life was in danger. I don't understand why he would have preferred to speak to a private detective instead of coming to the police, but then the rich have their own whims and fancies. And more often than not, these don't make any sense. Anyway, don't worry, Mr Maity. We are all aware of your reputation. I can only hope that we will be able to help each other.'

'I look forward to that,' Maity said calmly.

'But he did make a mistake by not coming to us, the old man,' said Inspector Sen, staring hard at Maity. 'Paid the price too.'

Maity did not say anything by way of a response. The Inspector's behaviour went through a sudden change, and he said: 'Anyway, what has happened has happened. This Lahiri—what's his name . . . yes, Abhijit Lahiri—he has been arrested. Seems he left Manikpur in a hurry, roughly the same time when the murder was committed. Well, he will be here soon. And I'm quite certain that it will not take more than one round of interrogation for my men to drag the truth out of him. What do you say, Mr Maity?'

'That would indeed be a remarkable achievement.'

Inspector Sen either did not catch the sarcasm in Maity's response or chose to ignore it. In any case, he turned towards Dr Sengupta and said, 'It seems you have announced the time of death, doctor?'

'Yes,' Prabhat Sengupta said as calmly and as briefly as possible, 'between midnight and three a.m. But a post-mortem is required to get the exact details.'

'Duly noted,' the Inspector said. 'By the way, you yourself have been staying in the same lodge as this Lahiri fellow, haven't you, doctor?'

'Yes, the Green View Lodge.'

'Did you notice anything unusual about him? Anything at all?'

Prabhat Sengupta stole a quick glance at Maity and said, 'No . . . I mean . . . we hardly spoke.'

'Hmm!' The Inspector stole a quick glance at Rafiq Ali, adding: 'Well, no worries. I might have a few more questions for you. Would you mind coming down to the police station in the afternoon? It's just a couple of miles from here.'

'Sure,' Prabhat Sengupta said, 'I'll be there.'

'Excellent, excellent,' said Inspector Sen. 'Well, is there anything else you can tell us about this case right now, Mr Maity?'

'You may want to look for a man named Shibnath Sarkhel,' Maity said as he raised his right palm to his chest. 'About this height. He was staying at the Green View Lodge too, in the room adjacent to Dr Sengupta here.'

'*This* height?' Inspector Sen scoffed. 'Shouldn't be too difficult to find then, eh? Heh, heh, heh! But do tell me, why should I look for him? What has he done? Is he a suspect too?'

Maity's response was extremely measured: 'He might be able to shed some light on whatever happened here last night. After all, Abhijit Lahiri was staying in the room right next to Sarkhel's.'

'Valid point,' Inspector Sen nodded thoughtfully. 'If that is true, then we most definitely need to speak to him. Any idea where I can find him?'

'He's not at the lodge,' said Maity. 'I can tell you that much.'

'No worries, we'll find him.'

'Has the murder weapon been found yet?' Maity asked.

'No, not yet. But we will find that too,' Inspector Sen cleared his throat.

Maity gave a nod and turned around to leave. I followed him.

'And Mr Maity!' the Inspector called out from behind, 'I'm going to have to ask you not to leave Manikpur till this gets over. As you very well know, everyone is a suspect right now. Including you and your friend here.'

'We will make ourselves available when you need us, Inspector,' Maity said.

As we were walking through the lawn and heading towards the gate, we saw Pele waving at us from outside the gate. He had brought the car around. Maity waved at the chowkidar to let the car through, and then turned around to face the bungalow itself.

'Maity,' I said, 'how did you know that it was Prabhat Sengupta whom I had seen Lahiri speaking to at the lodge last night?'

'That's easy,' Maity said, his eyes still scanning the bungalow and its surroundings. 'You saw this conversation happen inside one of the rooms, didn't you?'

'Yes, but it could have been Shibnath Sarkhel as well.'

'It could have been. Which is why I asked you if you had felt that there was anything unusual about the silhouettes you had seen at the window. Had it been Sarkhel arguing with Lahiri, then you would have been able to tell, on account of Sarkhel's height.'

How silly of me, I thought, it didn't strike me at all! It was Prabhat Sengupta, after all. The doctor was telling the truth. But what about the man in the bushes? Could that have been Sarkhel? I asked Maity.

'That is difficult to say, because you hardly saw the man. Although for the life of me, I don't understand why Sarkhel would want to hide in the bushes at that time of the night. Who would he want to hide from?'

'From Abhijit Lahiri perhaps?' I suggested. 'If he saw Lahiri commit the murder, then wouldn't it be natural for him to hide from the man?'

'Why?' Maity asked. 'Did he believe that Lahiri would kill him too?'

'If he was an eyewitness, then Lahiri might have wanted to. Don't you think?'

Maity looked at me for some time and said, 'Have you ever wondered why Sarkhel came to the bungalow last night?'

I thought for a second or two and said, 'For the same reason as the doctor did, I suppose. To see if Chowdhury was really dead?'

Maity shook his head and said: 'No, that's not possible. Because, according to him, he saw Lahiri commit the murder. Which means that *when* he decided to come here, he was certain that Chowdhury was alive.'

'Oh my god!' I said. 'So there could have been only one reason why he came to the bungalow. He himself wanted to kill Chowdhury! He wanted to finish him off as soon as possible, and leave Manikpur.'

Maity nodded a couple of times, although he looked like he was in deep thought. I went on, 'That is what must have happened. Lahiri tells the doctor and Sarkhel that he is going back to the city. Sarkhel realizes the doctor might leave too, and he will be left all alone in Manikpur. He comes to the bungalow later in the night. He wants to kill Chowdhury. He makes his way to the cabin, but finds Lahiri already present there. He sees Lahiri stabbing Chowdhury. He runs back to the lodge. He warns the doctor, tells him what he saw, asks him to run. Then leaves himself. And all of this could mean only one thing.'

Maity nodded, 'That Abhijit Lahiri came back last night. He came back to the bungalow after he pretended to leave. Which is not impossible. You saw him leaving towards Bagdogra. He could have asked his driver to take a left turn into the estate through the market entrance and drive towards the bungalow. Then he could have asked the driver to wait in the dark at a distance and made his way into the compound through the hedges, on foot. After finishing his business here, he could have made his way back to the car that was waiting for him. It was then that Rafiq Ali saw him. Do you remember? The man Ali saw was carrying a bag on his shoulder. And you had seen Lahiri carrying a bag too.'

'But hang on,' I said, 'why would he take the bag out of the car? He could have simply left it in the car, couldn't he?'

'He could,' said Maity thinking deeply. 'Unless . . . unless . . . unless he wanted to carry the knife in it. Carrying it on his person could be dangerous. If he was spotted, he would have no option but to drop the knife and run . . . '

Maity trailed off, and before I could say anything by way of a response, Pele screeched to a halt in front of us.

'Where were you, my friend?' Maity asked, his voice marked with slight irritation. 'We were waiting for you last night.'

'The garage on the highway was closed,' Pele said. 'I had no other choice but to go all the way to Sonarpur to get help. During the night, hardly any bus or truck passes on the highway. And it's not safe to walk along the highway, lots of wild animals all around. So had to wait a long time before a truck came through. Finally reached Sonarpur and woke up my mechanic friend. He had been drinking last night, so he had a hangover, and—'

'All right, all right, spare me,' Maity raised his hand. 'Come on now, we don't have much time, and we have several stops to make.'

'Fine,' said Pele, as we hopped in. 'Where to first?'

'*Mr Maity!*'

Someone yelled Maity's name just as he was about to respond to Pele's question. We looked out of the window to find Mohan Sharma rushing out of the bungalow, waving at us.

'Why is he running?' I asked.

'I think I have a pretty good idea why,' Maity murmured, as he watched Sharma hurrying down the path towards us. By the time the man had reached us, he was completely out of breath.

'It . . . it hadn't occurred to me so far,' Mohan Sharma said, gasping for air, 'amidst all the chaos . . .'

'But it did occur to *me*, Mr Sharma,' Maity said, slowly nodding his head. 'You see, it is my job to let things occur to me.'

What on earth was Maity talking about? And why was there a look of such intense terror and bewilderment on Mohan Sharma's face? What else could have happened now?

'It's the knife, isn't it?' said Maity, 'The one you had in your possession, the one the intruder had left behind a week ago?'

'Y-yes, Mr Maity,' said Mohan Sharma, his eyes wide in terror. 'I had kept the knife in the bungalow, in Mr Chowdhury's old bedroom. But it . . . it's not there any more! I suddenly had a doubt . . . so I went upstairs to check. I . . . I can't find the knife anywhere, Mr Maity! It's gone!'

[15]

Twenty minutes after Mohan Sharma had announced his startling discovery to us, we found ourselves standing in front of Ashu Babu's house. During these twenty minutes, I kept thinking about everything that had happened in this strange case so far. And although the solution was right in front of my eyes, it somehow seemed to me that there was something bizarre and mysterious about it all. As if there was something hidden from us, as if we were looking only at the things that were apparent, on the surface. Maity had gone quiet again, and I did not feel like asking him what was going through his mind. He simply stared out of the window, lost in his thoughts. Sometimes he would shut his eyes tight and open them again. Every now and then, he would twirl his fingers around in the air, as if to paint an invisible picture or draw a line that would connect all the dots. It seemed to me that all the facts of the case were bearing down heavily upon him, and he was struggling to establish the connection between them. There was indeed too much confusion all around. To cut through the clutter and arrive at the truth wouldn't be easy.

Up ahead, when we could see the turn near the water tank, Maity asked me a strange question.

'Prakash?'

'Yes, Maity?'

'If I were to remind you of an old school friend of yours—someone whom you have not seen or heard of in ages—and if I were to address him as Dr so-and-so, what would your first reaction be?'

I thought for a few seconds and said, 'Well, I'd probably want to know more about his profession. As in, I'd try to find out what kind of doctor he was.'

Our car had stopped in front of Ashu Babu's house by now. Before stepping out, Maity said: 'Exactly! Nine out of ten people would have the same reaction.'

Kanai had stepped out on to the veranda. His face was as calm and impassive as we had seen last evening. Before we could say anything, he asked us to come in with a gesture of his hand. Maity and I stepped in, crossed the sitting room and entered the next room, only to realize that even in broad daylight, Ashu Babu's bedroom didn't receive much light. Much of this seemed intentional, because there were as many as three windows on the walls, all of which were shut.

'I was expecting you.'

The voice came from somewhere within the darkness. Not that the room was totally dark, but having walked in from the broad daylight outside, I was having trouble adjusting my eyes. It took me a few moments to see anything, and even when I could, faint outlines were all I could make out. Something moved in the dark and I heard the creak of the bed. I squinted my eyes to find the veteran teacher lying on the bed, covered from chin to toe in the blanket I had seen last night.

'How come I didn't hear the eight o'clock siren from the factory this morning?' The shape shifted a little more in the dark. 'What news have you brought me, Mr Maity?'

Maity said, 'I'm afraid there's been a terrible tragedy, sir.'

There were a few moments of silence.

'Is it what I think it is?'

'Yes, sir.'

'Then why call it a tragedy?' The bed creaked under his weight as Ashu Babu tried to raise himself on his elbow, but he seemed too weak to sit up. His health seemed to have deteriorated since last night, even his voice was feeble, although each word was pronounced clearly and with as much emphasis as was possible under the circumstances.

Maity did not respond. I looked at Kanai. He was standing at a distance, watching the proceedings.

'Why have you come to me, Mr Maity? What do you expect me to do? Mourn?'

Maity was silent for a few seconds. Then he said: 'Last night, when I asked you about a young boy named Arjun Banerjee, you told me that you did not know anyone by that name. I was wondering if—'

'Correction!' The forefinger from Ashu Babu's trembling right hand went up in the air, but couldn't stay there for too long. 'I never said I didn't know anyone by that name. I said there was no one by that name in my school.'

Maity seemed confused, 'But then . . .'

'Arjun had come from outside. His father used to work here in Manikpur, but he used to study in a boarding school—I don't know where. I had only met him a couple of times, playing with the local boys in the school playground. He used to come to Manikpur for his holidays, spend time with his family and go back. It was on one of these visits that Chowdhury grabbed him and abused him. The poor boy was found unconscious in the woods. As always, the incident was hushed up. With threats and bullying from both Chowdhury and the police. A twelve-year-old boy, Mr Maity. A sweet little boy. Laughing, giggling, running around. Chowdhury scarred him for life. So don't you *dare* come into my home calling that brute's death a tragedy! Don't you dare do that!'

The last few words came almost in a growl, and the force with which they were spoken sent the old man wheezing and coughing. Kanai immediately rushed to the ailing man's side.

Maity watched them for some time and said, 'I'm going to take your leave now, sir. Thank you for all your help. I don't think I will be bothering you again.'

Maity turned around to leave and I followed him. When we had reached the doorway of the bedroom, we heard Ashu Babu's voice once again and were forced to turn around.

'Did he suffer?' the man asked, with great difficulty. 'Did he die in pain?'

I looked at Maity. He was staring at two glistening circles in the dark. Ashu Babu's glasses. The man had managed to lift his head from the pillow somehow.

'Probably,' Maity said. 'He was stabbed right through the heart.'

The circles disappeared. I realized the old man had collapsed on the bed again.

For the final time, his voice was heard again, gentler, calmer and more peaceful than ever: '*So foul and fair a day I have not seen!*'

We stepped out of the room and on to the veranda. Maity had a deep frown on his forehead. Something was bothering him.

'Can't we do anything for the poor old man, Maity?' I asked, in desperation. 'He seems to be in great pain.'

'If there is anything that will truly help him now,' said Maity, 'it's to leave him to himself.'

I wasn't too happy with what Maity said, and it must have shown on my face. Maity looked at me a couple of times and said, 'All right, all right, fine. We will ask Prabhat Sengupta to come and take a look at him.'

Our next stop was to be the police station. Maity glanced at his watch and remarked that in all likelihood, Abhijit Lahiri must have been brought there by now. We reached the highway and turned towards the right. Pele said that the police station was around a mile and a half from there. While passing by the Green View Lodge, we stared at the rooms where the three friends had put up. What a strange situation Maity and I were in right now!

'Too many threads,' I heard Maity mutter under his breath, 'way too many threads. Some twisted, some straight. Some dark, some fair. Some smooth, others crude and tattered. All intertwined with each other. I don't think I have ever come across such a fulfilling puzzle, Prakash.'

'Fulfilling?' I asked, confused.

'Of course! It has been a long time since I felt so alive! Exhausted, battered, no doubt—but alive! This is what one lives for, my friend! A puzzle that racks your brain and rattles you to the core, one that teases you with glimpses of a solution before plunging you back into darkness again. I can't tell you how enriching such an experience can be.'

'I don't know about you, Maity, but I can't make out head or tail of this entire affair.'

'That's because you are looking for the head in the head's place, and the tail in the tail's.'

'What do you mean?'

Maity took a moment to answer: 'Think of it as an artwork. A painting. Not one of those surreal works of modern art, no. A portrait. A face, a body, arms, legs—everything that ought to be recognizable. But you can't make out anything yet because parts of it are still unfinished, yet to be sketched, yet to be loaded with colours, yet to be given the final flourish. And in this specific case, there is a deliberate attempt to hide the colours, to stop the image from forming, to make you look for the face in the wrong place. Hence the warning letter, hence the attack on us in the garden, hence the lies.'

'Lies?' I asked. 'What lies?'

'Everybody is lying, Prakash, everybody. Either lying or hiding the truth.'

The conversation was beginning to take an interesting turn now. I said, 'Can you give me an example?'

'Certainly,' said Maity, 'take the doctor, for instance. Why didn't he—'

'*Watch out!*'

Before Maity could say anything further, I had yelled out at the top of my voice, because a child had come out of nowhere, tried to make a dash from the right side of the road to the left, botched up the calculation and fallen right in front of our car. Had Pele not slammed on the brakes in the nick of time, we would have had an extremely nasty and bloody mishap on our hands. As the rubber squealed against the road and the car came to a thudding halt, the poor kid was taken completely by surprise. The car hit him and threw him to the ground. A massive timber-carrying lorry zoomed past us, missing us by a whisker.

'It's a little boy, Maity!' I yelled.

'It's *not* a boy!' Maity muttered, as he jumped out of the car. Pele and I joined him. The afternoon sun had risen, and although summer was long over, the rays of the sun were strong enough to heat up the asphalt on the road. Lying on the fuming tar-pitched highway and writhing in pain was magician Shibnath Sarkhel!

'Of all the gin joints in all the world,' Maity shook his head, as Pele knelt next to the man to assess the injury. '*Khel khatam*, Sarkhel Babu. You need to stop running now.'

Other than a bruised elbow and a scratch on the knee, Shibnath Sarkhel had had a miraculous save. Our car was almost in the middle of the road; there were vehicles passing by, so we lifted Sarkhel off the road and moved him to the car. Pele drove the car off the road and parked it under the shade of a large tree.

'Bamboo groves make excellent mating spots for snakes,' said Maity. 'I'm sure you are aware of that. Whatever I am going to ask, you will answer truthfully. Or else we will tie your hands and legs behind your back and throw you into that bamboo grove over there. Understood?'

Shibnath Sarkhel had still not recovered from the shock of the accident. He stared blankly at Maity and me.

'Why are you running?' Maity said, his voice stern. 'Don't you know that a murder has been committed?'

'I didn't murder anyone,' said Sarkhel. Even his normal gestures seemed exaggerated for some reason.

'Let's assume for a second that you didn't. But running away from a crime scene is also a bad idea—I am sure that much you do understand? Where did you think you were going? You, of all people, would be nabbed by the police in a jiffy. The description they would send out would have to carry just one line.'

'I . . . I didn't kill Chowdhury. I swear I didn't. I just went to the bungalow. In fact, . . . in fact I saw who murdered him.'

Maity and I looked at each other. Maity asked, 'Whom did you see?'

'Abhi,' Sarkhel swallowed hard, 'Abhijit Lahiri. He said he was leaving, he said he wasn't interested in Chowdhury any more. That rich brat! He . . . he ditched us all. But I had my doubts, I knew him all too well. So later that night, I went to the bungalow, to check. And my suspicion was correct. I saw Abhi stab Chowdhury to death.'

'You saw the entire thing?'

'Yes, with my own eyes!'

'You saw his face?'

'I didn't have to. I am one hundred per cent sure it was him. He had a bag on his shoulder, he was carrying a knife in it.'

'How do you know he was carrying a knife in the bag?'

'Because I saw him bring the knife out of the bag. He went into the cabin, pulled the knife out, stabbed Chowdhury with it, put the knife back in the bag, opened the window and threw the bag out. Then he shut the window again, came out of the cabin, picked up the bag and ran away towards the gap in the hedge. From there, he made his way to the pebbled road and left for the airport.'

'What did you do then?' Maity asked.

'I waited for some time. Perhaps five minutes, perhaps fifteen—I don't know. I was . . . I was shaken. Never imagined in my wildest dreams that I would be so disturbed to see Chowdhury die. I came out of the bushes and peeped through one of the windows of the cabin. Saw Chowdhury's corpse lying there. It was . . . it was a horrible sight! I . . . I ran out of there and made my way back to the lodge. I met Prabhat and told him what had happened. Then I ran myself.'

Maity's face was still stern. He said, 'If you ran, then why did you come back? What are you doing here?'

'I ran all night. But couldn't make it too far. My feet are short. They don't carry me so well. At daybreak, I hid in the woods, I was exhausted. Then I began to think. About the entire thing. But most of all, I thought about Prabhat. Of all three of us who had come here, if there was anyone who I thought was least likely to kill Chowdhury, it was Prabhat. His resolve may have been strong, but murder is not everyone's cup of tea. Prabhat was not prepared for it at all, nor was he willing to admit that he didn't have the nerve for it. After I left, it began to seem to me that just like me, he too would want to go back to the bungalow one last time. And if he did, he was almost certain to get caught. And that bothered me. Poor chap had kept his vow, he had come to Manikpur. And I had abandoned him. I felt bad. By sunrise, I made up my mind. I would come back to Manikpur, and I would get Prabhat out of here. Of course, there was a possibility that I was being foolish, that he had left last night itself. But Prabhat and I were childhood friends, thick as thieves we were. I knew him all too well. And I knew he would need my help.'

Maity and I listened to Sarkhel with rapt attention. As did our driver. By now, even Pele had come to know that the owner of Manikpur Tea Estate had been murdered last night. And despite what he might have felt about Chowdhury's death, the way he had grabbed Sarkhel in his tight grip, it was evident that Pele was going to help Maity and me to the best of his abilities.

'If I ask my driver to let go of you,' Maity finally said, 'will you promise to behave?'

Shibnath Sarkhel nodded. Maity gestured to Pele, who let go of Sarkhel's arms.

Maity shook his head sadly and said, 'If only you would have listened to me, Mr Sarkhel, we would not have had to see this day. And just so you know, your dear friend Dr Prabhat Sengupta is also a suspect in Chowdhury's murder. In fact, he might be at the police station right now, which is exactly where we are taking you too.'

I had expected Sarkhel to vehemently protest being taken to the police, but strangely enough, he didn't. The question he asked instead was: 'And Abhi? He must have escaped by now?'

'No, Mr Sarkhel,' said Maity, 'you may not have much faith in the police, or in me for that matter, but I want you to know that Abhijit Lahiri has been arrested from Bagdogra Airport. We will see him, too, at the police station. Come on, Pele. Drive us to the station. It's time for a little reunion again.'

[16]

'Welcome, welcome, Mr Maity! Deeply honoured to have you at my station!'

Maity and I had just entered the Sonarpur police station. Inspector Sen grinned at us from his chair and extended a hand. Maity shook it and the Inspector offered us a couple of chairs. I glanced around the place and it looked decidedly run down. The walls had stains on them and the plaster was peeling off here and there. Although an obvious effort had been made in trying to whitewash over it, there was a 'Vote for' sign visible on one of the walls. There was one Nehru, one Tagore and two Subhas Bose's photo frames hanging on the walls around us. There was a dank stench in the air, probably coming from the only cell whose iron bars we could see. The lock on the cell door was so puny, so old and so rusty that it would take a strong man no more than a mere twist of his arm to break it open. The ceiling fan had two blades instead of three, which was why a green pedestal fan had been put on additional duty. The breeze from this fan was so strong that everything on Inspector's Sen desk had to be put under paperweights. I counted nine of them.

'Is Lahiri here already?' Maity went straight to the point.

'Yes,' said the Inspector, 'my men are interrogating him.'

Pele entered the station grabbing Sarkhel by his arm. Inspector Sen looked at Sarkhel and a red-stained, gum-baring grin spread across the former's face.

'Let me guess,' he said, 'this must be the magician fellow you were telling me about. Where did you find him?'

'Let's just say we bumped into him,' said Maity. 'My recommendation is that you keep him here for the time being, although I don't think he is planning on running away any more. Nor will he cause you any trouble.'

'Oh, we will take care of him all right,' said the Inspector, ringing a bell on his desk.

A constable walked in and made Sarkhel sit on a bench in the corner with a firm warning. Pele stepped outside and we turned to the Inspector again.

'Can I say something to you in all honesty, Mr Maity?' The Inspector lit a cigarette for himself after Maity and I declined his offer for a smoke. 'It seems to me that as of this moment, you know more about this case than I do. And to tell you the truth, that is making me rather uncomfortable. I am sure you will understand my position.'

'I do,' Maity nodded.

Inspector Sen smiled and said, 'The Green View Lodge lies vacant almost all throughout the year. The owner is a notorious man—has his fingers deep in several dubious business interests. Did you know that the Bangladesh border is merely 40 km from here? Extremely porous. There's a huge racket of ferrying people from that side over to this side, and from this side over to that side. This man I am talking about was the kingpin of this racket, used to be a local MLA too. He built the lodge as a love nest for his party boys, but after he lost the elections, he lost his clout too. Now, hardly anyone

goes to the lodge any more. Are you asking me to believe that
at this odd time of the year, all four rooms of the lodge being
occupied at the exact same time is a mere coincidence?'

Maity looked at the Inspector and said: 'One of them
is an American tourist. The other three men had arrived in
Manikpur to murder Jagat Narayan Chowdhury.'

Maity may have uttered the words quite casually, but the
effect they created was quite something. For the longest period
of time, Inspector Sen's mouth remained wide open and he
kept staring blankly at us, trying to digest the implications of
the information that Maity had so nonchalantly thrown at
him. Finally, he said, 'You mean . . . these men? The midget
magician, and that . . . Lahiri fellow?'

'The doctor too.'

'The doctor I saw at the bungalow this morning?' B.P.
Sen's voice was marked with a clear sense of disbelief. 'The
one who pronounced him dead?'

'Yes.'

'Good lord!' Inspector Sen was now on the edge of his
chair. 'But why?'

Maity explained everything to the Inspector in a clear
and concise manner. During the entire time, the Inspector
was so lost in what Maity had to say that he didn't puff on
his cigarette even a single time. I looked towards the far end
of the room and saw Shibnath Sarkhel sitting on the bench,
listening to everything, his face buried in his hands.

When Maity was done, Inspector Sen said, 'What are you
saying? I thought these things only happened in the movies!'

In his characteristic calm manner, Maity drew the
Inspector's attention to the fact that the ash of his cigarette
had almost reached his fingers and said, 'Prabhat Sengupta

is supposed to come here any minute. I would request your permission to send him to Ashu Babu's home for an hour or so. You can send one of your men with him, if you want. Once he is back from there, the doctor needs to be kept under observation too. Preferably here, at the station.'

'Ashu Babu as in Ashutosh Mukherjee?' B.P. Sen's bushy eyebrows had almost reached his hairline. 'The schoolmaster? Who lives in Manikpur village?'

'Yes,' said Maity. 'I'm not sure if you know, but he is quite unwell.'

By the looks of it, Inspector Sen was probably unaware of this fact as well, but he avoided admitting it by asking another question, 'How on earth did *you* come to know of all this?'

'Just keeping my eyes and ears open, Inspector,' Maity said. 'Would it be possible for me to have a word with Abhijit Lahiri?'

'Under normal circumstances, no,' pat came the reply. It was quite obvious that B.P. Sen was trying to establish his authority in the face of Maity's clear control over the situation in Manikpur. 'But if I wish to, I can make an exception for you. It entirely depends on the officer in charge, you see? And I am the officer in charge here.'

Maity softened his voice as much as possible and said, 'I completely understand. It's just a request, of course.'

Inspector Sen nodded his head contentedly and said, 'All right, come with me.'

As it turned out, Lahiri was being held in an adjacent room, not the barred cell. The room was hardly ten feet in length and eight feet in width, and almost a third of it was full of tea chests stacked high up against the wall, all the way to the ceiling. Even if there was a window in the wall behind those chests, it was not visible from where we stood. The chests themselves were light brown in colour, made of thin wood with aluminium foil covering the edges and the corners to prevent air or moisture from seeping in. The rest of the room hardly had any place to sit or stand around. There was a high-power bulb hanging from the ceiling by a long wire and it had no shade on it. It was virtually impossible for anyone to look at the light for more than two seconds but the two plain-clothes men who were present in the room had probably gotten used to it. The man sitting in the centre of the room on a stool was clearly having a tough time keeping his eyes open. I couldn't believe that this was the same smartly dressed and dapper young man whom we had seen in the guest house's living room last night. It seemed like a hurricane had blown over him.

'Anything?' Inspector Sen asked.

The two sturdily built men shook their heads. With a gesture of his head, B.P. Sen asked the men to leave the room. The door was shut behind us.

'So, Mr Lahiri?' said Inspector Sen. 'Have you made up your mind, after all? Are you willing to cooperate?'

With trembling lips, Abhijit Lahiri mumbled something. Inspector Sen put his ear uncomfortably close to Lahiri's face and said, 'What? Come again?'

'I want to speak to my lawyer,' came the feeble response.

B.P. Sen laughed so hard that the room shook to its core. Maity's face was serious; he was quietly staring at Abhijit Lahiri. Inspector Sen finally managed to control his bout of laughter and said: 'These are the United States of India, Mr Lahiri! Here, you don't have the right to remain silent.

Oh, and out here, the only Miranda you get from the police is orange in colour. Comes in a plastic bottle, costs twenty bucks. Tell me what I want to know, or you will be in a lot of trouble. The kind of trouble that no Hollywood movie can even think of showing you. Why did you murder Jagat Narayan Chowdhury?'

'I didn't.'

B.P. Sen looked at Maity and shook his head. Maity took a step forward and said, 'May I?'

Inspector Sen considered the situation for a few moments and said, 'Sure, go ahead and try, if you think you can do what we can't.'

Maity walked up to the spot where Lahiri was sitting, but did not speak to him right away. Instead, he grabbed the wire from which the bulb was hanging, walked towards one of the walls and looped the wire around a nail that I had not even noticed so far. Then he walked back to Lahiri, knelt in front of him, and simply said, 'What happened last night, Mr Lahiri?'

Abhijit Lahiri looked at Maity for a few seconds with a helpless look on his face. Then he said, 'After I said goodbye to you, I went back to the lodge, Mr Maity. I swear I did.'

'Go on,' Maity's voice was soft and calm.

'Shibu was nowhere to be seen,' Lahiri went on. 'I started to pack. I had arranged for a taxi to take me to the airport. It arrived at one o'clock sharp. On hearing the sound of the car, Prabhat came to my room. He tried to stop me. I told him that my mind was already made up. At around quarter past one, I locked my room, gave the keys to Prabhat and came down to the taxi. I sat in the car and left for Bagdogra.'

'You didn't stop in between?'

'No, not at all.'

'Nor did you come back to Manikpur?'

'Trust me, Mr Maity. I didn't.'

Maity nodded. I looked at B.P. Sen. He was clearly not happy with the fact that it had taken Maity not more than a minute to make his suspect talk. He intervened, 'How do we know that this man isn't lying?'

'He could be,' Maity rose to his feet and turned to face the Inspector. His voice had changed. 'But there are other methods to validate that.'

'Other methods?' The Inspector was clearly unhappy. 'What other methods?'

'It's a time-tested, efficient, and—most importantly—ethical method, Inspector Sen,' Maity's voice was firm, his eyes locked with the officer's. 'It's called an investigation.'

'Now look here, Mr Maity!' the Inspector growled.

'No, you look here, Inspector Sen,' said Maity, pointing towards me. 'You see my friend over here? He writes for the *Statesman*. I am leaving the three suspects in the Jagat Narayan Chowdhury murder case in your care. "Care" being the operative word here. They are to stay at the station overnight. All I need is one night—that's all. By tomorrow morning, I will have solved this case.'

Inspector Sen was so taken aback by Maity's audacity and confidence that he couldn't say anything in response. Maity wasn't finished.

'But if I come back tomorrow morning to find that there's so much as an ant bite on any of the suspects, I assure you that you will lose the stars that you have worked so hard to earn, Inspector. I will personally see to it that you do.'

Before Inspector Sen could say anything, a constable walked in and announced, 'Sir, one Dr Sengupta is here.'

My heart was thumping inside my chest. Never in my wildest dreams could I have imagined that Maity would stand up to B.P. Sen. And that too right in the middle of his own police station! The Inspector was still fuming, even as he stared hard at Maity. On the other hand, if one looked at Maity's face, one couldn't believe that he had said those words a moment ago. He was as calm as ever. His eyes, however, were still locked with the Inspector's.

'Narayan?' the Inspector finally said, and I shut my eyes in anticipation of the worst.

'Yes, sir?' the constable responded.

'Take the Jeep and escort the doctor to Ashutosh Mukherjee's house in Manikpur. The old man needs some medical attention . . . apparently!'

I breathed a sigh of relief. Maity gave a small nod and said, 'Thank you, Inspector. See you tomorrow morning.'

As we walked out of the station, I saw the two plain-clothes policemen standing in one corner and smoking away. Prabhat Sengupta came running towards us.

'What's going on, Mr Maity?' he asked. 'Where are they taking me?'

'It is said that the debt of a teacher can never be repaid,' said Maity, 'but you can at least try. Ashu Babu is very ill, doctor. I think he needs you. Please go with the constable, he will take you to the village.'

Prabhat Sengupta said, 'Oh! I . . . I didn't know. Yes, certainly, Mr Maity. I'll do the best I can. I . . . I just need to pick up my bag from the lodge.'

'Which reminds me,' said Maity, 'when you went to the bungalow last night, why were you carrying your bag with you?'

'My bag?' replied Dr Sengupta, 'but I wasn't! Why would I carry my bag with me?'

Maity stared at the doctor for a few seconds and asked, 'Why indeed?'

Prabhat Sengupta lowered his voice and said, 'Is everything all right, Mr Maity? What about Abhi and Shibu? Have they found them yet?'

'Nothing is fine as of now, Dr Sengupta. Everything is in a mess. And you are as much to blame for this situation as your other two friends are. But rest assured, everything will be fine tomorrow morning. I assure you that.'

Before the doctor could say anything, Maity walked away towards our car, and I followed him, leaving Dr Sengupta standing there with a strange expression on his face.

'It's almost three o'clock,' said Maity, after we had sat in the car. 'Let's get back to the guest house now. After a quick lunch, I need to do a bit of thinking.'

As we drove out of the police station compound, I opened my mouth for the first time since we had entered the station. 'You do know what I used to write for the *Statesman*, don't you, Maity?'

'I do,' Maity let out a massive yawn of exhaustion and said, 'Poetry!'

[17]

After we had reached the guest house and had a quick lunch, Maity said that he was feeling exhausted and wanted to lie down for a bit.

'I need to rest for a while, Prakash,' he said. 'An hour or so, perhaps. Why don't you ask Pele to drive you around the garden for a while?'

I realized Maity wanted to stay alone for some time, and I was more than willing to give him the time to think. Because although he had promised Inspector Sen that he would solve the mystery by tomorrow morning, it somehow seemed to me that he was nowhere near a solution. I wanted to check if my suspicion was correct, so I asked him.

'You are right, my friend,' he said, as he lay on his bed and stared at the ceiling. 'Everything is in its place, every single fact, every single character, everything that has happened. And yet, there's something missing. But so far, I can't seem to figure out what it is. I promised a big bang tomorrow. I had to; I had no other choice. But do I have what I need to produce that big bang? No, I don't. I have the gunpowder, I have the charge, the fuse is set, even the flint is in my hand. All I need now is a spark.'

After this, Maity turned to his side to face the wall and fell completely silent. My cue to exit. I came back to my room and stepped out on to the veranda. Pele had reclined his seat in the car, pulled his cap over his face and was taking a nap. I remembered the poor chap hadn't had any sleep last night, so I did not feel like disturbing him and decided to explore the garden on foot. In any case, a little bit of walking and fresh air would do me good, I thought. Things were moving at lightning speed and my head was in a mess.

As soon as I had come out of the guest house's compound, walked up to the post office and turned right towards the temple, my nerves began to calm down. The afternoon sun had begun slanting towards the western sky, although there were clouds forming towards the south-east. There was a strange stillness all around me. Other than the sweet sound of the rustling of the leaves in the breeze and the gnashing of pebbles under my feet, all other sounds seemed to have died down. I passed the temple on my right and walked another quarter of a mile or so. The owner of the estate had been murdered last night. There would probably have been no plucking in the garden today. Which perhaps explained why there was not a soul to be seen anywhere. Just me, and the unbesmirched beauty of nature all around me.

I suddenly stopped in my tracks because a strange sound had caught my attention. Somewhere up ahead, a goat was bleating. I had been hearing the sound for almost a minute or so, but hadn't paid much heed to it. That there would be cows and goats in such natural surroundings was only normal. But as I drew closer to the source of the sound, it somehow seemed to me that the call was one of distress. I quickly took a few steps ahead and saw a white goat in the distance, along the side of the barbed wire fence that lined the tea shrubs. I walked up to the animal. It was a baby goat—a kid. Bright white in colour, with swatches of light brown on its neck, back and hind legs. A tiny tail, writhing in pain and fear. Since plucking season was on, parts of the shrubs had stuck out of the fencing. The goat had probably tried to eat the leaves, and got its head stuck in the gap in the fence. The poor animal was doomed now: there was no way it was going to get its head out of there. It was bleating away in fear, and watching me with terrified eyes.

There was a deep ditch between the fence and the pebbled path on which I stood. The goat had probably made its way to the bottom and climbed out of it on the other side, but there was no way I would be able to do so. If I had to help the kid, I would have to jump over. I assessed the width of the ditch, instead. If I were to take a run-up before I jumped, there was a possibility that I could reach the other side and grab the fence before I fell into the ditch. I had to be careful though, because there was the risk of my feet slipping on the pebbles, or my miscalculating the jump. It had to be just right. Not too long, or I would fall against the razor-sharp barbs and hurt myself. And certainly not too short, as I would end up at the bottom, with a broken bone or two.

The goat was still watching me with its big black eyes. For a fleeting moment, I wondered if I should abandon my plan and walk away. Perhaps someone else would come along soon—a local passer-by maybe—and he would free the poor animal from its misery. But perhaps because it had sensed my thoughts somehow, or perhaps because of the sharp barbs that were sinking deeper into its hide with every passing second, the goat bleated once more. A heart-wrenching cry for help.

No way! I couldn't walk away. I made up my mind, walked back to the other edge of the path, hunched forward in readiness, filled my lungs with air, ran as fast as I could and threw myself into the air.

I banged my stomach against the fence, but managed to hang on to it. The goat was visibly terrified. The jump had rattled it further. I lifted my shirt to find that I had cut myself against the barbed wire just above my waist—there was a tiny amount of blood oozing out of the wound. A bit of Dettol would help. But first, I needed to set the animal free.

As I moved towards it, the kid started throwing its limbs around. Its fear wasn't unfounded. Humans have seldom been kind to other animals. I tried my best to calm it down, ran a soothing palm down its back to comfort it. Then I pulled the barbed wire apart just enough to allow the goat to pull its head out. The moment it was free, it leapt away. It turned around one last time to look at me from a distance, and I smiled at it. My heart was filled with a warm sense of joy! But it didn't last long because I soon realized that although I had managed to help the animal, I myself was in an extremely precarious situation now. Literally under my feet was the ditch, easily eight to nine feet deep. And there was no way I could jump the gap, because I didn't have the luxury of the run-up any more.

What was I to do now? I looked around helplessly, and quickly realized that the only way out of here was to climb the fence and enter the plantation—the actual plantation, where the tea shrubs were growing. Easier said than done. I had already cut myself once. I had no intention of letting that

happen again. I shimmied along the fence to find a suitable
spot where the barbs had worn out, and then climbed over. A
sense of relief came over me as my feet touched the ground
and I could stand up without the fear of falling over any more.
All that I had to do now was to find an exit and walk out of
the garden. But before I could do that, I took a moment to
admire the tea shrub itself from up close.

Two leaves and a bud, Maity had said. The perfect pluck!
I saw dozens of them around me, all perched prime on the
waist-high shrubs. How beautiful they looked! One leaf
slightly larger than the other in size, one slightly higher than
the other on the stem, and the pretty little bud in between,
like a tender baby fast asleep in the assuring protection of
its parents. Once again, my heart swelled up with a strange
sense of joy and bliss. I remembered the months of pain that
I had been through, the terrifying blankness of my mind,
the numbing inability to write even a single sentence that
made sense. I shut my eyes to feel the breeze on my skin
and breathed in the fresh smell of the leaves and the buds.
Somewhere out there, an unknown bird cooed from the
branch of a shade tree. And it seemed to me that everything
would be all right again.

Footsteps!

I quickly ducked under the shrubs. I was pretty sure that I
was trespassing, and although we were guests of the deceased
owner of the estate itself, the sheer embarrassment of being
discovered in the middle of what was clearly a prohibited
area was one that I was not willing to risk. Whoever it was,
he would be gone soon, and I could then come out of my
hiding place, quickly make my way out of here and head
back to Maity.

But as luck would have it, the footsteps began to draw closer and closer, until a time came when I began to wonder what would be more embarrassing: the fact that I had wandered into the middle of the plantation, or that I was trying to hide? I was considering my options when suddenly it seemed to me that the footsteps were moving away, the sound was getting fainter every other second. I tilted my head and raised just an eye to peep out of the shroud of green, and in doing so, caught a glimpse of the man who was walking away.

Mohan Sharma!

What on earth was he doing out here? And why was his manner so surreptitious and clandestine?

Something flicked inside my head and I decided to follow the man. Something was not right. I was determined to see where he went and what he did. I had not been of much help to Maity in this case, and this was my opportunity to change that. As quietly as possible, I tiptoed through the shrubs, minding where I stepped and staying as low as possible—just in case Sharma decided to look behind him. Although I was a good 50–60 yards behind him, in the middle of this rolling carpet of green, if I could see him, then that would mean he could see me too. Ducking behind a shade tree, I saw him walk towards a small iron gate in the distance. That must be the exit from this sector of the plantation, I figured. Where was he headed, after all? Mohan Sharma walked out of the gate, turned towards the west and disappeared behind a large bush. I came out from behind the shade tree and quickly made my way to the gate too.

The rows of trees that Maity and I had seen from the pebbled path were now in front of me, and this surprised me no end! In my pursuit, I hadn't realized how far I had come from the path. I was now standing on a patch of grassland and as I looked ahead, a sense of dread numbed my hands and feet.

Mohan Sharma had stopped walking and was now standing around 100 yards from where I was. And what stood before him, just beyond a dry nullah, could be nothing but the Chilapata forest! The forest front stretched away for miles towards the north as far as my eyes could see. Towards the south, it continued for a mile or so, before curving inward and merging with the plantation. Pele had said that there were leopards in the forest. Bears and wild boars too. Why on earth was Mohan Sharma headed towards it then? Although I could feel the rush of blood in my head, I hid behind the trunk of a massive jackfruit tree and tried to study the situation as patiently as I could.

Sharma was standing right at the edge of the forest. He looked here and there and entered the treeline. I found myself in a bit of a spot. Should I follow him into the forest? Or should I wait for him to come out? There was a single line of approach to the forest, and if Sharma decided to turn around and step out as I was moving towards him, I would find myself directly face to face with him. And something told me that that wouldn't be a desirable situation.

'*What are you doing here?*'

My heart leapt up to my mouth, and I almost slipped on the moss and fell. I thought I was following Sharma. Little did I know that I was being followed too. Someone had crept up right behind me and had scared the living daylights out of me. I swallowed hard and turned around to face the man.

'Didn't I tell you that the gardens are not safe to walk around?' exclaimed Rafiq Ali. 'And that there could be a number of wild animals around?'

'I . . . I was . . . just . . .' I stammered.

Ali looked in the direction of the forest and said, 'You weren't planning on going anywhere near there, were you?'

'No, no . . . I was just . . . admiring . . .'

'Well, come along with me.' Ali grabbed me by my arm and dragged me away. 'You can do all the admiring from my Jeep.'

I turned around to look back at the notorious Chilapata forest one last time. Had Mohan Sharma heard us? If he hadn't gone in too deep, he must have. Perhaps he was watching us from behind those trees. What was he doing in the middle of the forest? More importantly, what was Rafiq Ali doing here at this time of the day?

I hadn't noticed it so far, but by the time we reached the Jeep, it had become quite dark all around, and when I looked up, I found that the sky was overcast. A distant thunder rolled in the southern sky.

'There's a storm coming,' said Ali, as he thrust me into the passenger seat of his Jeep. 'All the more reason for you to stop wandering about. You are from the city; you aren't accustomed to the ways of the jungle.'

Ali walked around the front and sat in the driver's seat. By now, I had begun to tremble. I don't know if it was the sudden drop in temperature that was making me shiver or the sight of the double-barrelled rifle placed in the back of the vehicle. The gun was placed in such a way that the barrel stuck out into the space between Ali and me. It was hardly a foot away from my face, in fact.

'Where is Mr Maity?' he asked, as the car rolled out of the grassland and on to a bumpy dirt track.

'In the guest house,' I somehow managed to say. Tiny drops of rain had started falling on the windshield of the car. There was a strong wind blowing.

'Your being here is all wrong, you know?' he said.

'I'm sorry,' I said. 'I just wanted to take a closer look at the—'

'I'm not talking about you alone,' Ali shook his head. 'The two of you—you and your friend, being here, in Manikpur. It's all wrong.'

From the corner of my eye, I eyed the barrel of the gun once again. Beyond the barrel, all I could see was Rafiq Ali's rock-hard jaw, military-grade moustache and his fiery eyes. I turned my eyes to look forward. There was nothing to see, though. The rain had picked up, the windshield had become completely hazy. Ali had not turned on the wipers yet. How was he able to see through the rain? If the car took one wrong turn and fell into a hole or something, the gun could go off. I shut my eyes, and the next few words I heard only increased my fear.

'Don't think I don't know what the two of you are up to, you know?'

My left arm was getting drenched as the rain splashed through the window, and the wound on my stomach had suddenly begun to hurt. I clenched my teeth and held my breath. Ali took a sharp left turn. The barrel of the gun slid towards me, and stopped as the muzzle came and rested against my cheek, the cold touch of steel sending a shiver down my spine. Ali gently grabbed the barrel and put it back in the centre again.

'There's something going on between that doctor and you two, isn't it?' he said. 'I'm absolutely certain that you know each other from back in the city. Tell your sleuth friend that he needs to stop his games. I was never in favour of keeping this entire thing away from the police in the first place. Inspector Sen is a strict man. But that's exactly the kind of man that is needed to uphold the law in these parts. None of them listened to me—neither Mr Chowdhury nor Sharma. And now, look at the bloody mess we are in.'

To my left, I saw the temple and felt some semblance of relief. We had reached familiar territory, after all. The Jeep soon turned left once again and drove for a few more yards before coming to a halt in front of the guest house. The storm had fully developed by now. There were trees all around, and they were all swaying wildly in the strong winds. I saw the branch of a mango tree break off and collapse on the ground before getting swept away by the wind towards the gardens.

'I know Mr Chowdhury had asked you to come to Manikpur,' Rafiq Ali had to raise his voice over the howling wind, 'but he is dead now. As manager of Manikpur Tea Estate, I strongly advise you two to go back to the city tomorrow. There are three flights from Bagdogra to Kolkata, there are ample trains from Alipurduar Junction. If you can't find a seat in any of them, I will arrange a car for you, which will take you all the way to the city. But whatever you do, don't overstay your welcome. You had come to Manikpur to protect Mr Chowdhury. I don't have to tell you how that went. There's nothing left for you here any more. You give my message to your friend—loud and clear. It is the police who will find the murderer of Jagat Narayan Chowdhury.

In fact, they've already made remarkable progress in such a short time.'

Having said this much, Rafiq Ali extended his arm and flung my door open. I was almost forced to step out of the car into the storm.

'What do you mean?' I yelled at the top of my voice as the storm danced all around me and the rain lashed at my face. 'What progress?'

'Why, haven't you heard?' Ali yelled back before the Jeep started moving. 'They've found the murder weapon!'

'What!' I yelled out as loud as I could. 'Where did they find it?'

But by then, Rafiq Ali had already reversed his Jeep and driven away.

[18]

I ran inside to find Maity lying on his bed, staring out of the open window. The fact that splashes of rain were pouring in through the window and had left a significant portion of the floor completely wet, seemed to have no effect on him at all.

'Maity!' I yelled out in excitement.

'Catch your breath, my friend.'

I plonked down on the only chair in the room and said, 'They've found the murder weapon!'

Maity looked at me once, sat up in bed, stretched his back till the bones creaked and said, 'For heaven's sake, Prakash, please tell me something I don't know. There's nothing I would love more than that at the moment.'

'You know already?' I said, surprised. 'Who told you?'

'The Inspector called,' Maity winked.

'He called you?' I was surprised again. 'I thought he would have been furious with you till now?'

Maity smiled. He rose from the bed, shut the window and said, 'Those who have been consumed by greed, those who misuse their position of power, those who walk down the path of injustice—such people are perpetually afraid, Prakash. They may flex their muscles from time to time, but that's not because they are brave. That's only because they

203

are insecure, because they want to hide their weakness, cover their flaws. They live and breathe in the constant fear of being exposed, of being found out. On the other hand, those who are honest and upright, those who do their jobs well, with sincerity and dignity, they have nothing to fear.'

I smiled a little and asked, 'What did he say?'

Maity walked back to his bed and said, 'Well, he apologized for his behaviour, but not in the manner that you and I would expect. He was trying to cover up his act—more than anything else—giving all sorts of excuses and such. It was quite clear to me that he wasn't truly sorry. I don't think he is going to mend his ways. I let it go. We have other priorities right now.'

'Where was the knife found?' I asked.

'In the bushes behind the Green View Lodge. The police had searched the rooms too, but they didn't find anything there—anything important, that is. When they were combing the bushes, however, one of the constables found the knife lying there, covered in blood. The blood had dried up, but a sample has been sent to the doctor from Siliguri Medical College who is doing the post-mortem—just to ensure that the blood matches with Chowdhury's. I took the doctor's number from Inspector Sen, will give him a call later tonight.'

'Why?' I asked. 'Are you suspecting that the blood on the knife could be someone else's?'

Maity was now sitting on the bed with his back against the wall and the pillow on his lap. He said, 'The blood . . . the blood . . . it will probably match . . . but . . . just a small doubt . . . about the blood . . .'

Having said this much, he fell silent.

'What doubt, Maity?' I asked impatiently.

Maity stared into the void for some time and then seemed to shake off the thought. 'Nothing, you go and put on some dry clothes, or you are going to catch a cold.'

'But I have something else to tell you, Maity,' I said. 'And I assure you, you can't possibly know this already.'

'Ah, finally!' his face lit up.

In as accurate a manner as possible, I gave Maity a detailed account of whatever had happened earlier that evening. Starting from my entering the plantation itself, to my following Mohan Sharma all the way to the edge of the forest and finally, my encounter with Rafiq Ali and his asking us to leave Manikpur. Maity listened with rapt attention, without interrupting me even once. When I was done speaking, he asked me if it was Rafiq Ali who had told me that the murder weapon had been found. When I said yes, Maity nodded a couple of times and then asked me to give him an accurate description of the spot where Ali had found me, and I did that as best I could. Maity smiled and then said: 'Very interesting! Excellent job, Prakash, you held your nerve. Well, I think a strong cup of tea might help us think better, what do you say? You go and change, I'll tell Gangadhar. I need to make a few phone calls too. Let's meet in the living room in ten minutes.'

Maity walked out of the room and I stepped into the bathroom. As I got out of the wet clothes and splashed some warm water on my face, I realized how exhausted I was. I had gone to bed pretty late last night, and Maity had woken me up at the crack of dawn. My face looked haggard in the mirror and my eyes were bloodshot. I decided to ask Maity if we could have an early dinner tonight. I would probably not be able to sleep off soon; just like Maity had had his rest, I needed mine. As I combed my hair, my mind went back to Mohan Sharma. What was he doing inside the forest? Had he gone there to meet someone? Was there someone waiting for him in there? Who could it be? And what about Rafiq Ali? Was he following me too? The man had clearly seen through Maity's pretence of not being acquainted with Dr Sengupta beforehand. Why was he so hell-bent on sending us away from Manikpur? It was true that in Jagat Narayan Chowdhury's absence, his was the final word of authority in the estate. This was a private property after all, and if he wanted us to leave, there was very little that Maity and I could do.

Maity didn't seem too bothered about all this though. For some strange reason, at the moment, all his attention seemed to be focused on the knife, especially on the blood that had been found on it. And I just couldn't understand why. It had to be Chowdhury's blood—who else could it have come from? Who else had been murdered or wounded in Manikpur, after all?

I took care of my wound, put on a shirt and walked into the drawing room. Maity had just finished a call and put the receiver back on the cradle. He was thinking deeply. I sat in an armchair and waited for him to speak. Meanwhile, good old Gangadhar had brought us our tea, along with some fried cashews. Both tasted delicious, especially after my getting soaked in the rain. The storm was still raging outside, and the howling and whistling sounds of the wind could be heard even from the safe confines of the room. As a thunderbolt struck somewhere nearby, I suddenly remembered that Pele was still sitting in his car outside the guest house, and with all the large trees all around, it was extremely unsafe for him to do so. I told Maity as much.

But it almost seemed like he hadn't heard me at all. After almost a minute, when I asked him again, he came out of his trance. 'Huh? No, no . . . let him stay.'

'But Maity,' I said, 'the storm has really picked up. I myself saw a large branch—'

'I . . . I need to go,' Maity mumbled.

'Where?' I asked, completely taken aback. 'Who did you call? What happened?'

One more lightning strike somewhere extremely close by. The room shook to its core. The glass showcase standing in the corner rattled from top to bottom. My eyes were on Maity though.

'Ashu Babu is dead!'

'What?' I jumped out of my chair. 'When? I mean, how?'

Maity rubbed his chin and said, 'Inspector Sen called again just now. He said that the old man was more or less stable when Dr Sengupta had visited him around noon. The doctor prescribed a couple of medicines too, apparently. But after he left, the old man's condition worsened in the afternoon. The escorting constable had left the police station's number with Kanai. When Ashu Babu's situation continued to deteriorate, Kanai called from a neighbour's place, and Inspector Sen immediately sent the doctor back to Ashu Babu's house. But by the time he reached, the old man had passed away. Apparently, he had been suffering from respiratory problems for quite some time now.'

'Oh God!' I said. 'If only we could have . . . where are you off to?'

The tea remained untouched; Maity headed back to his room and I followed him.

'I have to go,' he said, as he picked up his phone and wallet. 'The cremation is supposed to happen later tonight. But with this storm . . . I'm not sure. In any case, I want to be there. You stay here, there's absolutely no need for you to come with me. You've gotten drenched once, and I don't want you to come down with a fever. Don't wait up for me, I might be late.'

Despite my repeated requests, Maity refused to take me along. In less than two minutes, he was out of the door and I was left all by myself in the guest house. I don't know if it was just my mind playing tricks on me or if the storm had indeed intensified even further. I was really worried about Maity now. I paced around in my room for some time, feeling extremely impatient. Two deaths in the gardens—one after the other. Although one was quite different from the other, inasmuch as one was a murder and the other had occurred due to natural causes. But the fact remained that so many things happening at the same time had completely thrown my sanity off balance. I simply could not think straight any more. And now, even my strength was leaving me. My calf muscles hurt and my shoulders were giving way. I decided to lie down in my bed for a while. And, as soon as I did, my eyelids involuntarily shut in on themselves.

As I slept, I had a strange dream. I saw that Maity and I were sitting at two opposite ends of an extremely long and ornate dining table. Spread along the length of the table was a wide variety of scrumptious-looking food and beverages. I looked across the table and saw Maity hunched over his food, a white napkin neatly tucked into his collar, cutlery clinking against each other in his hands, as he quietly ate his meal. I noticed that despite there being ample food on the table, there was no plate before me.

'Maity?' I called out, in a voice that echoed back to me. 'Where are we? What are we doing here?'

Maity didn't respond. Perhaps he hadn't heard me. It seemed to me that he was too far away. I pushed my chair back and rose to my feet, feeling extremely light-headed. The sound of the chair dragging against the floor seemed to attract Maity's attention. He raised his head and looked here and there, and as if he had not seen me at all. He simply went back to his meal.

'Is everything all right?' I asked again. There was no response.

I looked around. The regal table was set in a large hall. Other than the table itself, there was nothing else in the room, it was stark naked. No chandeliers, no paintings, no curtains—nothing. And then I realized that there was no light in the room either. A strange twilight seemed to wax and wane outside, and in its faint light, I saw a few shadowy figures sitting in various places at the table, all far from each other, all quietly eating their meals. Among all the people in the room, the only face I could see was Maity's.

'Why is it so dark in here?' I said, squinting my eyes and minding my steps, as I slowly walked towards my friend. 'What place is this? And who are all these people?'

'Come, Prakash,' Maity's baritone echoed through the room. 'Come join us.'

I looked at Maity. He was still eating away. Although the voice was his, it wasn't he who was speaking!

'You must be hungry,' the voice said. 'You don't want to come down with a fever.'

As lightning flashed outside the room, the faces of the other people appeared before me for a second or two.

They were not men!

Boys! Young boys, barely into their teens!

Four of them! And they had all stopped eating and were now looking at me.

I reached out in the dark and grabbed the back of a chair to steady myself.

'M-Maity?' I croaked, as my voice began to fail. 'A-are they . . . who I think they are?'

Maity extended his hand and gestured to the chair next to him.

'Come, Prakash,' he said, his voice calm, 'sit by my side.'

Gathering all my strength, I ran up to the chair and sat down.

'Now let's eat,' he said. 'Would you like a fork and a knife?'

Lightning struck outside the room and I looked down to find that the knife that Maity had extended towards me wasn't a table knife at all. It was a dagger—with blood dripping from it!

I woke up with a start, to find the room completely dark. What a nasty nightmare! For the better part of a minute, I kept breathing heavily. I had broken into a cold sweat and on trying to reach for my phone beside the pillow, I realized that even my pillow was completely drenched in my sweat. I looked at the screen of my phone, still no signal. My eyes fell on the clock. Almost three o'clock! Had I been asleep for so long? Why was it so dark in here?

I held up the backlight of the phone and peered into the adjoining room. Maity was not in his bed. In the large table in the centre of my room, a few new items had appeared. Plates, bowls, glasses and a few hot cases. The caretaker Gangadhar had probably tried to wake me and having failed to do so, had left my dinner on the table. There were a couple of wax candles and a matchbox placed near the plates, which probably meant that the storm had taken out the power. From the sound of it, it seemed to me that although the storm had subsided, it was still raining heavily outside.

I was starving, so I made my way to the table to light the candles, but no sooner had I taken a few steps than I saw something in the corner, let out a choking gasp and dropped the phone from my hand. The room was instantly plunged back into darkness again.

There was someone in the room! Standing in the corner by the window!

My hands and feet had turned numb, and I fumbled around in the dark to find my way back to the bed.

'Stop dropping things, will you?' said a voice in the dark. 'Which reminds me, we need to find that iron rod and give it back to Pele.'

'Maity?' I somehow managed to say, 'Is that you?'

'Sorry, Prakash,' Maity said, 'I seem to have given you a bit of a scare!'

'Why are you standing around in the dark like that?' I made no attempt to hide the irritation in my voice.

Maity's voice was calm though. He said, 'As I have often told you, my friend, in order to see the light, you must first witness the dark.'

'Oh, enough of your philosophical balderdash!' I said, wiping the sweat off my face. 'Will you please stop creeping me out and light the candle?'

'Very well!'

'How long have you been standing there like that?' I asked. 'And what about the cremation?'

I heard Maity's footsteps in the dark. And then I heard his voice again, 'The rain had stopped for a couple of hours, so the cremation was duly completed. Everything was over by midnight.'

'Midnight?' I was now truly surprised. 'So what took you so long?'

'I was looking for something,' he said, his voice marked with a strange and unmistakable hint of contentment, 'and it took some time and a bit of effort to find it.'

'What were you looking for?' I asked. 'What did you find?'

A couple of matches struck the box and a flame flared up in the dark. In the dancing light of the flame, I saw Maity standing in the centre of the room, casting a large shadow on the wall behind him. He was soaked to the bone, his hair was ruffled, and yet, a familiar smile was gently floating on his lips. With a twinkle of excitement that seemed to burn brightly in his eyes, he uttered a single word in response to my question.

'Spark!'

[19]

The next morning, I woke up to find that the storm had completely died down and the rain had stopped. The sun was shining brightly again, and I glanced at my watch to find that it was well past eight o'clock. I had overslept. I walked into Maity's room, but didn't find him there. There were faint voices outside the guest house. The door that led from Maity's room to the veranda was open, and through it, I saw Maity standing outside the compound's gate, talking to someone. As the person was standing right in front of him, and Maity's back was turned towards me, I couldn't see who the other person was. To get a better view, I stepped on to the veranda and as soon as Maity heard me, he quickly turned around.

'You're up?' he smiled. 'Let's get ready. I've called Inspector Sen and asked him to gather everyone in Chowdhury's cabin.'

I could now see who Maity was speaking to. Kanai looked at me with those calm, beautiful eyes of his. What was he doing here at this time of the morning? I suddenly remembered that with Ashu Babu gone, the poor boy probably didn't have a place to live any more. I figured Maity must be speaking to him to find out if arrangements could be made for him and had probably given him some money too. Meanwhile, having patted Kanai's back a couple of times, Maity sent him away and walked back to me.

'What is he going to do, Maity?' I asked.

'Who, Kanai?' Maity asked, as he sat in the cane chair in the veranda and picked up the morning's newspaper. 'He has a distant uncle living in Siliguri. He will probably go and live with him, go to school there. Ashu Babu has left him some money. Nothing much, but it's his money now. I've spoken to the Inspector and asked him to see that he never wants for anything. Come on now, we must hurry. We're supposed to be at the cabin by ten o'clock.'

I knew Maity was a stickler for punctuality. Ten meant ten for him, so without wasting any more time, I quickly took a shower, got ready and met him in the dining room. Pele had arrived by now. After a quick breakfast, the entire duration of which Maity kept his face buried in the newspaper, we set out for Chowdhury's bungalow again. On the way, I wanted to ask him if he had finally managed to find a solution to the puzzle, but he seemed so engrossed in his thoughts that I decided against it.

As our car rolled in and stopped under the portico, the first person we met after stepping out was Rafiq Ali.

'I think I had told you clearly enough . . .' he began, but was immediately cut short as Maity raised a hand.

'Not now, Mr Ali,' Maity said, his voice firm, 'I will listen to everything you have to say. But only after you have listened to everything that I have to say. As of now, I request you to let Mr Sharma know that I have arrived. Please ask him to meet me at the cabin. And I expect you to be there too. It's important.'

The way Maity had said those words, Rafiq Ali couldn't say anything further. With a grim face, he looked at Maity and me in turn for a few seconds. Then, he simply turned around and stepped inside the bungalow. Maity and I made our way towards the cabin.

At exactly ten o'clock, Maity stood up and scanned the room before beginning his speech. We had all gathered in the living room of the cabin by the pond in the Chowdhury compound. We—as in Maity and I, Dr Prabhat Sengupta, Abhijit Lahiri, Shibnath Sarkhel, Rafiq Ali, Mohan Sharma and Inspector B.P. Sen. A couple of constables stood near the door, as did Pele and Charan.

Having looked around the room and ensured that everyone was present, Maity began to speak, 'As you are all aware, in the early hours of yesterday morning, the owner of the Manikpur Tea Estate—Mr Jagat Narayan Chowdhury— was found dead in his bed in the next room. He had been stabbed through the heart, although the murder weapon itself was nowhere to be seen. Later in the day, Inspector Sen's men discovered the weapon—a knife—lying in the bushes behind the Green View Lodge on the highway.

'My association with this case began five days ago— when Mr Chowdhury came to see me at my home in Kolkata along with his secretary Mohan Sharma, and asked me to investigate an intrusion that had happened in his bungalow on the sixteenth of this month. Mr Chowdhury had reason to believe that his life was in danger. At that point of time, I expressed my inability to take his case—a fact that I began to regret later, when I received another visitor the same night.

'As you all know, the gentleman sitting over there by the window is Dr Prabhat Sengupta, and it was his wife who came to see me later that night, and told me a fascinating story. A story about four boys from Manikpur who had been wronged by a powerful man—a man who had ruined their lives forever. These four boys were hardly into their teens when these incidents had happened, so there was no way for them to raise their voices against the injustice meted out to them. No one would have heard them. Which was why the four boys had vowed that they would take their revenge when they had grown up. They had promised each other that on a specific date twenty years hence, they would all return to Manikpur and avenge themselves by murdering the man who had altered the course of their lives. That man was none other than Jagat Narayan Chowdhury, and the four boys were Dr Prabhat Sengupta, investment banker Abhijit Lahiri, magician Shibnath Sarkhel and one other friend of theirs who failed to keep his promise and who never turned up in Manikpur. On the insistence of Dr Sengupta's wife, I came to Manikpur—as much to protect Chowdhury, as to prevent the doctor and his friends from committing a crime that was sure to send them to the gallows.'

Maity paused for a moment, and I looked around the room to find everyone's eyes fixed on him. Inspector Sen, in particular, was listening with rapt attention—so much so that his mouth was wide open.

'After arriving in Manikpur, I took two steps. First and foremost, I asked Mohan Sharma to ensure that Mr Chowdhury always be kept under observation—that no one be allowed to meet him. Second, I tried to speak to each of the men who had arrived in Manikpur with the intent of killing Chowdhury. I tried to convince them to abandon their plans. While Dr Sengupta and Mr Sarkhel summarily refused to listen to me, I realized—much to my surprise, no less— that better sense had prevailed upon Abhijit Lahiri, and that he had already made up his mind to return to the city. I didn't have to say a thing to him. In fact, it was he who told me that he was going back, and that he had tried to move on from the traumatic experience that had occurred twenty years ago—his sister's rape by Chowdhury and his men.'

There was a gasp or two across the room, and everyone reacted to Maity's words with varying levels of discomfort. Maity now began to pace around the room, as he resumed speaking.

'I understand,' he said. 'Don't speak ill of the dead, they say. But today, standing merely a few feet away from the bed where he slept and died, I must speak of the crimes that the deceased Jagat Narayan Chowdhury had committed during his lifetime. And I must speak of those crimes for two reasons. One, because *someone* has to. So what if they were committed twenty years ago? So what if Chowdhury had managed to escape the law back then? What of the immeasurable amount of pain and hurt he had caused to those four boys? What of the innumerable other crimes that he must have committed—that no one even knows of? Or that no one dared to raise their voices against? Who knows how many lives he must have destroyed by his deeds? Are the memories of those men, women and children supposed to die a silent death with Chowdhury's demise? Is death truly the one great exoneration? One that is awarded to the deceased on a platter, sans any semblance of repentance? No, one can't allow that to happen. At least *I* can't.'

Mohan Sharma had been fidgeting around uncomfortably for quite some time. He now said: 'But Mr Maity, what proof do you have that all these crimes have been committed? They may be mere accusations, after all.

Mr Chowdhury enjoyed a great reputation in all of Manikpur, and beyond. I've told you how—'

'I have seen the kind of reputation that Mr Chowdhury enjoyed in Manikpur, Mr Sharma. I appreciate the fact that you have the courage to stand up for your former employer, but I urge you to guide your loyalty towards a more deserving person next time. As for proof, I will give you proof. I do not say anything without evidence. When the time is right, rest assured that I will give you enough evidence to back my claims.'

Although he seemed utterly unconvinced, Mohan Sharma sat back in his seat and remained silent. Rafiq Ali was visibly upset too, but he didn't say anything.

'The second reason,' Maity continued, 'why I must speak of all the crimes that Chowdhury had committed against those four boys, is because they have a direct bearing on his murder. It is impossible to understand the nature of the crime that was committed in Manikpur yesterday without truly understanding the nature of the crimes that had been committed in Manikpur twenty years ago. Take the doctor, for instance. Prabhat Sengupta's father had raised his voice against Chowdhury's injustice. Chowdhury silenced him by killing him and making it look like suicide. I have already told you about the brutal crime committed against Abhijit Lahiri's sister. Shibnath Sarkhel's mother was falsely accused of stealing from the Chowdhury household—an accusation that drove her to commit suicide. And finally, a young boy named Arjun Banerjee—who came home to Manikpur during his vacations to spend time with his parents, but ended up being sexually abused by Chowdhury himself. As I found out in the course of my investigation, Chowdhury was a heinous man—a murderer, a rapist and a paedophile. A man not worth saving, and a man who didn't care for penance.

'But despite that, my work was cut out. I had to protect Chowdhury. It was a difficult decision for me, but I simply had to stop the three men sitting in this room from committing one crime to avenge another. Because in the eyes of the law—which ought to see everyone equally, but hardly ends up doing so—a murder is a murder. It doesn't matter what the reason behind it is. Unless, of course, it has been committed in self-defence, and clearly that eventuality is ruled out in this case. Which is why I began to study the three men and their past, in order to understand them. That was my only hope to try and stop them. And it was while doing this that one question kept bothering me. It was a simple question, but it kept coming back to me over and over again: Why didn't the fourth friend ever turn up in Manikpur?

'It was a question that had many possible answers. For instance, we had already seen one of the friends—Mr Lahiri over here—have a change of heart, after he had arrived in Manikpur. Perhaps that's what happened to Arjun Banerjee too, *before* coming to Manikpur? Or perhaps he was too afraid to carry out an immensely difficult job like murder? Was it also possible that he had completely forgotten about it all and gone on to make peace with his life—just as thousands of children who are victims of sexual abuse all around the world every day end up doing?

'But no! We must not forget that only a few days ago, Arjun Banerjee had called up all three of his friends and reminded them of the vow they had taken, the pact they had made. Clearly then, he had not forgotten. Nor did it seem to me that he had had a change of heart or that he was too afraid of executing the plan. No, what it did seem to me was far more sinister, far more devious, and in many ways, far more tragic. It seemed to me that Arjun Banerjee was already in Manikpur, and was living here under an assumed name.'

There was pin-drop silence in the room. Everyone looked at each other with a strange sense of dread and fear in their eyes. The tension in the room was palpable, but Maity was in no mood to slow down.

'In order to reveal the true identity of this mysterious man, though, I first had to understand the nature of the crime committed against another man, who is with us here today. Because you see, it had always seemed to me that the crime committed by Chowdhury against one of the four boys in question was not as vile as the others he had been accused of. Think about it—murder, rape, child molestation. All heinous, unpardonable crimes. Even the law has serious punishments for these crimes. As opposed to the fourth one—slander!'

I looked at Shibnath Sarkhel. And it seemed to me that he was almost about to pounce at Maity and choke the life out of him. It was perhaps the presence of the Inspector and his men that made Sarkhel remain in his seat, fuming nonetheless.

'What are you trying to say, Mr Maity?' he asked.

'I am saying, Mr Sarkhel, that Chowdhury didn't have a direct hand in your mother's death. There is not even an iota of doubt in my mind that what happened to your mother was very tragic. And what happened to you as a result was also something certainly no child should have to go through. But the fact remains that in your case, the crime committed by Chowdhury was a lesser crime. I don't know how else to put it.'

Having known Maity for so many years, I knew that he could think of a dozen other ways to say what he was trying to say. Far more sensitive ways, in fact. Which could mean only one thing—he was trying to incite Sarkhel! When I quickly looked at Sarkhel, I realized Maity's clever plan was working.

'You, you, you!' The man's entire face had contorted devilishly and turned red. 'You think you can say whatever you want and get away with it, eh? How dare you insult the memory of my mother? Do you know what she had to go through in order to bring me up? In order to give me an education, a good life? You say Chowdhury only slandered my mother? Do you know that like many other planters, he deliberately allowed the free flow of hooch and opium through his own tea gardens? Just so that labourers remained addicted and never had the power to rise in rebellion against his oppression? Do you know that it was this addiction that took my father—my poor, innocent father—from me? And from my mother? One labourer less in the garden didn't mean a thing to Chowdhury. But it meant everything to us— everything! My father would be found lying drunk in the ditches every other day. And all the burden of the family fell on my mother's shoulders. Imagine her plight, when she had to go and work in the same household which had brought about her husband's ruin! Have you ever had to see your mother shed tears as she washed the dishes of a man who had practically made her a widow? Have you ever had to wake up in the middle of the night to find her weeping, and feel helpless? No, Mr Maity, you've probably led a life of luxury and security yourself. Which is why you are so smug, so full of yourself. Which is why you know nothing about what poverty looks like, what poverty can do to you, and what poverty can make you do.'

'Stealing this, for instance?'

Maity's words silenced Shibnath Sarkhel in an instant, as he—like everyone else in the room—looked at the small, shiny thing that Maity had placed on the table in the centre of the room. Despite the extensive wear and tear that it had clearly gone through over the years, there was still an unmistakable and regal shine on it. From the corner of the room, I heard old Charan draw a sharp breath.

A Rolex! Jagat Narayan Chowdhury's Rolex!

'Your mother had indeed stolen the wristwatch, hadn't she, Mr Sarkhel? She had done it out of sheer desperation, and perhaps in a momentary lapse of judgement. To see one's only child's future getting ruined right in front of one's own eyes is perhaps one of the greatest tragedies of a parent's life. I, of all people, understand that, Mr Sarkhel. Especially when that child is mocked and laughed at for being a dwarf. No word in this world is as misused and misunderstood as "normal", isn't it, Mr Sarkhel? And *you*, of all people, must have known that all your life. All that your mother wanted was to give you a "normal" life, a fair chance, just like everyone else. Which is why she stole the watch, picked it up from Chowdhury's bedroom when no one was looking. One might even wonder if it was indeed a crime, after all. But do you know what is worse, what is more unfortunate, what is truly more tragic than having to steal an expensive wristwatch to fend for your child, Mr Sarkhel?'

Shibnath Sarkhel had buried his face in his palms by now, and was on the edge of breaking down.

'What is far, far more tragic is to be discovered stealing by the same child!' said Maity.

Sarkhel was weeping bitterly by now. It seemed to me that someone had wrung my heart and squeezed all the blood out of it. I had never seen Maity so emotional in all these years. His lips were trembling, and although he was putting up a grave face, his eyes betrayed the feelings that were going through his mind.

'You had stumbled upon the watch in her belongings, hadn't you, Mr Sarkhel?' Maity went on.

'And she had seen you discover the watch. By then, the entire village of Manikpur was aware of the accusations against her, but no one believed that she could steal. She was one of their own after all, and they thought fondly of her. But you? You had just chanced upon an ugly truth. And you couldn't face this truth. Your first impression was that she had betrayed the trust of the very people who had supported her. You insulted her, called her a thief and ran away. But in your frustration, you never stopped to think of your mother. She had already lost her husband to alcohol and opium. Now she had lost you too. She had nothing to live for any more. Everything was over. Out of sheer shame, frustration and fear, she set herself on fire.'

'I ran, ran, ran,' Sarkhel's words came in chokes and gasps, as the rest of the room looked on in stunned silence. 'When I saw the smoke from the top of the trees in the orchard and heard her piercing shrieks, I ran as fast as I could, believe me. *But these legs!* These damned, blasted legs! I . . . I just couldn't . . .'

Prabhat Sengupta quickly hugged his friend and pulled him into his arms. Shibnath Sarkhel wept silently, and Maity gave him a few moments to calm down. After some time, Maity addressed him again.

'It was you who had entered Chowdhury's bedroom in the bungalow on the sixteenth of this month. You had spent enough time on the streets to learn how to pick a lock. But you had no intention of killing Chowdhury. No, all that you wanted to do was to replace the watch in the room, make it seem like it had been misplaced all those years ago, not stolen. You did what no "normal" son would ever think of doing. You risked your life to clear your mother's name.'

Sarkhel looked up at Maity with tears in his eyes.

'But,' Maity continued, 'you were seen by the chowkidar. In your rush to escape, you left a knife behind. You were carrying it on your person, just in case you were caught and had to scare your way out. But in all the scurry, you dropped it and it remained in the bungalow. And most unfortunately, it was this knife that was used to murder Jagat Narayan Chowdhury last night.'

'But . . . but . . . I don't understand,' Mohan Sharma spoke out. 'Who stole the knife from Mr Chowdhury's old bedroom in the bungalow, Mr Maity? And how on earth did you get the watch? If Mr Sarkhel had indeed put the watch back in Mr Chowdhury's bedroom, how did it end up with you? Did you remove it from there?'

'No, Mr Sharma,' Maity said calmly. 'I didn't.'

'Then who did?'

Maity took a step closer to Mohan Sharma and said, '*You* did, Mr Sharma! *You* removed the watch from the bedroom. And the knife was never in the bedroom, in the first place. Why would it be there, of all places in the house? No one lives in that room any more, remember? You yourself had said as much to me when we had first met. No, it was in your office, in your custody, and *you* removed it. It was *you* who stabbed Jagat Narayan Chowdhury. It was *you* all along, Mr Sharma! Or shall I call you by your real name from now on?'

[20]

The reaction that Maity's words had on those present in the room had to be seen to be believed. Never before had I seen a group of people in such a state of pure, paralysing shock. Even the most calm and reserved man in the room—Abhijit Lahiri—clutched his hair and looked at Mohan Sharma in disbelief. Prabhat Sengupta and Shibnath Sarkhel seemed utterly incapable of saying or doing anything. And the Inspector's jaw was almost on the floor.

'Trying to look for your old friend in that face, doctor?' asked Maity. 'That wouldn't be too easy. A man's facial features may not completely change with age, but you will be surprised to know what baldness can do to a face. Indeed, this man is none other than Arjun Banerjee, who came to Manikpur to work for the very man who had plucked the innocence out of him. The three of you thought he was too scared to keep his promise, didn't you? But he wasn't—he did keep his promise, although he didn't keep the time. He came six years too early!'

'Arjun?' Dr Sengupta finally managed to utter his first words. 'I can't believe this! Is it really you?'

Arjun Banerjee didn't say a single word. He simply stared at the floor and remained silent.

'All four of you have burnt in the fire of vengeance over the last twenty years,' Maity continued, 'but imagine the pain that this man must have gone through! Just sit back and imagine! For six long years, he served Chowdhury. Followed his commands, managed his office, took dictation from him, helped him up and down stairs, followed him to places, stood beside him. For six years, he allowed Chowdhury to mistreat him, shout at him, shut him up, treat him like an animal. All so that he could keep his promise. He wasn't willing to let any of you kill Chowdhury—no! It had to be *him*! Because of all the crimes that Chowdhury had committed against the four of you, the one against him was the most personal. It was so brutal, so heinous, so vile, that it had left behind not just a violated body, but a sick mind too. A mind that was capable of infinite patience, careful planning, and—something that made this bizarre case even more bizarre—a sheer sense of malevolence.'

'What do you mean, Mr Maity?' said Inspector Sen, 'I don't understand.'

Maity took a moment or two to respond: 'I don't blame you, Inspector. It's not so easy to understand. Let me try and explain it to you with an example from the old days of hunting. Back in the day, in some parts of Western Europe, there was a much-known lore that when a group of friends went hunting for game, there used to be a pact between them—an unwritten code of honour—that in the race to hunt down their prey, in the zeal of getting to it first, they would refrain from harming each other in any way. But every now and then, there would be someone—some rogue hunter—who would break the code. You stumble out of the woods to discover that your friend has taken aim at the animal that you have been tracking for hours. And your desire for the prey is so strong, you have worked so hard to get to it, to claim it for yourself, that you do the unthinkable.'

'You shoot your friend!' A whisper of absolute awe escaped the Inspector's lips.

'You shoot your friend,' nodded Maity. 'Something similar was going through Arjun Banerjee's mind. His hatred for Chowdhury was so intense, and it had grown so much over the years as he began to understand things, that he could never allow any of his three friends to get to the target first. Chowdhury had to die, and by *his* hands. At the same time, he was faced with another problem. A rather serious problem. You see, hunting for game is a different matter altogether, you could not only get away with it back in those days, you would, in fact, be considered a champion after killing the animal. But the murder of a human being had consequences! No matter how vile the man was, the law was sure to catch up with Banerjee had he murdered Chowdhury in blind fury. No, Arjun Banerjee was far too clever for that. Not only did he plan to murder Chowdhury, he planned to frame someone else for the act.'

Everyone turned their attention to Arjun Banerjee for a moment. The man was still sitting in his chair, staring at the floor with a calm gaze.

'Which is exactly why,' continued Maity, 'he called up each of them and reminded them of their vows. Which is exactly why he waited for six long years. Think about it! Can there be anyone better to pin a murder on than someone who has vowed to kill? The stage was set for Banerjee, and all that he had to do now was to let the three friends into the property, one by one. When everything was ready, he took his first step, an utterly easy one.'

Maity now turned around to face the man himself, 'Yes, Mr Banerjee, I personally called up the resident doctor of the garden, Dr Kishore in Bhagalpur, and he confirmed to me that in an inconspicuous manner, it was you who offered him his leave. In his absence, you welcomed Dr Sengupta into this cabin, and the doctor came, completely unaware of the fact that he was walking into a trap. And despite my repeated warnings to you to ensure the safety and security of your employer, you didn't do a thing about the gap in the hedge fence.'

Old Charan clutched his head and sat down on the floor. Prabhat Sengupta was dumbstruck. But Maity was unfazed. He spoke on: 'It was you who sent those two thugs after Prakash and me, wasn't it, Mr Banerjee? And it was you threw the rock into the doctor's room, with the warning letter along with it. You thought you could scare Prakash and me enough to make us leave Manikpur. Because you hadn't succeeded in stopping your employer from coming to me in Kolkata and hiring me—he was far too arrogant to take your advice on that. But when the letter didn't have its intended effect, and the thugs failed, things began to go out of your hands, and you realized that you would have to act quickly. That night, when Abhijit Lahiri was arguing with Dr Sengupta at the lodge, telling him that he had decided to go back to the city, you were nearby, listening to the conversation. Prakash had seen you from the guest house's terrace, but hadn't realized that it was you who was hiding in the bushes. When you saw Lahiri leave, you panicked. You realized that the others might also leave. You couldn't let that happen—because with everyone gone, and me being present in Manikpur, you knew that the murder of Chowdhury would without doubt be looked upon as an inside job. One out of the three men had gone, but the other two were still here. You rushed back to the bungalow, picked up the knife from your office and hid it in a bag. Your objective was to build a story—the calm and calculating Lahiri tells everyone that he doesn't want his revenge any more, but before he leaves, he murders Chowdhury. You would use the knife dropped by the intruder to stab your employer as he slept, and then throw the knife in the bushes behind the guest house. It would all add up, and Lahiri would be blamed for the murder that you had committed.'

An expression of disgust spread across Abhijit Lahiri and Shibnath Sarkhel's faces as they looked at their old friend. Dr Sengupta stared blankly at him, perhaps unable to believe the man's devious plan. Despite all this, Arjun Banerjee did not react in any way whatsoever.

'But there were two things that you hadn't accounted for, Mr Banerjee,' said Maity. 'Two remarkable coincidences that made this strange puzzle even more difficult for me. One of these actually ended up working in your favour. But the other spelt your doom.'

'And what are those, Mr Maity?' asked Inspector Sen. He was almost at the edge of his seat, and it was clear from his expression that he was eager to find out what had actually happened in Manikpur. For the first time since he had been exposed, even Arjun Banerjee looked up at Janardan Maity with a frown of curiosity on his face. What coincidences was Maity talking about?

'At the exact moment when you entered the cabin and stabbed Chowdhury, there were two people who were nearby—both of whom had seen you, but in an extraordinary twist of fate, both of whom had thought that they had seen someone else. One was Shibnath Sarkhel—who, having failed to replace the Rolex in Chowdhury's old bedroom in the bungalow in his first attempt a few days ago, had no other choice but to try and do so again the night of the murder. Because he was planning to leave, you see? And before he left, he simply had to put the watch back in the bedroom. This time, he succeeded. But as luck would have it, when he was coming out of the bungalow and making his way towards the gap in the hedge, he saw a shadowy figure approach the cabin in the dark. He had no other option but to hide. And from his hiding place, he saw a man with a bag on his shoulder enter the cabin. His first impression was that it was none other than Abhijit Lahiri who had lied to him and Dr Sengupta, and that he had come back to murder Chowdhury.'

'But . . . but . . .' Shibnath Sarkhel almost stood up.

'Allow me to finish, Mr Sarkhel,' Maity raised his hand, 'I will explain why, despite not seeing the face of the murderer clearly, you were *so* sure that it was Abhijit Lahiri. It's truly fascinating how the human mind works! You were upset with Lahiri, you thought he had tricked you. You saw the bag on the murderer's shoulder, you saw the knife, and you thought that it could be Lahiri. But it is my firm belief—and you can correct me if I am wrong—that up until then, you were not entirely sure. What truly reinforced your belief that it was Lahiri who killed Chowdhury was the presence of a second man nearby at that exact moment.'

'Rafiq Ali!' I exclaimed.

'Yes, Prakash,' Maity nodded. 'In an incredible stroke of luck, the manager of Manikpur Tea Estate, Mr Rafiq Ali, was returning from a party and passing by the bungalow at that exact moment when Arjun Banerjee was on his way to plant the murder weapon in the bushes behind the lodge. Mr Ali saw someone leave the bungalow and disappear in the shrubbery. He stopped his car, looked for the man and, on not finding him anywhere, drove away towards his own home.'

'Oh my god!' Shibnath Sarkhel clutched his hair and exclaimed in a manner that did not seem exaggerated to me at all.

'Yes!' Maity said. 'Sarkhel was still hiding in the lawns of the bungalow, and it is the sound of Rafiq Ali's car that made Sarkhel think that it was Lahiri who had left for the airport. Remember, Sarkhel was panicking at that moment. In his mind, his friend had tricked him, he had just witnessed a murder. In the dead of the night, the sound of a car in the middle of a secluded place like a tea garden must have sounded decidedly unnatural and odd to him. His panicky mind immediately put two and two together and came up with a convenient answer—that the car was waiting for Abhijit Lahiri, and that it was Abhijit Lahiri who murdered Jagat Narayan Chowdhury.'

'What a remarkable case!' Inspector Sen shook his head, flashing a thoroughly impressed smile. 'And hats off to your deduction, Mr Maity!'

'I am not done yet!'

Maity's words silenced the soft whispers that had begun to spread across the room. I was surprised too! There was more?

'Indeed, this case is remarkable,' Maity said, 'but the story doesn't end here.'

Once again, there was a hushed silence in the room. From the open window, I could see ripples on the waters of the pond. Last night's storm had left its effect on various parts of the lawn. Right from here, I could see at least two broken branches that had fallen into the waters, taking down a number of beautiful flowers and water plants with them. It would take quite a bit of doing to get those two massive branches out of the waters. Although I knew that the bungalow had witnessed much more than a storm in the last few days. And as Maity had himself said a moment ago, he was not yet done.

'While I have the deepest sympathy towards what happened to you twenty years ago, Mr Banerjee,' Maity resumed his speech, 'it is this vile act of trying to frame your friends that I cannot condone. They trusted you. No matter how grave and flawed the plan that all of you had hatched all those years ago, one thing was true—you were all in it together. There ought to be a sense of honour and dignity, Mr Banerjee— even in crime. You are not worthy of that honour. And the fact remains that you stabbed Jagat Narayan Chowdhury in your full consciousness and you tried to pin the blame on not one, not two, but *all* your friends.'

'All of them?' Inspector Sen asked.

'Yes, all of them,' Maity nodded. 'You see, Inspector, at first glance, it may seem that Banerjee's plan was perfect. But there was one problem that he simply hadn't considered, in all the mad rush of panic-fuelled adrenaline. And that was the murder weapon itself. Arjun Banerjee had told me that the knife was in his possession. How, then, was he to explain its disappearance? Banerjee realized that he was in deep trouble, and that he had not considered this variable in his equation at all. Which was why, it became imperative for him to distance himself from the knife. In order to do that, he built a story around the knife being stolen from Mr Chowdhury's old bedroom in the bungalow, not from the office downstairs. To strengthen his story further, he decided to stage a break-in in the bedroom. But when he reached the spot, he found that the lock to the bedroom door that led to the balcony was already open. He must have been completely baffled on seeing this, until a little investigation around the room revealed the watch itself. And at that moment, everything became clear to him. Fate had dealt him a winning hand, with not one, not two, but three aces. He realized that Sarkhel had broken into the bedroom, and in order to frame him too, all that he had to do was to remove the watch from the room, to move it as far from the scene as possible. He had already made the mistake of keeping the knife close to him, and that had put him in a tight spot. He was not about to make the same mistake again. To get rid of the watch, he threw it away in the forest, from where I retrieved it last night.'

'But . . . how did you know that he had thrown the watch in the forest?' Abhijit Lahiri asked.

Maity turned towards me and smiled: 'Because, as always, my most trusted friend showed me the way! Prakash had seen Mohan Sharma, that is, Arjun Banerjee, head into the forest last evening, and no one can give a more vivid description of a place than Prakash Ray can.'

I felt a little embarrassed as everyone turned to me with a twinkle of appreciation in their eyes. Even Rafiq Ali smiled at me and gave me a gentle nod.

'You tried everything, Mr Banerjee,' Maity's voice was firm again, 'but it all came to nothing. And do you know why? Because breaking your friends' trust is a far worse crime than taking revenge on your enemy. Bad things happen to us—all of us. But so do good things. And we need to find strength in the good things in life to forgive and forget the bad ones. You didn't. You were so blinded by your hatred towards the man who had wronged you that you ended up wronging your own friends. And in doing so, not only did you lose your friends, you lost your chance at revenge too.'

What!

What on earth was Maity saying? Arjun Banerjee was frowning deeply; his eyes were wide in shock and disbelief. Everyone else in the room was waiting with bated breath to hear the next bombshell that Janardan Maity was about to explode in the room.

'Dr Sengupta?' Maity finally said.

'Y-yes?'

'Would you consider yourself a good doctor?'

I looked at the doctor and found his lips trembling. He was clearly in no position to answer the question. Maity's penchant for theatricals was not unknown to me, but this was too much! How many shockers was he hiding up his sleeve, really?

'I would presume you do,' Maity stared at him for the longest time and then fired his question: 'Then why didn't it occur to you that there was very little blood on the sheets on which the corpse of Jagat Narayan Chowdhury lay?'

The doctor hung his head and pinched his forehead. Maity was not ready to let him off so easily. He said, 'Much less than a man of Chowdhury's height and weight ought to have? Can you explain that? With your knowledge of medical science?'

No words came out of Dr Sengupta's mouth. Maity walked away from him and stood in the centre of the room again.

'If you don't tell everyone, doctor, then I will. The fact that you were repeatedly insisting on a post-mortem may have escaped everyone else's attention, but it hadn't escaped mine. Mr Arjun Banerjee, I regret to tell you that all those years of planning, all those years of tolerating the man who abused you, of remaining in his shadow, of working for him like a slave—all of that has finally come to nothing. You may go to prison for trying to frame your friends, Mr Banerjee; you may even go to prison for attempting to murder Jagat Narayan Chowdhury, but while I am around, you will not be punished for a crime you haven't committed. And let me tell you that you have certainly not committed the murder of Jagat Narayan Chowdhury. Because he was already dead when you stabbed him. Yes, I had a doubt about this when I first saw the blood, so I spoke to the doctor conducting the post-mortem last night. Later today, when the report arrives, you will learn that Jagat Narayan Chowdhury's heart had stopped a little after midnight, well before you had stabbed him. He had died of perfectly natural causes. It was his old age that had killed him. Not you.'

'No!' Arjun Banerjee sprung up from his chair, and the two constables came running towards him. 'No, no, no, no, no!'

As the two constables grabbed him from both sides, Arjun Banerjee's deafening cries rung through the cabin that had once seen dozens of British merchants suffer in quarantine out of fear of a disease that was not contagious at all.

'I killed him! I . . . I tore through that dark, vicious heart of his. I killed him, no one else. He couldn't have been dead, that's not possible, I know for sure! *I* killed him!'

Maity nodded at Inspector Sen, and the latter asked the two constables to take Arjun Banerjee out of the room. As he was being dragged out, Banerjee suddenly pushed the two constables away in an unexpected show of inhuman strength and ran for the door. But before he could reach the door, a loud thud echoed through the room and Arjun Banerjee swung around and collapsed on the floor like a felled tree. Pushing his greaser cap up with a toothpick and placing the pick back between his lips again, our beloved friend from the hills calmly resumed his place in the corner after knocking the fugitive straight out with a perfect right hook.

'Thanks, Pele!' Maity smiled.

'No problem!' The young man nodded calmly, the toothpick once again dancing between his lips as he looked towards me and said, 'Just make sure you write my name in that book of yours!'

[21]

Maity was right. The post-mortem report arrived around noon, and it did say that Jagat Narayan Chowdhury died of a cardiac arrest. Arjun Banerjee—whom we had known as Mohan Sharma all along—had been taken into custody, and Inspector Sen had personally assured Maity that despite everything that the man had done, Banerjee would be treated with care.

'I am amazed to see how your mind works!' he said, as he shook Maity's hand. 'It's incredible! It's almost as if it's not possible . . . and yet, I saw it happen right in front of my eyes! How, how, how do you think like that? How did you come up with the solution?'

Maity and I had a quick exchange of glances. Maity cleared his throat and said, 'As I've told you before, Inspector, I just keep my eyes and ears open. And my mind too—I can't emphasize the importance of the second bit enough.'

'You called up Dr Kishore in Bhagalpur, you spoke to the doctor who conducted the post-mortem, you interrogated so many people, you listened to them, you memorized every single thing they told you—you even went into the forest in the middle of a stormy night! That's just . . . marvellous!'

'It's not marvellous, Inspector,' said Maity, 'it's investigation!'

'Yes, yes, of course,' the Inspector seemed embarrassed. 'But what made you suspect Mohan Sharma—I mean Arjun Banerjee—in the first place?'

'Well,' Maity said, 'there were several things. But the most important among them was Charan.'

'You mean the old butler?'

'Yes. I found it very surprising that a stranger would be entering the cabin, moving around and then leaving—all with Charan lying right there, just outside Chowdhury's bedroom. So what if he was asleep? If you think about it from the murderer's point of view, he wouldn't risk being discovered by Charan, would he? And this led me to think: Who was the only man who Charan would be not at all surprised to find moving around the cabin, *even if he were to wake up all of a sudden*? And the answer was clear—it had to be Mohan Sharma. He was right there, and had promised to spend the night in the cabin too. Charan knew that.'

'I see, I see!' Inspector Sen nodded, understanding the logic of what Maity had just told him. 'It's so simple when you explain it like that.'

'The second thing that aroused my suspicion was, as I said before, the knife. The moment I heard Sharma tell me that he had gone to Chowdhury's old bedroom to look for it, I had my doubts. Because that seemed like an unnecessary bit of information he was giving me. In that tense moment, when he had just discovered that the probable murder weapon had disappeared from his custody, where it had disappeared from seemed to me like a detail he was trying a bit too hard to

plant in my mind. Moreover, there was absolutely no reason
for him to leave the knife in an unused bedroom. If at all, he
would want to keep it nearby, and in a safe place, probably
under lock and key. But instead, he claimed that he had kept
it in Chowdhury's old bedroom, just so he could dissociate
himself from it. That was one grave mistake that he made.
And later, when Prakash saw him walking into the forest,
I realized he was trying to hide something. But by then, I had
already come to know that the knife had been found behind
the lodge. So, I began to wonder: What *else* could it be that he
was trying to get rid of? There was only one way to find out.
I had to go to the spot and look for it.'

Inspector Sen was all smiles. 'Remarkable! And I think
you have to admit that you owe a lot of your success in
solving this case to your friend here, eh Mr Maity? Heh heh,
Mr Ray, what do you say? No, no, no, no, no . . . there's no
point being humble about it. You two are a team, and *you*, in
particular, Mr Ray, are . . . are . . . are . . . like Dr Watson was
to Sherlock Holmes!'

I looked at Maity, he winked at me mischievously.
Inspector Sen took a step closer to me and said in a low
voice, 'I'm sure you didn't mind the . . . you know . . . the little
incident that happened at the station, did you, Mr Ray? You
aren't really going to . . . write about it or anything, are you?'

'Not at all, Inspector,' I smiled as I replied confidently.
'You needn't worry about that.'

Inspector Sen grinned from ear to ear, thanked me
profusely and walked away to the other side of the room,
but from the way he was still stealing anxious glances at me,
I realized how true Maity's words were. The dishonest always
live under the constant shadow of fear.

Abhijit Lahiri walked up to us. It seemed to me that a big load had been taken off his mind.

'Thank you for everything, Mr Maity,' he said.

'No, thank *you*,' said Maity. 'You are the only sensible man I have come across in Manikpur over the last few days. And the bravest one, too. It takes a lot of courage to move on, Mr Lahiri. I admire you in ways that I cannot even begin to describe.'

Abhijit Lahiri smiled and shook Maity's hand firmly.

'I do have one question though,' said Maity. 'Just before leaving the lodge for the airport, you had told Dr Sengupta, "It's all over now." You were referring to your own state of mind, weren't you? You were trying to say that twenty years of seething in vengeance was all over for you. It had nothing to do with Chowdhury, right?'

'Right again,' Lahiri smiled. 'But with everything that Arjun had done, no one would have believed me, not even Prabhat. If you wouldn't have been in Manikpur, I would have been in big trouble.'

'And that would have been tragic, because you were the only one among the four who had genuinely walked away from Manikpur, who was absolutely clear in his mind as to what was the right thing to do. And that's extremely commendable, Mr Lahiri.'

Abhijit Lahiri thanked Maity again and said his goodbyes. On seeing Shibnath Sarkhel standing quietly in one corner, Maity and I walked up to him.

'So, Mr Sarkhel?' Maity said. 'When are you planning to leave?'

Shibnath Sarkhel turned around to face us with a sad smile. 'In a day or two, I guess. I was thinking of going back to the village once.'

Maity watched him hang his head and said, 'I want you to understand something, Mr Sarkhel. I want you to know that within the periphery of what her circumstances permitted her, your mother did the best she could do. Let alone being ashamed, you should be proud of her. Don't let her memory afflict you, don't let it cause you pain and grief. Cherish her. Think of her as someone who, with absolutely no help and support from anyone, tried to do the most difficult job in the world—raising a child!'

Shibnath Sarkhel's eyes had welled up again. Maity placed a soft hand on his shoulder and said, 'In the absence of your father, it was your mother who was your hero, your idol. To see her fall from the pedestal you had set her up on was not an ordinary thing to happen to you. And just like her, you too had a momentary lapse of judgement. Instead of treating her with kindness at a time when she probably needed it the most, you left her to deal with her own shame. And I know that this plays on your mind even today. I know that you hold yourself responsible for her death. But remember that you were just a child when all this happened. And you shouldn't blame yourself for it at all. It wasn't your fault.'

Sarkhel grabbed Maity's hand as tears rolled down his cheeks. Maity's next few words seemed to comfort him to a great extent, 'When you go back to your village, Mr Sarkhel, hold your head high. And you will see that everything is fine.'

Before we left, Rafiq Ali came and spoke to us.

'You are leaving?' he asked, with an embarrassed smile on his face.

Maity smiled back at him and said: 'There are three flights from Bagdogra to Kolkata every day. Prakash and I are planning to take the evening one. We just have to go back to the guest house to pick up our luggage. '

Rafiq Ali couldn't take it any more. He stepped forward and said, 'I am so sorry, Mr Maity. I made a mistake. I am truly ashamed, I don't know what to say . . .'

In a gentle voice, Maity said: 'You have nothing to be ashamed of, Mr Ali. Very rarely do we come across people who speak as honestly as you do. I have seen the papers; I know how difficult it must be to manage the affairs of the estate. The fact that you do so with such sincerity and with such loyalty towards your garden and its people only speaks volumes about your integrity. Do you think that I haven't noticed that the same people who spoke ill of your employer are all praises for you? If that's not the greatest test of your nature as a human being, I don't know what is.'

Ali thanked Maity profusely, but despite his repeated pleas, Maity politely declined to stay for a few more days in Manikpur. Pele was waiting for us. As we sat in the car, Prabhat Sengupta came running towards us.

'Heading back home, Mr Maity?' he asked, with a look of genuine admiration in his eyes.

'Yes, doctor,' Maity smiled. 'As should you.'

'I . . .' the doctor hesitated for a second, 'I couldn't save Ashu Sir, Mr Maity. I . . . I tried, but there was very little to be done. His lungs were completely . . .'

'I understand,' interrupted Maity. 'But I want you to make a promise to me.'

'Sure, please tell me.'

Maity extended his hand out of the car's window and said, 'Promise me, that from now on, you will stop worrying about things that can't be undone. Promise me that from now on, you will only look ahead.'

Prabhat Sengupta was taken aback for a moment, but when he understood what Maity was trying to say, he simply placed his hand on Maity's hand and smiled a little.

'In mourning the dead, Dr Sengupta,' said Maity, before our car moved out of Jagat Narayan Chowdhury's massive compound for the final time, 'never ever forget the ones who are alive. Go back to your wife. She needs you more than anyone else does!'

We reached the guest house at around two o'clock in the afternoon. Maity had already called his friend in the airline and arranged for our tickets, and he said that if we hoped to catch the flight, we would need to start off immediately.

'We don't have much time, Prakash. Pack up your stuff and meet me outside in ten minutes. We'll get something to eat on the way. I will see if I can find Gangadhar, I need to speak to him.'

Having said this much, Maity pulled out a five-hundred-rupee note from his wallet, put the wallet back in his jacket pocket, threw the jacket on the bed and walked out of the room. I quickly pulled my suitcase on my bed and started putting my stuff back in it. The wet clothes from last night had dried by now. I got them out of the bathroom and packed them too.

What a fascinating case, I thought! As always, Maity's intelligence had ensured that even the most baffling puzzle was finally solved. Arjun Banerjee had been caught—I was sure he would be punished for what he did. Dr Sengupta would go back to his wife, and both Shibnath Sarkhel and

Abhijit Lahiri would probably find their peace and move on in their respective lives. As I shut my suitcase and locked it, I couldn't help but smile at the ingenuity of my dear friend. I could hear his voice at the far end of the veranda. He was probably handing Gangadhar a tip.

My eyes suddenly fell on Maity's jacket. Something was sticking out from its pocket. Not the wallet, something else. Where had I seen that brown thing before? I took a couple of steps towards Maity's bed to catch a better glimpse, and as soon as I did, a sudden jolt of shock seemed to run through my body.

An envelope!

A small brown envelope. In a flash, I remembered where I had seen it before. It was this envelope that Maity had in his hands this morning, when he was speaking to Kanai! As soon as he had seen me on the veranda, he had quickly put the envelope in his pocket. I had not thought much of it at that time, but now that I thought about it, his actions seemed decidedly strange to me. Was he trying to hide the envelope? Why would he want to do that? Why would he want to hide something from *me*?

Maity was still speaking to Gangadhar; I could hear his voice in the veranda. I had an irrepressible urge to find out what the envelope contained. The door leading from Maity's room to the veranda was shut, but the bolt was unlocked. If I had to do something, I would have to do it right this instant or it would be too late. I quickly plucked the envelope out of the jacket's pocket and brought out a folded sheet of paper from inside. A letter!

There wasn't much time to think, Maity would be back any time now. I began reading the letter.

Dear Mr Maity,

By the time you have the opportunity to read this letter, I will be dead. If you are even half as intelligent as I think you are, you will have probably realized by now that it was not the blade of a knife that killed Jagat Narayan Chowdhury. Nor do I need to tell you that he was already dead before the knife struck him. But there are some things in life that even an enlightened mind such as yours is incapable of knowing, Mr Maity. And it is to tell you about a few such things that I am writing to you today.

It all happened on a particularly stormy afternoon twenty years ago, right here in Manikpur. School had been suspended, because part of the thatched roof had collapsed. Students had been sent home but I had stayed back to get some important papers out of the office. I had retrieved the papers and was almost about to head back home, when I heard a noise from one of the classrooms. Wondering who could have been left behind, I made my way to the classroom, only to witness a strange sight.

Yes, Mr Maity, I am aware of the vow that Prabhat, Shibu and Abhijit had taken along with their friend Arjun twenty years ago. And despite their young age, I knew at that very instant that they would honour their vow. I could see it in their eyes. For twenty long years, I wished that they would never come back to Manikpur, that they would forget, that they would move on with their lives. But for twenty years, those four sets of eyes kept haunting me. Because what I had seen in those eyes, I pray that no teacher in the world should ever have to see.

A teacher's mind is a strange entity, Mr Maity. A man like you would perhaps understand that. Every year, dozens of students come to learn from a teacher. Is it just Math and History and Grammar and Science that a teacher teaches his students? No. A good teacher teaches far more than that. He teaches ethics, values, the ability to distinguish the right from the wrong. But more often than not, it seems to us teachers that it is a lost cause. What kind of a world are we preparing our students for, really? What value do traits like honesty and integrity have in this world, after all? Which is why, we are often faced with the dilemma: Are we making our students stronger or weaker before sending them out into the world to fight their battles?

But every time, every single time we have self-doubt, we shake that feeling off. And we pick up our chalk pieces and start writing on that blackboard again, teaching those little minds what is right and what is wrong. Because what is wrong, will forever remain wrong, no matter how much the world changes. And what is right, what is good, what is pure—yes—that will sail those young minds through. It is with this simple yet crucial assumption, it is with this hope, that we perform our duties every day.

Which is why, when I saw the four boys that day, I knew that I had to do something, that I had to stop them. Unfortunately, though, before I could, all four of them left Manikpur and went their own ways, and I was left behind thinking of the curse that had befallen them. The curse of vengeance!

I wondered if they would come back, sincerely hoping that they wouldn't. But a week or so ago, when Kanai told me that three men had come to stay in the lodge on the highway and one of them had dwarfism, I realized that my worst fears had come true. I realized that the boys had returned, that they would murder Chowdhury, and in doing so, would end up ruining whatever life they had built for themselves. And it was then that I decided that as a teacher, I couldn't let that happen.

Yes, Mr Maity. It was I who murdered Jagat Narayan Chowdhury. It took a bit of doing, but I had a perfect weapon available to me right outside my house. Did you know, Mr Maity, that the seeds of a garden croton have a small amount of poison in them? And that the consumption of a sufficient number of these seeds can be fatal to a child? Or to an old man? I remember when we used to be younger, we used to tell children never to put those seeds in their mouths. It's strange how a poisonous plant such as this is commonly available within everyone's reach.

Even when he was a younger man, Chowdhury liked to have his breakfast out in the open, beside that garden pond of his. I knew this from back in the day, when I used to go to his bungalow to give tuitions to his kids. The day before you arrived in Manikpur, I went to see Chowdhury in the morning. In my pocket were over a hundred croton seeds, crushed to a fine, tasteless and odourless powder. His breakfast had been served by the pond, but he had not arrived yet. As I was waiting for him, I slipped a small portion of the powder into his food. Small enough to leave no trace in his bloodstream, but large enough to kill him.

Do I regret what I did? Not one bit. A man like Chowdhury deserved the end he met. And I—who ensured that he met his maker—am about to go away soon. Everything will be fine now. Yes, perhaps the people of Manikpur who have given me their love and respect over the years will henceforth know me as a murderer. But I hope they will realize why I did it. Those young boys, Mr Maity! Those precious souls! I had had the misfortune of seeing them getting ruthlessly crushed all those years ago. I couldn't see them getting wrecked once again, could I? No, not on my watch.

You came across to me as an intelligent man. But you also seemed like a man whose compassion was still intact. I hope, then, that you will understand why I chose to do what I did. And I hope that you will see to it that the boys find their peace. Just as I have found mine.

Sincerely,
Ashutosh Mukherjee

There was a soft creak from the door, and I looked up from the letter to find Maity standing at the doorway staring at me. The curtains were blowing in the breeze. Gangadhar walked into my room to take the suitcases outside. Pele sounded the horn a couple of times. We were getting late for our flight. But I had to ask Maity one last question before we left Manikpur.

'You knew this?' I asked in a whisper.

Maity sighed.

And nodded his head.

Epilogue

More than a year had passed by since we had come back to Kolkata.

That day, on the way to Bagdogra, at the airport, or on the flight, Maity and I did not say a single word to each other. When I reached home, I went into a hole, locked myself up in my room, trying to cope with the many emotions that were battling with each other in my mind. On the one hand, I was sad that Maity had lied to everyone, claiming that Chowdhury's death had been a natural one. I felt that as someone who had spent his entire life in the pursuit of truth, and as someone who always upheld the law, Janardan Maity had no right to hide the contents of the letter from being made public. If his logic was that in keeping the truth from everyone, he wanted to prevent a much-respected man such as Ashu Babu from being thought of as a murderer, then I was not willing to buy that argument at all. Ashu Babu had himself written in his letter that the people of Manikpur had always showered him with love and respect. And everyone in Manikpur knew what a heinous man Jagat Narayan Chowdhury was. Even if they were to be told the truth, they would never think poorly of Ashutosh Mukherjee. It was simply not possible. Maity's fears were unfounded, and for once, his judgement had turned out to be wrong.

But on the other hand, I also realized that Janardan Maity was only human, and he could make mistakes. He may have taken a questionable decision, but one thing was true, and even I had no doubt in my mind about it. And it was that his intentions were honest. I knew my friend well enough to say that with absolute certainty.

What truly hurt me, then, was to know that he had hidden the letter from *me*. Granted, that he did not want anyone else to know. But why keep the truth from me? Had I ever said or done anything to make him believe that I wouldn't understand him? That I wouldn't have faith in him? Did he not believe that his secret was safe with me? It was this one question that completely devastated me. I have always believed that one of the fundamental requirements in any friendship is reciprocation. If Maity couldn't trust me, how could he expect me to trust him?

For one whole year, I did not meet him, nor did I call him even once. And what hurt me further was that he did not call me either. I am sure he had enough sense in him to realize that it was he who had made the mistake. Despite that, if he hadn't had the common courtesy to reach out to me and apologize, if he did not even bother to make amends, or to explain his position to me, then there was very little that I could do.

For the first few months, I was very depressed that things had turned out this way. I don't know what Maity thought of me, but I had genuinely thought of him as a true friend. And I was sad to have lost his friendship. In order to cope with my grief, I began to do the only thing I knew how to do. I began to write. One fine morning, just like that, the words started flowing. And then a time came when I just couldn't stop. In as little as three months, I finished my novel. The sense of contentment I felt was something that no words can describe. I sent the manuscript off to my good friend and editor Snigdha Chatterjee, and within a few hours, she woke me up with a phone call in the middle of the night to tell me that she had finished reading it in one sitting, that she loved it, and that she was going to publish it. After several months, I went back to sleep with a smile on my face.

A few months later, one fine morning, I was busy with the final edits of my novel. It was supposed to go to press in a couple of weeks, when I received an unexpected visitor. It was Mahadev—Janardan Maity's old manservant.

'What's the matter, Mahadev?' I asked him as I welcomed him in. 'Is everything all right?'

'You need to come with me,' he said, his face grim and overcast with a sadness that I had never seen nor expected to see on Mahadev's face. 'You need to come see him.'

'See whom?' I asked. 'Maity?'

Mahadev looked at me and said, 'Something is wrong with him, Dada Babu. Please come and see for yourself.'

Mahadev had known Maity ever since he was born. He had stayed with him all his life. On seeing his eyes glistening with tears, I couldn't take it any more. I immediately called a taxi, put Mahadev in it, jumped in myself and reached Maity's house in Bhowanipore. The same gate, the same flower garden, the same baroque stairwell. Hundreds of fond memories came rushing back to me. But the moment I entered Maity's living room, I was aghast.

What on earth had happened here? I had spent such wonderful times in this very room, in lively discussions and enriching debates with Maity. Pot after pot of tea had been supplied in this room by Mahadev himself, as the reminiscences of our adventures or the analysis of a good movie or the argument on who made the best biryani in Kolkata just wouldn't end. We listened to Bach, we played chess, we read, we chatted, we even sat quietly and listened to the rain. All in this room. And look at it now!

All the windows had been shut tight, letting almost no light in. There was a dank and musty smell in the air. As I tried to find my way in the dark, I stumbled upon books and cutlery strewn around on the floor without care. And amidst all this, I found Janardan Maity himself sitting on his favourite couch by the window, almost invisible in the darkness.

'Open the windows, Mahadev,' I ordered.

'No, no, no!' Maity yelled out. '*Don't!*'

But paying no heed to his master, Mahadev did the needful, sending a rush of daylight into the dusty room and forcing Maity to curl his feet up on the couch and cover his face in agony.

'How many days has it been, Maity?' I asked, as I knelt before him. 'How many days has it been since you have seen light?'

It took Maity almost a minute to take his palms off his face and look at me. The first words he spoke to me wrenched my heart and sent a lump of emotion up my throat.

'I knew you would come, my friend!'

I shook my head in disbelief and said, 'Look what you've done to yourself.'

Maity ran his palms along his cheeks. I had never seen him with a beard up until that day.

'I need a shave, don't I?'

I tried to fight back my tears and said, 'Why, Maity? Why did you keep the truth from me?'

Maity thought for a few seconds and then looked away in a childlike huff, 'I had my reasons.'

I shook my head. The man was clearly in a mess. And although he probably didn't think of me as a worthy friend to him, it was my responsibility to bring him out of this hellhole that he had created for himself. I asked Mahadev to run a hot bath for him, and in a stern voice, commanded Maity to shave and shower.

'I will do that,' Maity said, his voice marked with a sense of impish mischief, 'but you have to promise me something.'

'Promise?' I asked, irritated. 'Promise what?'

Maity looked at me and said, 'That you will come along with me on one final journey!'

'Final journey?' I asked. 'Where to?'

As he bent forward to answer my question, I saw the same twinkle of intelligence in his eyes that was so, so familiar to me.

'The Victoria Memorial!'

Without waiting for me to respond, Maity rushed out of the room. And in less than an hour, I found myself sitting in a cab, heading towards the Maidan. It was a Sunday, and the afternoon traffic was on the lighter side. Maity was sitting beside me, and although he was silent, it seemed to me that he was in good spirits.

I had come to the Memorial after almost three years, but the place was as beautiful as ever. I knew that there were some fascinating exhibits in the museum inside, but Maity showed no interest in going in. He seemed to be enjoying the afternoon air, as was evident from the way he was breathing in lungfuls of it. We strolled on the lawns on the eastern side of the building, talking about the good old times again. I told him about my new novel, and he was very happy to know that I had written it. He spoke at length about a few delicacies that he would love to try out after all these days, and seeing him talk animatedly about food and cinema and books once again, only one thought came to my mind. That although he had never said so in as many words, my friend was happy to see me.

'Let's sit here for a while,' he said, as he glanced at his watch. 'It's nice and quiet in this part of the garden.'

'What are we doing here, Maity?' I asked. 'And why do you keep looking at your watch?'

'Ah! Good observation!' he exclaimed. 'I see that these last few months have not dulled the effect I have had on you!'

Maity's behaviour seemed odd to me, but there was nothing new in that. The man had some strange habits, and to those who didn't know him closely enough, most of these habits could come across as rather annoying. I had gotten used to them by now, so I looked around to admire how green and peaceful the gardens were. And as soon as I did, my heart stopped in an instant.

'And . . . as if on cue,' Maity's voice reached my ears.

Dr Sengupta!

The man had put on a bit of weight in all these months, but even from so far away, I didn't have any problem recognizing him. He was walking out from behind a row of gladioli, pushing something along the walkway, and there was someone along with him. His wife, Mitali Sengupta. The doctor was pushing a pram. Had the doctor and his wife had a baby, then? How lovely, I thought! I looked at Maity and found him quietly staring at the couple.

Dr Sengupta now pecked his wife on her cheeks, hunched over the pram for some time and then walked away towards the southern gates. Mitali Sengupta watched her husband's retreating figure for some time, and then made her way to the canal with the pram. She dusted a bench with a handkerchief, sat on it and opened a book.

'Come with me, Prakash,' Maity rose from his seat and walked towards the canal. I followed him. There was a gentle breeze blowing from the side of the Maidan, and it was making the afternoon even more pleasant. Down by the edge of the canal, a few students from the Art College nearby were sitting and sketching a profile view of the Memorial building.

'Mrs Sengupta?'

Mitali Sengupta looked up from her book. She looked more beautiful than she had the last time. There was a radiant smile on her face, and she seemed truly happy.

'Oh, Mr Maity!' her face glowed. 'What a pleasant surprise!'

'Please, madam,' Maity said, 'please don't get up. In fact, I was wondering if we could sit down instead?'

'Certainly,' she said, making room for us on the bench. We took our seats. Maity placed his jacket on his lap and said with a warm smile, 'What have you named her?'

'Poorna!' Mitali Sengupta said with a proud smile on her face, as she adjusted the wrapper to cover the baby's ears, making her coo in delight. I had never seen something so beautiful in my life! The little girl could not have been more than a couple of months old. With her big, dark eyes, she watched us in surprise, perhaps wondering who these two strangers were. Maity stared at the little girl fondly for a long time.

'I had tried to reach you several times on your phone, Mr Maity,' said the baby's mother. 'Not sure if you have changed your number or something, but no one responded. I had even come to your home once, along with my husband. But the elderly gentleman who opened the door said that you weren't in. There is, of course, the matter of your compensation, and I can't thank you enough for everything that—'

'I don't need any compensation from you, madam,' Maity raised a hand to interrupt Mitali Sengupta. 'But I do need to ask you a few questions. And if, indeed, you are as grateful to me as you say you are, then I will expect that you give honest and truthful answers to my questions.'

'Certainly, Mr Maity,' she said. 'What questions, though?'

Maity stared at Mitali Sengupta for some time and said: 'When Jagat Narayan Chowdhury came to see me at my home for the first time, he said something strange. At that point of time, his words had seemed trivial to me, the mere ranting of an old and senile man. But I would like to ask you today, if they mean anything to you.'

Mitali Sengupta was listening to Maity with rapt attention. Maity went on.

'Chowdhury had felt that it wasn't the first time he had come to my house that night. "We've been here before, haven't we?" Those were his exact words. Could you tell me, madam, why he must have felt so?'

Mrs Sengupta smiled and said, 'I'm not quite sure why you are asking *me* that question, Mr Maity? I don't see how I am supposed to know that.'

'No problem at all,' Maity shut his eyes and shook his head. 'See if you can answer my second question instead. When I was in Manikpur, I had met your husband's schoolteacher Ashutosh Mukherjee, fondly known in the village as Ashu Babu. When I met him the first time, the old man had told me that none of the four boys—including your husband—had come to see him after they had left Manikpur. And yet, when I referred to your husband as Dr Prabhat Sengupta, he never asked me what kind of a doctor he'd become. I found it rather strange, given the fact that little Prabhat used to be Ashu Babu's favourite student. Why do you think he never asked me that question, madam?'

The breeze had picked up. Mitali Sengupta's smile was slowly fading away. This time, she didn't even respond to Maity's question.

'No?' Maity shook his head again. 'No problem, here's my final question, and I promise you that there won't be any more after this one. In a letter that Ashu Babu had written to me before he passed away, he had mentioned that he used to give private tuitions to Chowdhury's children. I was also told by Chowdhury's secretary that his children now live in London. But when I made inquiries, I could only account for his son, who does live there. No one could tell me anything about the daughter, except that she had completed her studies from the University of London. Apparently, she left London after finishing her studies, and has never been seen again. Would you be so kind as to tell me, madam, where did Jagat Narayan Chowdhury's daughter disappear to after she left London?'

A very familiar feeling was beginning to send shivers down my spine again. The rapid thumping inside my heart and the rush of blood in my head that I had missed so much in the last one year was now back. And boy, what a feeling it was!

'Chowdhury was your father, wasn't he, madam?' Maity asked gently.

Mitali Sengupta had started trembling. Maity took his jacket from his lap, put it around the lady's shoulders and said, 'And would I be wrong, Mrs Sengupta, if I were to say that you committed the gravest crime a woman can possibly commit? Just so that you could save your husband? You committed patricide! You murdered your own father!'

Mitali Sengupta was finding it difficult to look Maity in the eye. She had clutched her book so tight that its spine was about to snap. Maity gently pulled the book away from her hands, set it aside on the bench and continued speaking.

'When I learnt that Ashu Babu used to tutor Chowdhury's children, and that his daughter had disappeared from London after finishing her studies, Chowdhury's words instantly rushed back to me. "We've been here before, haven't we?" he had asked his secretary, referring to my home. But that wasn't true. He had never come to my place before. Why then did he feel that way? It was then that I remembered that your father had started his career as a tea-taster. As you—of all people—very well know, madam, the job of a tea-taster is to taste hundreds of varieties of tea every day, and one must be formally trained to be able to do so. And as we all know, the sense of smell is an integral part of the act of tasting. Yes—smell! Half an hour before Chowdhury had stepped into my home, *you* were sitting there, waiting for me. And along with you, you had a gift for me. A box of freshly baked cookies and muffins, whose aroma had not faded even till later in the night. An untrained person like Prakash or I hadn't noticed the smell in the air after you had left, but your father had no ordinary nose, did he? He immediately caught the smell, because he had smelt the same aroma earlier that day, when he had visited you in your bakery.'

Mitali Sengupta was now visibly afraid. Her face had turned pale and from the way she clutched the pram and drew it closer to herself, I understood the thoughts that must have been going through her mind.

'Unfortunately,' Maity was in no mood to relent, 'Chowdhury simply couldn't make the connection between you and me. He could never imagine that such a remarkable coincidence could occur. He never thought that that very night, you would come to me to seek my help in stopping your husband from murdering your father.

'When I realized that Chowdhury was your father, my first impression was that you were trying to save him out of love for him. But then I asked myself: Why would you hide that fact from me? More importantly, why would you hide that fact from me and *still* ask me to go to Manikpur? Weren't you afraid that your husband might tell me about your relationship with your father? And then it all became clear to me. I realized that Prabhat Sengupta did not know that you were Jagat Narayan Chowdhury's daughter. Yes, Mrs Sengupta—there might have been many coincidences in this story, but the fact that seven years ago, at a party thrown by a common friend, you merely bumped into the man whose entire life had been destroyed by your father wasn't a coincidence at all. Was it? No, you came back from London

and sought Prabhat Sengupta out. Because you knew what
had happened to Prabhat's father, and because Prabhat and
you were good friends in school. A fact that your father had
no way of knowing.'

'Father?' Mitali Sengupta finally spoke, her face lined
with an expression of sheer revulsion. 'What that man did to
me were not the actions of a father, Mr Maity. What do you
know about what my mother and I had to go through? Bit
by bit, I saw my mother wither away, and finally perish from
her illness. That monster did nothing to help her—*nothing!* I
was just a little girl. I begged him to call a doctor, I pleaded
with him to save my mother. But he didn't. Not because he
couldn't. But because he didn't want to. I still remember the
nights when my mother used to lie in bed writhing in pain,
and my father would sit on a couch, merely a few feet away,
simply watching her and sipping his whisky. I will never
forget the sadistic look in those eyes, Mr Maity. Night after
night after night, he just watched her die, bit by bit. He . . . he
derived pleasure from her pain. And not just my mother, his
vicious urges didn't spare anyone. *Anyone!*'

Little Poorna whimpered a bit, perhaps she had never
heard her mother speak in such a voice. Mitali Sengupta
immediately took her child in her arms and rocked her gently.

'Prabhat and I were good friends in school,' she said. 'In
fact, he was the only friend I had. My brother was several
years older than me, and he soon left for London for his
higher studies. Other than my mother, no one at home so
much as dared to take me in their arms. All out of fear of
my father. Throughout my childhood, no one had spoken a
kind word to me. Prabhat came to my life like a blessing. He
was so kind and gentle. A genuine friend. The day he lost his

father, I was devastated. Because the rumours had already started flying thick. He didn't want to talk to me any more, he even stopped looking at me. I realized that thanks to the actions of my father, I had lost the only friend I had.'

'Which was why,' Maity said, 'when you came back from London, you sought him out?'

Mrs Sengupta nodded, 'I did. It was not just he who had been troubled by the memories of Manikpur for twenty long years, Mr Maity. But unlike him, I had no one I could share my pain with. When I approached him at the party, he couldn't recognize me at all. How could he? Our circumstances had changed, we had changed. And unlike me, he wasn't looking for his old friend! He seemed happy to meet me, simply because he didn't know who I was. And I just didn't have the heart to tell him. I thought I would, when the time was right. But the more I kept meeting him, the more I realized I was falling in love with him. And I just didn't want to lose him again. The possibility of having him in my life was far more important to me, and I could do anything—*anything*— to be close to him. Imagine my plight, then, Mr Maity, when five years after our wedding, I learnt that he and his friends had vowed to kill my father. I tried to persuade him, reason with him, not out of any love for my father. But out of concern for him.'

'Allow me to tell the rest of the story, Mrs Sengupta,' said Maity. 'And please feel free to correct me if I go wrong anywhere. When you couldn't convince your husband to give up his plan, you went to Manikpur, to see your old teacher, to seek his guidance. Ashu Babu heard you and told you that the only solution to this problem was if you were to tell your husband the truth—that you were Jagat

Narayan Chowdhury's daughter. But you couldn't bear
the thought of earning your husband's wrath and hatred.
You had seen him burn in the fire of vengeance after all.
You refused to reveal your identity to your husband, and you
told Ashu Babu that you would murder your father instead.
You even showed him the croton seeds and reminded him
how he used to tell his students never to put the seeds in
their mouths. You told him that it was with those seeds that
you were going to poison your father. Needless to say, Ashu
Babu severely disapproved of this idea, and was extremely
concerned about you. He tried to talk you out of it and sent
you back to Kolkata.'

Mrs Sengupta nodded her head and said, 'But a couple
of days later, my father came to my bakery, looking for me.
Apparently, his lawyers had had me traced down to Kolkata,
and he had come to see me. I remember a rather strange
feeling had overpowered me that evening. Even when I was
almost about to give up on my plan, he had walked right into
my bakery! What would you call that, Mr Maity? Other than
a sign from god? And perhaps you won't believe me, but for
as long as he stayed in my bakery, he continued to speak ill
of my mother. And I . . . I don't know what snapped within
me. I saw a remarkable opportunity. I figured if I poisoned
my father then and there, and he died in Kolkata, then my
husband would not be suspected at all. Because he was in
Manikpur at that time! I still had the seeds with me. And I
crushed them and mixed them in his tea.'

Maity said: 'The moment he left, you realized your
mistake. You realized your father hadn't been administered
even half as much poison as was enough to kill him. And if,
as a result of this, he went back to Manikpur and died *there*,

your husband would be a prime suspect. It was then that you immediately rushed to see me and asked me to bring your husband back from Manikpur.'

I asked a question that had been going around in my mind for some time, 'Wait a second, Maity, are you saying that Chowdhury wasn't poisoned in Manikpur at all?'

'No,' said Maity, his eyes still fixed on Mitali Sengupta, 'he was poisoned here, in Kolkata. By his daughter. The poison killed him three days later.'

'But . . . but I don't understand,' I said. 'Chowdhury never drank any tea other than the one from his own garden. Why did he—?'

'That is precisely the point, Prakash,' said Maity. 'You see, Jagat Narayan Chowdhury was proud of the tea from his garden. But with this pride came a sense of arrogance too. All Mrs Sengupta had to tell him was that the tea she was offering him was sourced from Manikpur.'

'But how come he couldn't recognize his own garden's tea when he drank it?' I asked, still confused.

'He did!' Mrs Sengupta said softly.

'Yes, and that was the most pivotal moment in this entire story,' Maity added. 'The fulcrum around which this entire mystery revolves. The key to the puzzle! Had Chowdhury drunk the whole cup of tea that evening, he would have probably been dead that very night itself, even before he could reach me. But all that he took was one sip. And he immediately realized that there was something wrong with it. He went back to Manikpur, feeling sick all along. And he knew that somehow or the other, his sickness had something to do with the tea his daughter had served him. Remember his words from the morning he passed away, Prakash?

"No one is to be trusted, Mohan", he had said. "Not even your own shadow. You won't see the arrow before it hits you!'"

Mrs Sengupta's eyes had welled up. The little child's eyelids had become heavy, so the mother gently placed her on her shoulder and rocked her. Maity continued, 'The moment I inquired about the four boys, Ashu Babu realized that you had sent me to Manikpur. Because other than him and the boys themselves, only you knew of the pact. He immediately called you in Kolkata, and you told him what you had done. The news devastated Ashu Babu. And he realized that there were now five—not four, but *five*—young lives which could be potentially ruined because of a simple act of vengeance. Which was why, he had no other choice but to write that letter to me and take the blame himself. You should take solace in knowing, Mrs Sengupta, that your teacher did everything he could to save your life.'

Tears rolled down Mitali Sengupta's cheeks, and she shut her eyes in pain. After some time, she opened her eyes and said, 'But despite Ashu Sir's best efforts, despite my careful planning, despite every single thing that happened in Manikpur, you saw through *everything*, Mr Maity!'

Maity did not respond.

Mitali Sengupta looked deep into Maity's eyes and said: 'And that's nothing short of a miracle! I had only heard about your brilliance. But now I have witnessed it myself. Which makes me wonder. It's been so many months. Why haven't you handed me over to the police yet? Why don't you let the law punish me for what I have done?'

I looked at Maity. And he simply held his head high and said, 'I have my reasons.'

Mitali Sengupta breathed a sigh of relief, as did I. But Maity wasn't done yet. He rose from the bench, took the coat off Mrs Sengupta's shoulders and said, 'But before I leave you today, madam, I must tell you that I have only one regret in this entire story. I so, so wish that you would have showered your husband with a little more love. Just enough for him to realize how precious his life already was, how fortunate he was. If only you would have done that, madam, you would not have had to go through the rest of your life knowing that on every street corner you turn, in every market that you shop, in every festival that you celebrate and every tragedy that you mourn, in every single moment that you spend being a happy wife and a proud mother, one thought would be your constant companion. And it is that there will always, inevitably be someone who knows that you committed murder. Yes, Mrs Sengupta. *That* is your punishment. The burden of the knowledge—*that I know*! Goodbye, madam. Come, Prakash.'

Maity walked away and I followed him. When we had gone some distance, I turned around one last time to find Mitali Sengupta still sitting on the bench by the canal gently rocking her baby to sleep. I turned back and said, 'So this is why you hadn't told me about the letter?'

'Remember what I had said, Prakash?' Maity said. 'That as long as I am around, no one would be punished for a crime they haven't committed. *No one!*'

I smiled at Maity and said, 'I'm sorry I misunderstood you, Maity!'

We had reached the gates of the Victoria Memorial. Maity turned around to face me. He said, 'There's no apology needed here, Prakash. And thanks for coming. I . . . I really appreciate it.'

I smiled. Then I said, 'I need to head home now, I have an important phone call to make. Shall I drop you on the way?'

Maity looked towards the setting sun and said, 'You go ahead, Prakash. I think I'll sit here for some time. I think after all these days, a bit of fresh air and sunlight might do me some good.'

I nodded. We promised to meet again the next day. Then I hailed a cab to head home. As the cab started moving, I saw a familiar figure sitting on one of the benches of the Victoria Memorial garden. His eyes were shut, his face was calm and he was in deep contemplation. A fond feeling warmed up inside me as I looked at the man. Janardan Maity was back again!

As soon as Maity had disappeared from my view, I whipped out my cell phone and placed a call.

'Hello, Snigdha? Yes, it's me. Listen, about the novel . . . I would like to add a chapter to it before you send it to press.'

'A chapter?' she sounded surprised. 'Why? It's just fine the way it is right now. Adding a whole new chapter might ruin everything, don't you think?'

'On the contrary,' I said, 'it will give the story a whole new dimension.'

'This is too last-minute, Prakash,' said Snigdha. 'Is it important?'

I paused for a second and said, 'I can't tell you how important it is. Trust me on this, and give me a couple of days, I'll send it to you.'

'Fine then,' she said. 'Oh, by the way, have you thought of a title yet?'

My cab was now speeding along Red Road. The wind was in my hair and it seemed to wash away the gloom that I had lived with over the last year. As I leant back in my seat, a sense of calm prevailed over me and a fond smile spread across my face.

'Yes, I have.'

* * *

Acknowledgements

My sincere thanks to:
Shri. Manash Banerjee
Smt. Tilottama Chakraborty
Miss Reya Banerjee
and
Pele

Scan QR code to access the
Penguin Random House India website